The LOST ONES

BOOKS BY DANA PERRY

Jessie Tucker Mystery series
The Silent Victim
The Golden Girl

Detective Abby Pearce series
Her Ocean Grave
Silent Island

Detective Nikki Cassidy series
The Nowhere Girls
Last One to Die

DETECTIVE NIKKI CASSIDY BOOK 3

The LOST ONES

DANA PERRY

bookouture

Published by Bookouture in 2024

An imprint of Storyfire Ltd.
Carmelite House
50 Victoria Embankment
London EC4Y 0DZ

www.bookouture.com

ISBN: 978-1-83790-439-6
eBook ISBN: 978-1-83790-438-9

PROLOGUE

I've been running so much.

I've been running so far.

I've been running for so long.

All I want to do now is come home again.

Please help me do that.

If you're reading this, you probably know what happened to me fifteen years ago when I was abducted and "murdered." What you don't know is what has happened to me since. I want to tell everyone my story.

I am not dead.

I am not really even missing any more.

I am here.

I am right here in front of you to find, and I am real.

Like the sky above this house where I once lived is real, and the trees and grass around it are real too—that's just like me, no matter what else you have heard or talked about in the past.

I want to come home again...

Caitlin Cassidy

ONE

"Your sister Caitlin died fifteen years ago, Agent Cassidy," said Dave Blanton, my boss at the FBI.

"I know."

"Your father was the one who handled her murder case."

"I know that too."

"And you caught the man who killed her."

"Right."

"Then this note claiming to be from your sister now can't possibly be true."

"Of course not."

"Then why do you want to go back to Huntsdale to investigate it?"

"Because I need to be sure."

My name is Nikki Cassidy, and I'm an agent for the Violent Crimes Against Children department of the FBI in Washington.

I've made front-page headlines recently by breaking some big cases, including uncovering one of the FBI's own agents as a secret serial killer who had murdered numerous teenaged girls over the years. I've seen plenty of strange things, and it takes a lot to shake me up. But I was still in a state of shock and disbelief over the events which had transpired in my hometown of Huntsdale, Ohio in the past several days.

A young woman showed up at the door of the house where I grew up in Huntsdale and announced to the occupant that she used to live there. With her mother and her father and her older sister Nikki, she claimed. The woman identified herself as Caitlin Cassidy, who was my sister.

This did not seem possible for a number of reasons, the most obvious being that my sister Caitlin was dead. She had been abducted and then found murdered when she was only twelve years old.

My mother had told me to watch my twelve-year-old sister at home that day while she was out. Instead, I took Caitlin to a summer carnival with me because I wanted to go with my friends to meet boys. Caitlin disappeared when I wasn't paying attention to her, and she was later found murdered. A bouquet of roses was left on her body, which turned out to be a calling card from the killer.

He left roses with other victims too until I finally stopped him in a shoot-out. But even that wasn't enough to ease the pain for me. No, I still carry the wounds of my guilt from that long-ago summer day when I allowed my sister to die.

So why was someone opening up those wounds again by claiming Caitlin was somehow still alive?

Adding to the incongruity of it all was the fact that the young woman at the door of my old house was a teenager herself. She was described as no more than sixteen or seventeen years old, maybe even younger than that. My sister would be a grown woman in her late twenties by now if she had lived.

When the person now living in the house pointed this out to the young woman, she got very agitated, burst into tears and ran away. But later the woman in the house discovered the girl had left a note behind. The note now in our possession saying she had been on the run for a long time, and she wanted someone to help her "get home again." That note had my sister's name on the bottom, Caitlin Cassidy.

The woman living in the house later identified the girl she had seen on her doorstep from a missing child poster as a sixteen-year-old runaway girl named Laurie Reddick from another part of Ohio. The Reddick girl had disappeared from her home outside of Dayton, on the other side of the state, several weeks earlier and had not been heard from since. Until she showed up at the front door of my old house in Huntsdale claiming to be my long-dead sister.

But why?

What was her reason for doing something like this?

How did she even know about my sister?

I had no idea, but I wanted some answers. The local authorities and state police were supposedly looking for the girl. But it wasn't a big priority for any of them. She was simply another runaway as far as they were concerned, they were treating her the same as any other teenaged girl—who, as far as they knew, was in no imminent danger—so it was no big deal for them to find Laurie Reddick.

But it was a big deal for me.

Which is why I was sitting in Dave Blanton's office right now telling him how I wanted to go back to Huntsdale—where I'd just been and broken the case involving the murderous FBI agent.

"I've always had some questions that never got answered in my sister's case," I said. "Even though I eventually found the man who did it, I've had these questions about her death. Now I have this other big question: Who is doing this and why are they doing it? Who got this girl to show up at my old house with a story that she was really Caitlin? I want to know. Boss, I need to know."

Dave Blanton was an old-school, by the book FBI guy who wanted us to call him "boss" or "chief" instead of using his name. He, in return, always referred to me as Agent Cassidy, not Nikki or Cassidy.

It seemed silly and annoying to me most of the time.

But I was sticking to the "boss" terminology right now to help get him on my side to accomplish what I wanted: let me investigate this latest bizarre incident in my hometown of Huntsdale.

Except it wasn't working.

"There's nothing really illegal for us to pursue here, is there, Agent Cassidy," Blanton said.

"A teenaged girl—this Laurie Reddick—is going around and posing as my dead sister Caitlin."

"It's weird, I admit—but not exactly a crime."

"Well, she is a runaway."

"There's a lot of runaway teenaged girls out there, you know that better than anyone. We don't chase after all of them."

"The rest of them don't say they're Caitlin Cassidy."

"You're making this personal. I understand why it's personal for you, but I need you to remain professional about your job. Chasing after a young woman simply because she claims to be your dead sister is not professional."

"Then I'll do it on my own. Take some vacation days and go back to Huntsdale that way to check it out."

"I can't let you do that either. Whether you're on duty or not, you're one of my agents and you carry a badge and you carry a gun. If you get into any kind of trouble there, the bureau—and specifically me—is still going to be responsible for you. And you will get into trouble if you go back to Huntsdale, I'm pretty sure of that."

"Why would you say that?"

"As I recall, you're not exactly popular with the Huntsdale Police Department and its chief. Plus, one of their own got killed because of us the last time you were there. You really need to leave Huntsdale and all of this alone for now, Agent Cassidy."

I'm not sure what would have happened if events hadn't worked out the way they did. I mean I wasn't prepared to quit the FBI or anything and throw away my career over this. But I had to find out about the girl posing as my sister. There were still too many questions out there about Caitlin's murder, and I needed answers.

But everything changed a few minutes later when Alex Del Vecchio, my partner at the bureau, burst into Blanton's office and announced to us:

"You're not going to believe this! That girl—the runaway who claimed to be Nikki's sister—they just found her body! Someone strangled her to death!"

TWO

Laurie Reddick had been found at a rest area of the Ohio Turnpike, just north of Columbus.

Her body was found inside the women's bathroom at about three a.m., slumped over a sink with her arms and legs out to each side. It was almost like someone had deliberately positioned her that way. Staging the scene is what we call it when a murderer does that to the victim. The Laurie Reddick death scene sure seemed staged.

The body was discovered by a woman and her teenaged daughter.

At first, they thought Laurie Reddick was drunk or simply sleeping. Until they got closer. That's when they saw her bulging eyes, her lifeless face and—even more importantly—the rope that someone had twisted around her neck. They realized she was dead and ran screaming out of the bathroom looking for help.

Once the victim was identified through items found in her handbag as a runaway from the Dayton area—in western Ohio, on the other side of the state from Huntsdale—the police came up with what seemed to be a reasonable scenario of what happened to her.

She was on the run so she was hitchhiking along the turnpike to get further away from her home near Dayton. Someone picked her up, assaulted her, eventually strangled her and then left the body in the rest stop bathroom.

The problem with this was there was no evidence that the girl had been assaulted—sexually or otherwise—from the lack of bruises or scars and other physical evidence on her body.

But the rest of it—the theory it was a hitchhiking that turned bad—was still what authorities were pursuing until the new connection emerged: the connection between Laurie Reddick and her visit to my old house in Huntsdale—about seventy-five miles away in the other direction from where her body was found—when she pretended to be my dead sister.

And that's what left me with so many questions.

I mean Laurie Reddick had showed up at the house where I used to live and pretended she was Caitlin Cassidy, then left behind a note purporting to be from Caitlin claiming she was still alive.

Then, sometime after all this, someone had strangled her to death.

The idea that the two incidents could be completely unrelated—she shows up at my house claiming to be Caitlin Cassidy and her being strangled to death a short time later—was too much of a reach to believe.

Instead, a new theory emerged by cops and FBI and me too.

Someone had put the Reddick girl up to the visit to my former house in Huntsdale as Caitlin, then strangled her to death afterward. But why? To keep quiet about what she had done? Why would anyone find it was worth murder to keep this secret? Why even send her in the first place? Why was any of this happening to me—bringing back the past about my dead sister—all over again?

The woman who found Laurie Reddick was very traumatized by the experience, police on the scene said. Not just for herself, but also distraught that her daughter—who was close to the same age as the dead girl—had witnessed the results of such a horrible crime. She said she feared it might be a nightmarish memory that stayed with her daughter all her life. I hoped she was wrong about that, but I wasn't sure she was. I'd been about the daughter's age fifteen years ago when my sister was murdered. And I'd never quite put that nightmare behind me in the time since.

The autopsy provided no surprises. Laurie Reddick had been killed by the rope around her neck. It was tied into a knot, almost like a hangman's noose, then pulled tighter and tighter until the girl was dead. There was also evidence that the killer had loosened it several times during the process, then tightened it around her neck again—keeping the girl alive long enough to maybe enjoy her struggles to breathe.

Did all this happen in the women's bathroom? It seemed unlikely since this all would have taken some time, and anyone could have walked in on the horrific scene going on there. No, it seemed more logical than she had been strangled somewhere else, possibly in the car she was in after hitchhiking, and then her body placed in the washroom to be found. But not simply dropped there. Positioned over the sink in dramatic fashion to satisfy the killer's sick fantasies or whatever caused him to do this.

But then there was more.

More than I could imagine when I first heard the news from Alex about this girl being dead.

Shortly after the body was found, and before the news of Laurie Reddick's murder was spread anywhere on the media, police received an email from someone who already knew all the details about the crime.

So they were certain it had come from the actual killer.

In the email, the writer painstakingly described the scene in the bathroom at the rest stop—including a graphic description of how Laurie Reddick looked lying dead on the sink with arms and legs spread out from her and with a noose around her neck.

The emailer then talked about savoring the moments of the kill—enjoying Laurie's death struggles—and how he drew it out as long as possible to satisfy the maximum thrill for him before finally strangling her to death.

And then—in an even more bizarre twist—the email included a series of quotes from Ted Bundy, one of the most infamous serial killers ever who murdered at least thirty women and possibly as many as a hundred before he was caught and eventually executed.

The quotes from Bundy were:

"Murder is not just a crime of lust or violence. It becomes possession. The victim becomes a part of you, and you two are forever one."

"When you feel the last bit of breath leaving their body, you're looking into their eyes. A person in that situation is God."

"Society wants to believe it can identify evil people or bad or harmful people, but it's not practical. There are no stereotypes."

"We serial killers are your sons, we are your husbands, we are everywhere. And there will be more of your children dead tomorrow."

The note then ended in a bizarre way, with some words that were particularly haunting to me.

The police were mystified at first by the significance of the concluding words, but later were able to determine where they came from.

It was a song lyric.

From a song by Bette Midler called "The Rose".

The killer quoted her line about a rose blooming in the spring after a long winter.

There was no mistaking that message to me.

Roses again.

Just like with my sister Caitlin and the other victims before.

Someone—another deadly killer—was still taunting me with more roses.

THREE

"What do you think is going on here with this Reddick girl's murder?" I asked Alex. We were in a car driving from Dayton Airport—where we'd landed a few hours earlier—on our way to the home of Laurie Reddick in the town of Groveton, which was about twenty-five miles north of Dayton.

"I think it's about someone who doesn't want to let go of this thing with your sister. Someone who gets off on this as some kind of sexual thrill or whatever. So he gets this girl Laurie Reddick to get your attention by doing what she did in Huntsdale. And, once she's done that, he kills her."

"How sick and twisted and crazy does a person have to be to do something like that?" I asked, shaking my head.

"We deal with a lot of sick and twisted and crazy people in this job, Nikki."

"But this one made it so personal with me."

"Look, it's not hard to figure out what happened here. You've been all over the papers and TV and the internet, especially since the last case. You're a very easy target for someone like this. The star woman FBI agent who catches serial killers even though she's haunted by the one who killed her sister: the sister who disappeared from a carnival fifteen years ago right in front of the future agent's eyes and—"

"Yeah, yeah, I know the story of what happened."

"Sorry."

I looked out the window as we passed through a small town on the way to the Reddick place in Groveton. There were a lot of small towns in Ohio. Just like the small town where I grew up in Huntsdale, Ohio. But I'd found out since then that these small towns sometimes held secrets. Deadly secrets.

I'd been involved in a lot of big cases trying to uncover those kinds of secrets since I joined the FBI. The Highway Killer. The Singles Slayer. The Psychic. The Bone Hacker. The Greenfield Rapist. And, of course, everything I'd done to solve my sister's long-ago murder and the more recent killings in Huntsdale. I'd gotten a lot of media notoriety from all this along the way. I wasn't sure if that notoriety was a good thing or bad. Because the notoriety was very likely the reason someone was doing all this involving the memory of Caitlin now.

"So I guess your hot romance with that police chief in Dorchester from our last case has cooled off, huh?" Alex asked me now, changing the subject as we drove.

"You might say that."

"When's the last time you talked to him."

"Not since I left Dorchester."

"That's definitely cooled off."

"Ice cold," I said.

I wanted to keep focused on the case, but Alex seemed more focused on my love life. She was married—happily married, as far as I knew—and the mother of a four-year-old boy. Still, she got some kind of vicarious delight in knowing all about the twists and turns and highs and lows of my romantic life. Which at the moment wasn't very interesting at all.

"What about your fiancé?" she asked.

"Ex-fiancé."

"That's definitely over?"

"Definitely."

Greg Ellroy and I had planned to be married in the fall, until I had second thoughts about it. Or cold feet. Wedding jitters or whatever you want to call it. I canceled the plans, and I pretty much ended our romance too. I simply decided I didn't want to spend the rest of my life with him.

Hey, Greg is a great guy—good-looking, personable, a successful Washington, D.C. attorney. He'll make some woman a wonderful husband. But not me.

"So you don't have any regrets about ending it with Greg?"

"No regrets at all," I said.

The only thing I had regrets about was my relationship—or lack of a real meaningful relationship—with a cop in Ohio named Billy Weller.

Weller and I had gone to the same high school together in Huntsdale. Even though I didn't remember him, he remembered me, and there were sexual sparks flying between us that could have led to a long-term relationship. Maybe even marriage. But Billy Weller died in the same shoot-out with the man who murdered my sister. He died while saving my life as I eventually captured the killer.

And he died in my arms.

I've had a hard time dealing with that memory since it happened.

Maybe I always will.

"How do we handle things when we get to the parents' house?" I asked Alex, hoping to switch topics and get her off the conversation about my sex life.

"You spoke to the mother on the phone, right?"

"Yeah, she was reluctant to even talk to us at first. She said she'd already talked to police, why did she have to do it all over again with the FBI? She finally agreed to see us after I did some tough talking about the powers of the FBI in a murder investigation, working with the police like this. But she wasn't too happy with me. So..."

"We play good cop and bad cop with her?"

"Right."

"And I'm the good cop?"

"The role fits you better than me, Alex.'

We were passing through another town now and getting closer to Groveton. It was only a few miles down the road, according to our GPS. I looked out again at the houses on the road as they whizzed by and wondered if there were other teenaged girls living in them like Laurie Reddick. Troubled teenagers looking for a way out. Troubled enough to run away from home. So troubled that they might get into the same kind of deadly situation that Reddick did.

But there was something else bothering me.

More than just Laurie Reddick.

The most frightening aspect of this whole case.

"If someone murdered the Reddick girl so casually like this for almost no reason at all, you know what that means?"

She knew.

We both knew.

Even before the letter he sent quoting Ted Bundy about the thrill of murder and the verse taunting me about roses.

"He's done it before," Alex said. "Killed other girls like this."

"Maybe a lot of them.'

"And he's not going to stop, he's going to keep doing it."

"Until we catch him," I said.

FOUR

It didn't take long for us to figure out why Laurie Reddick ran away from home once we met her parents.

I probably would have run away at sixteen too if I had parents like them.

Maybe I wouldn't even have waited until I was sixteen to leave.

The house where the Reddicks lived was in obvious bad shape on the outside—peeling paint, overgrown weeds on the lawn and a broken window on the front. Inside, once we walked through the door, it was even worse. Clothes and other belongings scattered around the living room; dust and dirt everywhere you looked; and a pile of unwashed dishes in the kitchen sink. Good housekeeping was clearly not a priority for these people.

Carl and Helen Reddick sat at a table in the cluttered kitchen talking to us. They were both drinking from cans of beer even though it was only 10:30 a.m. An almost empty bag of garlic potato chips lay on the table in front of them. Beer and potato chips. The Breakfast of Champions. Neither of them offered me or Alex any beer or the remaining potato chips in the bag. More for them that way, I guess.

Carl Reddick was a big hulking man. He wasn't exactly obese, just huge all over with a big gut in front. He was wearing a sleeveless T-shirt and a pair of Bermuda shorts with bare feet. We had told them we were coming to interview them, but I guess they didn't feel it was worth it to dress up for anyone. Even if it was people here to talk about their dead daughter and maybe find out who killed her.

His wife Helen was dressed in a tattered nightgown that looked like it had seen better days. She looked like she had too. Helen Reddick might have been pretty once, but the years, and God knows what else, had taken its toll on her. She had frazzled blonde hair, a tired look on her face and her eyes seemed glazed when she looked at us. I had a feeling Mr. and Mrs. Reddick had been up drinking long before we arrived.

They were still reluctant to talk to us, just like Mrs. Reddick had been when I spoke to her on the phone.

"We already talked to a bunch of police about Laurie," Carl Reddick said. "Talked to them on and on. They kept asking us questions about Laurie and why she might have run away."

"Why did she run away?" I asked.

"No idea," he grunted, belching loudly as he did so.

"Was she unhappy in school?"

"Beats me."

"Anything else that was bothering her before she left?"

He just shrugged.

I turned to Mrs. Reddick and asked her.

Another shrug from her.

"Nothing I know about."

"Sixteen-year-old girls don't run away from home for no reason," Alex said, in what sounded like an accusatory voice.

I guess she had already given up on playing the role of good cop with these two.

"Goddamned Laurie did," the husband said.

"But why?" I asked. "You must have some idea."

"That girl was just a bad seed."

"A bad seed?"

"Yes. I mean she was always causing trouble. Me and Helen did our best to deal with her. God knows, we tried. Just like we've tried with the rest of our kids."

It turned out they had four other children besides Laurie. Their ages ranged from eleven to seventeen. Three boys and a girl. We asked if we could talk to them about their sister in the hopes Laurie might have talked to them about her plans before she left. But the couple said none of the other children were around now.

"Where are they?" Alex asked.

"No idea," Carl Reddick said.

"Doing something somewhere, I guess," was all we got from his wife on the whereabouts of the other four kids.

No, Carl and Helen Reddick weren't exactly going to be candidates for Parents of the Year.

I thought about what it must have been like for Laurie growing up in this house with these people. I mean my house wasn't perfect, but I had a much different upbringing. My father had been a great guy who taught me so much, inspiring me in his job as a small-town police chief in Huntsdale to go into law enforcement myself. My mother was difficult to deal with for both me and Caitlin at times—but it was still a good home. At least until Caitlin died, and by then I was on my way to college. I couldn't even imagine having parents like this pair. I think Alex—who was a mother herself—was even more appalled. I knew her well enough that I could tell from the expression on her face as she questioned them that she was having a hard time keeping it together and remaining professional.

But we needed answers from these people so we kept pressing on.

"Mr. and Mrs. Reddick, your daughter was last seen at a

house in Huntsdale, Ohio," I said. "A house where I used to live with my sister Caitlin until she was murdered fifteen years ago. Your daughter claimed to be Caitlin to the current occupant of the house. And she left a note behind saying she was Caitlin. Do you know anything about why she would have done this?"

"I have no idea what you're talking about," Carl Reddick said.

"Did she ever mention my sister's name to you for any reason?"

"No."

"Do you know if she watched something on TV about my sister's case?"

"No."

"Did she ever tell you about someone trying to convince her to go to that house and play the part of my sister?"

Another no from both of them.

I looked over again at Alex. I think we both realized we were wasting our time talking to this couple. They didn't know anything about their daughter. They didn't know anything about their other kids. They didn't really seem to care about any of them.

"Can you help us to find some of Laurie's friends she might have talked to before she left?" Alex said.

"I don't really know much about who her friends were," the mother said with a shrug.

Of course, you don't.

"Are you sure you can't think of anyone? It would really help us if you could."

"There was one girl that used to come around here," the husband said. "What was her name again, Helen?"

"Sarah... or Sheila... or something with an S. Or Shirley. Yeah, that was it. There was some girl named Shirley she was friends with."

"Any idea what Shirley's last name was?"

"Nope."

"Do you know how we might contact Shirley?"

They did not.

Before we left, we asked to see whatever possessions Laurie had left behind. They took us to her room. It was a small room, and there weren't a lot of things in there. No cell phone, tablet or laptop computer—she probably would have taken those things with her if she had them. There were a few clothes, books and other items that had belonged to her. On one of the walls was a picture of a young woman in a swimsuit running on a beach in Southern California. I wondered if Laurie looked at that picture and dreamed of a life like that somewhere outside this house.

Alex and I were just about to give up when we found something.

Two things.

The first was a small book with a list of names and phone numbers and email addresses. People she presumably knew. One of them was the name Shirley Hunsaker. That was very likely the friend Shirley the parents had mentioned. I called the number next to the name, confirmed it was her and made arrangements to talk to her in person later.

But then, before we left, we found something else.

Something that was really shocking to me.

It was a picture of my sister Caitlin.

And a newspaper clipping about her abduction and murder.

There was more too.

Another newspaper clipping which was an article about me.

The headline said:

STAR FBI AGENT STILL HAUNTED BY SISTER'S LONG-AGO MURDER

FIVE

"Why would a sixteen-year-old girl specifically target you with a charade like this involving your dead sister?" Dave Blanton said from Washington when we told him what we'd found in Laurie Reddick's room. "How would she know about you? Why would she care? It doesn't make any sense."

"Sure, it does."

"If someone else put her up to it."

"Exactly."

"But who?"

"Someone—and I have no idea who that might be—who enjoys playing this kind of game with me. With us. Sending the girl to my old house in Huntsdale, killing her afterward, sending all those Ted Bundy quotes and the rose stuff to remind me again about my sister. He's trying to get our attention with all this. And he damn sure has done that!"

Alex and I were talking to Blanton on a speakerphone from the car.

"Did the parents know any more about the picture of you and the newspaper clipping about your sister that you found there?" he asked.

"No, they said they had no idea why Laurie might have had that."

"Do you believe them?"

"Yes."

"They seemed truthful to you about it?'

"They seemed oblivious. These people had no idea about anything their daughter was doing. And they didn't care. We can't get any information out of the mother and father, as sad as that might be."

Alex then described for Blanton in some detail about the state of the Reddick house, the fact that they didn't even know where their other children were and the rest.

"Is there anything we can do about this?" she asked him.

"Like what?"

"I'm concerned about the state of the four other children living there. These are the parents from hell."

"We're not the moral police, Agent Del Vecchio."

I realized now how upset Alex had been by our interaction with the Reddicks. Sure, it bothered me too. But I mostly just wanted to find out who killed Laurie Reddick and why. As a mother herself, Alex was worried about the safety and well-being of the remaining Reddick children.

"There's got to be something we can do," Alex said. "An agency that looks after child welfare? Some federal bureau or branch out here who looks into this kind of thing?"

"I'll look into it." Blanton sighed.

Before we left the Reddick house, we'd managed to get them to find a picture of Laurie for us.

It wasn't easy. They told us they didn't have many pictures of their daughter, and it would be a lot of trouble to find one. But eventually they did. It was from a year or so earlier—a class photo from her school. So she probably looked a little older when she died. But it still gave us a graphic image of the girl.

I looked at the photo in my hand of Laurie Reddick. She

had short, dusky blonde hair, a few freckles on her face and nice blue eyes. She was an attractive teenager, just starting to grow into a woman. Until someone prevented that from happening. Would she have grown up to be a beautiful woman? Would she have broken out of the nightmare of that house for a better life? We'd never know now.

We took the picture and showed it to people around the town of Groveton. A lot of people recognized her. Many of them had heard about her murder from the news. Everyone pretty much thought she was a nice kid who had drawn the short straw when it came to a family.

No real surprise there.

But the surprise did come from a few people we talked to who had encountered Laurie in the days before she disappeared from Groveton.

The owner of a jewelry store said she had bought a ring there. Not a particularly expensive ring. But one worth more than he thought the girl could afford until she paid him for it in cash.

A clothing store reported a mini-shopping spree by her there. Again, nothing too gaudy. But several pairs of jeans, some T-shirts and blouses and even a designer jacket.

Shirley Hunsaker—the friend of Laurie's we'd found out about at the Reddick house—confirmed this spending spree too when we interviewed her.

"Laurie clearly had come into some kind of money," the Hunsaker girl told us when we met with her at a coffee shop where she was working a part-time job as a barista. "I was surprised. I mean Laurie never had any money. If we went any place, I usually had to pay. But suddenly she had more money than I did. Even though I was working this job, and she wasn't working anywhere."

"Did you ask her where the money came from?"

"Of course, I did.'

"And?"

"She wouldn't tell me. She said it was a secret. All she'd say was: 'I guess I struck it rich!'"

So Laurie Reddick had suddenly come into a financial windfall before she disappeared.

Presumably the money came from someone who had paid her to later pull off the Caitlin charade in Huntsdale.

But she'd paid for that money in the end with her life.

"When was the last time you saw her?" I asked.

"Just a day or two before she left town. We went to a shopping mall together. Laurie began buying a lot of stuff for herself, and a few things for me too. Like she got me a pair of running shoes I wanted. That's when I knew for sure something was going on with her. Especially the way that shopping trip ended."

"What happened?" Alex asked.

"Someone approached us in the mall. Someone Laurie knew. Laurie said she had to talk to this person, and she needed to do it in private. She said she'd see me later. But that never happened. I left the mall, and I never heard from her again."

"Do you have any idea who this person was?"

"No, not at all."

"Or the connection with Laurie?"

"I assumed it had something to do with the money Laurie was suddenly flashing around and spending."

This was big. This girl had seen the man who very likely had sent Laurie to pose in Huntsdale as my sister, and then murdered her afterward. It could be the lead—the big breakthrough in the case—we were looking for.

"Can you describe him for us?" I said.

"Him?"

"The man who met with Laurie at the mall."

"There was no man."

"But you said..."

"It was a woman."

I looked over at Alex. She was as surprised as I was. Neither of us saw that one coming.

"Okay, describe the woman for us," I said.

"Oh, she was older," Shirley Hunsaker said to me. "Maybe your age. Or a few years younger, in her late twenties. But very similar to you. In fact, she looked like you too. A lot like you, Agent Cassidy. I mean she looked so much like you she could have been your sister or something."

SIX

I spent a lot more time talking to Shirley Hunsaker, trying to find out more details about the woman she thought looked so much like me. Asking her more specific questions about how the woman looked, what she wore, the sound of her voice—and anything else I could think of.

But Hunsaker wasn't of much help. All she remembered is that the woman knew Laurie, Laurie said she wanted to talk to the woman alone and that was the last time she saw Laurie. She told me nothing more about the mysterious woman in the mall. Except that she looked like me.

I asked her if she'd be willing to sit down with a police artist and try to draw a picture of the woman she saw, based on whatever memories she did have. She agreed. I set up a meeting for her with a police artist, telling the local authorities I wanted it done as soon as possible.

I wasn't sure how long I'd be in Groveton. Probably not much longer. I'd talked to the dead girl's parents and the only friend of hers I could find. There were other places besides Groveton for me to go with the investigation, other things to do.

First, the crime scene at the turnpike rest stop where

Laurie's body had been found. Then I knew I needed to go back to my hometown of Huntsdale to talk to the woman living in my family's old house to see what else she remembered about her encounter at the door with Laurie Reddick.

Before I left Hunsaker, I asked her to tell me the specific store where they'd been when the mystery woman who looked like me showed up. Then I went back to the mall and asked the people in that store if they recognized the description or knew anything else about this woman. I went to several other stores nearby too in case she might have gone in one of them after the meeting with Laurie.

But no one knew anything about her.

It didn't help that I had no picture of her to show them. Or even any specific description. I resorted to asking people if they'd seen anyone that looked like me. It seemed like the simplest thing to do. But it certainly raised questions from the people that I interviewed.

"You're looking for someone who looks like you?" one store owner asked.

"Yes."

"Exactly like you?"

"More or less. I'm not sure."

"Do you have a twin sister or something?"

"I don't."

"Then who is she and why are you looking for her?"

I'd shown my FBI credentials at the beginning of the interview, but hadn't gotten into anything specific. I told him now that I was conducting a murder investigation, I thought this woman might be involved somehow and I wanted to find and talk to her.

"So an FBI agent is looking for a murder suspect who looks exactly like her. Wow!"

"She's not necessarily a suspect. Not yet. But yes, well... you're right."

"Sounds crazy to me."

"It sure does," I said.

I left my card and contact information with him and everyone else I talked to before I left the mall. I asked them to call me if anyone ever did see the woman there.

But I didn't really expect to hear back from any of them.

I checked also to see if she might have appeared on any mall security video, but she hadn't.

No, the mysterious woman had disappeared from the mall as quickly as she had emerged that day with Laurie.

"What do you make of all this?" Alex asked me later.

"You tell me."

We were eating lunch at a diner in downtown Groveton. I was munching on a greasy cheeseburger and French fries. I always preferred diner hamburgers to the ones at places like McDonald's or Wendy's or Burger King. I don't think that I've ever really had a bad cheeseburger and fries meal at a diner, wherever I've traveled. Alex was eating a Caesar salad with some kind of low-calorie dressing. Alex ate better than me. She did a lot of things better than me.

"The way I see it, there are three possibilities to explain this," she said.

"Okay, go. Let me hear them."

"Possibility number one: This really is you. You're the woman who met the girl in the mall that day. And somehow blacked it out and don't remember being there. Or you're trying to hide it from me and everyone else for some unknown reason."

"That makes no sense at all, Alex."

"I know. Because I know you. But, if someone from the outside looked at this series of events totally objectively, that's one possible theory they would have to consider in the big picture of things. So I just thought I'd throw it out there."

"Let's move on to possibility number two," I said, nibbling on one of my French fries.

"All right, the second possibility is she's a doppelgänger."

"A doppelgänger?"

"Someone who just happens to look very much like you. Almost identical. It does happen. People—not sisters—who have someone else that looks like they do."

"And this doppelgänger—whoever she is—just happened to show up here in Groveton as part of a murder investigation we're conducting?"

"That does seem pretty far-fetched."

"It sure does."

I finished off my cheeseburger and ate some more of the fries. I offered Alex a few fries, but she said no. She seemed content with her salad. I was fine with that. More French fries for me that way.

"Let's hear possibility number three," I said. "And it better make more sense than the first two."

"Someone deliberately made themselves up to look like you. Like a character might for a part in a movie or TV show. Same hair color, same kind of clothes you wear, maybe even some kind of plastic surgery—all to play the part of you. So there's a second Nikki Cassidy out there besides you."

"But why?"

"Maybe she's working with whoever killed Laurie Reddick. And wrote those notes about Ted Bundy and a lot of other murders of young women."

"Or else she is the killer," I said.

"A woman serial killer?"

"Why not? We've come a long way, baby."

"I am woman, hear me roar," Alex muttered.

Alex and I liked to make jokes like this sometimes, even in the most grisly murder investigations. I guess it helped us deal with all the horror and violence and everything we encountered in this job.

She was right though.

The idea of someone deliberately posing as me made the most sense of any other answer.

Still, there was one possible answer she'd left out.

The possibility that the woman at the mall who looked so much like me was my sister.

I mean my sister would probably look like me—a lot like me —as a woman in her late twenties.

Of course, that was impossible.

My sister was long dead.

SEVEN

The official investigation into Laurie Reddick's murder was being handled by the Ohio State Police, based in Columbus. Local police authorities were involved, too. But, because the killing had occurred on the Ohio Turnpike at a rest stop, the state troopers had jumped into the investigation. I found out very quickly that they were running the show.

"You want to see my crime scene?" said Lieutenant Bonnie Tatarko from the Columbus area barracks, when I asked her to take me to the spot on the turnpike where Laurie's body had been found.

Lt. Tatarko was a pretty imposing woman. I'd discovered that when I arrived at the barracks and asked to see her. She was tall—probably over six feet—and big overall besides that. Not fat, she just had a formidable-looking body. She had blonde hair pulled back in a tight bun; was wearing a neatly pressed state trooper uniform; and definitely had a no-nonsense look on her face. I decided right then and there that I didn't want to get on the wrong side of Bonnie Tatarko.

I'd driven to Columbus from Groveton, a trip which only took about an hour and a half. Alex stayed behind in Groveton to see if she could find out any more from people who knew Laurie Reddick there—at her school, any other friends, people in the town. We'd get together again later.

After Columbus, I planned on going back to Huntsdale to talk to the woman living in my old house who had seen and talked with Laurie Reddick. But first I wanted to visit the crime scene. Lt. Tatarko agreed to take me there. But she had questions for me, just like I had questions for her.

"Why is the FBI interested in this case anyway?" she asked.

I told her everything I knew, including the connection with my sister and everything we'd found out about Laurie Reddick in Groveton.

"Your sister, huh?" she said when I was finished giving her the rundown. "Now I know who you are. The one I saw on all the TV news recently. That was a helluva bust thing you did. You must be a damned good investigator."

I shrugged. "I had a lot of help from local authorities," I told her, even though that wasn't true in Huntsdale with its Police Chief Frank Earnshaw.

"And now you want to solve the Laurie Reddick case?"

"Well, that's obviously the idea."

"So do you and the other FBI plan to try and take this case away from me?"

"We want to work with you, Lieutenant Tatarko."

This could still go either way. I knew that was how it worked out when the FBI interacted with local law enforcement agencies.

Maybe it would be like Huntsdale where Chief Frank Earnshaw did everything he could to throw obstacles in front of me when I was there. Or else maybe like Chief Connor Nolan in Dorchester, Pa. where we worked together well. So well that I wound up sleeping with him. I wasn't planning on sleeping with Bonnie Tatarko. But I did want to have a comfortable working relationship with her.

I guess in the end she had the same idea.

"Let's go," she said. "The rest stop where it happened is only about fifteen minutes away from here."

We drove there in a state trooper vehicle. She had on her state trooper's hat now too. I wanted to make some joke about how she looked a bit like Smokey the Bear wearing it. But instead I kept my mouth shut. She was definitely a formidable presence to be around. And dressed in full uniform, with her gun on her side, I could see why she could easily intimidate people she was dealing with—not just criminals, but people in her own unit too.

We talked on the ride a bit about our respective careers in law enforcement. She told me about rising up through the ranks of the Ohio State Police to her rank of lieutenant in the Columbus barracks—despite running into a lot of sexism along the way because she was a woman.

I told her about growing up with my father as the local police chief and more about my career at the FBI.

Tatarko knew about all my big cases, and she ran through the names of them as we drove. The names I knew all too well: The Highway Killer. The Psychic. The Bone Hacker. The Greenfield Rapist. And, of course, my most memorable case of all, The Singles Slayer.

"You seem to always catch the killer," she said.

That wasn't exactly true.

"Not always. Sometimes they still get away, no matter what you do."

"Well, you can't win them all."

"I want to try."

I liked Bonnie Tatarko. I hoped she liked me too. We definitely seemed to be developing a relationship, at least a professional one. She was much more like Connor Nolan than like that jerk Earnshaw.

When we got to the rest stop, we found that the women's bathroom there was still closed. It was no longer a crime scene officially. But someone—either the local police who first investigated, the turnpike people, or maybe other state troopers—had kept it off-limits to anyone. I imagine that didn't sit too well with travelers on the turnpike who stopped at the rest area to use it. But I was glad. It gave me a better opportunity to see it the way it was when Laurie Reddick's body had been found.

I was surprised to see there was no door on the restroom area. And it was bigger than I expected. Making it more likely, it seemed to me, that she had been killed somewhere else and then the body was dumped here. Otherwise, someone could have just walked in while it was happening.

But Tatarko said that didn't seem to be the case.

"We think she was strangled in one of the stalls—that one at the end," she said, pointing to a stall. "We got fragments of fibers from her clothes in that stall which matched what she was wearing when she died."

"So the killer strangled her in the stall and then placed the body in here?"

"That's the scenario we're looking at."

"But the killer—wasn't he taking a chance that someone would walk in on them?"

"Not if they were in the stall. And we've placed the time of death—based on the medical examiner's report—at around three a.m. So it happened in the middle of the night when the traffic going in and out of here would be very low."

"Still, if someone did come in, a man inside the woman's restroom—even if they didn't know what he was doing in here—it would get a lot of attention. He couldn't take a chance on that happening."

"That's what we thought too. Until we found the evidence she'd died in the stall. And now we know something else too, don't we? Thanks to you. We know that the last person seen with the Reddick girl was this woman she met at the mall in Groveton. That changes everything. Do you understand what I'm saying here, Cassidy? Maybe there never was a man in this restroom with Laurie Reddick. Because—"

"The killer could be a woman," I said.

EIGHT

I had checked into a motel on the outskirts of Columbus when I arrived earlier. Before I went to see Tatarko at the state trooper headquarters. I figured it would be late before I finished my business with her, and I really didn't want to drive all the way to Huntsdale tonight when it was dark.

Besides, I was bushed. It had been a long day. All I wanted now was a drink, a meal and a good night's sleep.

It was a reasonably large motel, eight stories high with lots of rooms, so there was a restaurant off of the lobby. I probably could have found some other better places if I looked. But I didn't want to go through the effort. Instead, I settled in at the bar here where I ordered a vodka tonic and some kind of chicken pasta that was the special of the night.

While I waited for the food, I sipped on the vodka tonic and thought about everything I'd found out—along with what I still didn't know—from my time in Groveton.

There were three things I was certain about:

1) Laurie Reddick was a troubled teenager from a horrible family situation who would probably have done anything to get away from that house.

2) Someone had given Laurie money—quite a great deal of money, according to Shirley Hunsaker—to do something for them: which apparently was to pose as my sister at our old family home.

3) The person who gave her the money—at least the only obvious one based on what we knew about the case—was a woman. A woman who looked like me. Maybe not exactly like me, but similar enough that Shirley Hunsaker thought that this woman could even have been my sister.

The things I didn't know were:

1) Who was this mystery woman in the mall that Laurie had gone off to talk to in private without her friend Shirley?

2) How did this woman look so much like me? Was it just a bizarre coincidence? Some kind of elaborate acting job? Or... or, well, something else.

3) And then, of course, came the biggest question of all: Why? Why did someone pay the girl to pose as my sister? Why did they kill her after she finished the job? Why was any of this happening to me after all I'd been through with my sister's long-ago murder?

The chicken pasta arrived, and I dug into it, hoping that might help spur my thinking process as I sought these answers. But it didn't. The pasta was kind of disappointing. Not enough sauce, chewy pieces of chicken and not particularly tasty when I did manage to eat some. I left half of it on the plate, and I ordered another vodka tonic.

I sipped on that, a lot quicker than I sipped on the first one, and continued trying to come up with some brilliant solution to all this.

But the vodka didn't help.

Nothing—no solution or inspiration or Hercule Poirot like deduction—popped into my mind.

All I knew was that I was very tired and needed some sleep.

I headed upstairs to the eighth floor where my room was.

When I got there, I had a strange feeling something was wrong. Nothing I could exactly put my finger on. More like a feeling. A feeling that someone else had been in this room since I left it.

That's when I noticed the papers and documents I'd piled up on a table. Stuff from Groveton that I left there when I first arrived after the check-in. They were still there. Except they looked different. The item on top wasn't the one that was on top before. It had been a Q&A I'd written up about our conversation with Shirley Hunsaker and Laurie's parents. But the top item was a newspaper clipping. The newspaper clipping we'd found in Laurie's room at the Reddick house.

Did I unintentionally leave it that way?

No, I didn't.

I'm very serious about things I'm working on for a case, and I remembered exactly how I had ordered stuff in that pile.

My suitcase wasn't in the same place either. It had been on a stand by the door. But now it was on top of the bed. And it was open. Like someone had been going through it. Except that someone wasn't me.

Suddenly, I heard a noise. It was coming from the bathroom. That's when I noticed for the first time that the bathroom door was closed, too. I had left it open before. I was sure about that.

The intruder was still here!

I was pretty sure of that now.

And I might be trapped by whoever it was in this hotel room.

"Is someone there?" I yelled out.

No answer.

"I'm with the FBI!" I said.

Still nothing.

I took out my Glock 19M and pointed it at the closed door.

"I'm armed, I'm warning you!"

Everything was quiet now. Maybe it had been my imagination. But I didn't think so. Somebody else was in my hotel room. Somebody else was hiding there in my bathroom. I was pretty sure of that.

I moved slowly toward the bathroom door with the Glock in front of me.

Should I wait for the police to arrive?

I heard another noise now from the bathroom.

It sounded like footsteps.

Footsteps moving toward the door.

I was almost at the door now.

Everything was silent again now.

What in the hell was going on? Who was hiding in my bathroom? And why? There was only one way to find out that answer.

I reached for the knob, turned it and pushed the door open.

A figure suddenly came running out of the bathroom.

He crashed into me, knocking me to the floor.

He hit me so hard that it knocked the gun out of my hand, which went skittering off to the side.

I thought the guy might go for the gun.

But he was more interested in getting away.

I tried to stop him, but he was strong and he managed to knock me back down onto the floor.

That gave me a chance to recover my gun.

Now I was armed, and he wasn't.

That gave me the advantage.

I chased after him, then tripped him before he could get to the door of my room.

He fell to the floor face down.

I jumped on top of him, pressed my Glock to the back of his head and quickly had him under control.

"FBI," I shouted to him. "Don't goddamn move!"

He stopped struggling.

"Let me go," he screamed.

"You are under arrest. For trespassing, assaulting a federal officer and probably a lot more as soon as I think of it."

Then I put a pair of handcuffs on him, and it was all over.

NINE

I held him down with my knee in his back and his hands cuffed behind him while I checked him for weapons. There were none. I put my own Glock back in my holster.

I called the front desk and told them to call the police to come deal with this guy.

Then I rolled him over and started to question him.

"Okay, tell me who you are and why you were in here trying to rob my room?"

"No, no, you've got it all wrong!"

"How do I have it wrong?"

"I'm not a thief."

"Then who are you."

He hesitated before answering.

"I don't want any more trouble," he finally said.

"Look, the police are going to be here any minute to deal with you. I'm a special agent with the FBI. You're already in about as much trouble as a person can be. Your only option is to tell me who you are, why you are in my room and why you're so bad at being a burglar or a sex pervert or whatever other reason you were in here. So start talking."

"I'm a reporter," he blurted out.

"A reporter?"

"Yes. I'm working on a story."

"And you simply mistook my room as the site of a press conference? That's kind of hard to believe."

"My wallet and press card are in my pocket. You can check."

I reached into his pocket and took out the wallet and what looked like a press ID card. It said his name was Brett Anson. There was a picture with it. I compared the picture with the face of the guy in front of me. A middle-aged guy, probably about forty, with sandy long hair. It was the same person.

"All right, you're a reporter. That still doesn't explain what you're doing here in my hotel room."

"I'm working on a story."

"What kind of story?"

"A story about you."

"Me?"

"Yes. You're big news, Agent Cassidy."

"Who are you doing this story for?"

"The *National Investigator*."

I threw his press card and wallet down next to him.

"Do you know about the *National Investigator*?"

"Yeah, I know all about it."

The *National Investigator* was one of those sensational, tabloid-like media outlets. Like the *National Enquirer* used to be. Only now it wasn't just gossipy magazines people were buying in a supermarket. The *National Investigator* had a show on TV and a hugely popular website, which drew big online traffic for its scoops about famous and newsworthy people. And they were notorious for the outrageous lengths they would go to for a juicy story that might go viral. It was sort of like *TMZ* on steroids.

"Why are you interested in me?"

"Are you kidding? The star FBI agent haunted by her sister's murder. Now trying to crack the case of a girl posing as her sister who was murdered. This is great stuff. People want to know about Nikki Cassidy. And that's what we do at the *National Investigator*. We tell people what they want to hear about celebrities."

"I'm not a celebrity."

"Sure you are."

"What do you mean?"

"You're the celebrity FBI agent. The hottest name in law enforcement right now."

"So what did you think you were going to find in my room here?"

"I was looking for anything about your progress on the Laurie Reddick case or the stuff with your sister. I needed an edge—something more than anyone else in the media had—to break a big story. That's how we operate at the *National Investigator*. By breaking the journalistic rules sometimes everyone else is afraid of doing."

"And you just figured out a way to get in my room? You were taking a big chance, weren't you? What if I was here?"

"I knew you were out of the room. I found out you were working with the state troopers looking at the crime site where the girl was found murdered. I have a source who told me that. I convinced one of the cleaning people to open the door for me, saying I'd forgotten my key. Once I was inside, I figured you'd be gone longer. That I had time to go through some of your stuff, looking for something that might contain possible evidence you've uncovered so far. But then I heard you at the door. I didn't know what else to do so I ran into the bathroom to hide. I figured my only chance was that you would go out again quickly without going into the bathroom. That way I could make my escape. Except it didn't work out like that."

"Not very smart for the hotshot reporter you claim to be."

"Hey, I didn't really do anything wrong here. You're fine, I'm fine. No harm, no foul. Let's move on and forget about this. Just let me go, okay?"

"You did nothing wrong? You've interfered with a federal murder case. You've assaulted a federal agent too. This kind of interference from you could scuttle my chances to solve this case—as well as my search to find out more about what happened to my sister Caitlin. You could have caused a lot of damage here."

"But I could have also come away with a big story," he replied with a smirk.

"Getting a big story is that important to you?"

"Sure. That's my job. I'm very good at my job, just like you're good at your job. There's nothing wrong with being ambitious to get ahead. Okay, I have ambition to become a media star. But a lot of people have ambition. Even you, Agent Cassidy. So now that we understand each other—take these handcuffs off. I'll leave quietly then, and I promise I'll never hide in your bathroom again."

I looked down at him on the floor. I'd put the handcuffs on him as tightly as I could, and he kept struggling with them as he talked to me. Looking more closely at him now, I realized he wasn't a bad-looking guy. And I could just tell he was the type who got by a lot of the time by charming people. Especially women.

There was a knock at the door.

I opened it and the police the front desk clerk had called were there. Two uniformed officers from the Columbus force. I introduced myself, showed them my FBI credentials and let them in.

Then I pointed to Brett Anson in the handcuffs and told them about how I'd found him hiding here when I walked into the room and what happened after that. I also told them how I'd learned afterward he was a reporter looking for a story—and not a burglar or sex fiend.

"Do you want to press charges against the guy?" one of the cops asked me when I was finished.

"We can book him on a couple of charges—at least unlawful entry and assault—as long as you're willing to sign a complaint against him," the other one said.

I looked over at Anson lying on the floor.

"C'mon, this doesn't have to go any further," he said. "You're not going to really put me in jail, are you?"

It wasn't a difficult decision for me to do what I did next.

It was easy.

I never had a moment of hesitation.

"Book the son of a bitch," I told the cops. "And I'll sign the complaint against him."

TEN

Huntsdale Police Chief Frank Earnshaw was as unhappy to see me when I walked into his office the next day as I was unhappy to be there.

I never liked coming back to my hometown of Huntsdale.

Too many bad memories.

But somehow I'd been spending a lot of time here with the cases I was working—my sister's long-ago murder as well as a series of other killings of young girls.

Now I was back talking again to my arch-nemesis over the past few months during my time here—Chief Earnshaw.

"Goddamn it, you're like a bad penny," Earnshaw said to me now. "No matter how many times I think I'm finally rid of you, you keep coming back here."

"Good to see you too, Chief."

"If you're here about the girl who was posing as your sister, I'll tell you exactly what I've told the media and everyone else who asks: The girl was obviously not your sister, she was someone claiming to be her for some unknown reason, she was not from Huntsdale, she was only in Huntsdale a very short time as far as we can determine and—most importantly of all—

when she turned up dead, it happened in another jurisdiction from here. Which means neither I or the Huntsdale Police Department have any reason to be involved in the matter. End of story. Are we done here, Cassidy?"

"It seems like you could have put a little more effort into this."

"For Christ's sakes, Cassidy, it wasn't even a crime what the girl did here. Pretending to be your dead sister. Bizarre, yes. But not really a crime. And the girl's murder didn't happen here. Like I said, this is about Huntsdale. We have crime cases of our own to solve here. Maybe not big crime cases to you, but they keep us pretty busy."

"Well, I'm going to go talk to Maureen Wilcox—the woman living in my old house—after I leave here," I told him.

"I'm sure you will."

"Any objection to that?"

"I object to you even being here."

I sighed. "Is all this anger coming from you because I'm a woman? Or because I'm the daughter of the man who used to be police chief here, a man that did a better job as chief than you could ever do? Or is this the same sparkling personality you have for everyone you meet on the job, Chief Earnshaw?"

He glowered at me. Okay, I was baiting him. But he deserved it. What the hell, it was him who started it by attacking me the minute I walked in his door.

"Do you want to know why I don't like you?" Earnshaw said. "Let me count the ways. You've been a pain in the ass ever since you arrived in this town to investigate your sister's murder. Big-footing us with your FBI badge. But the last time you were here you did something even worse. You cost the life of a good police officer. A good man. Edgar Daniels was my friend as well as a valued member of my force. And you're responsible for his death. You and the rest of the damned FBI."

I didn't have any answer for that. He was right. Because we

had screwed up, and that was why Edgar Daniels was dead. It wasn't my fault. Not directly. But a rogue FBI agent named Phil Girard had shot Daniels to death and tried to blame him for a series of murders Girard had committed himself.

I'd walked in past the empty desk where Daniels once sat when I came in here. The desk had previously been occupied by Billy Weller, another Huntsdale police officer and the man I was falling in love with. Maybe Earnshaw was right to want me to get the hell out of Huntsdale. Maybe I was bad news for him and for the town.

"Edgar Daniels had a family, you know," he said now. "No wife or kids, but a brother and a sister. A mother who is still alive too. I had to tell all of them about everything that happened and how he died and how stupid it all was. All because you thought he was some kind of killer instead of being the fine police officer and fine man that he was. So pardon me if I don't think you're the heroic law enforcement officer you make yourself out to be in the media and everywhere else."

Earnshaw didn't say it out loud, but I was sure that the other thing he had against me and the FBI—besides the death of Daniels—is that we believed at one point that he might be part of the murder conspiracy. So we kept him out of our investigation and instead targeted him as a potential suspect. That was a tough one for me to make up for with this guy.

"Okay, it's been fun," I said, standing up from the chair where I'd been sitting in front of his desk.

"Just be careful what you do in Huntsdale."

"What does that mean?"

"Just what it sounds like. If I hear you've been harassing anyone here, I'll arrest you for it. FBI or no FBI. This is still my town. Remember that."

It was a bluff, of course. He wasn't going to arrest me for anything. I knew that, and I'm sure he knew it too. But I guess it made him feel better, more macho or something, to pretend he had a lot of authority in his job.

"I was hoping you'd be a lot more cooperative," I said. "I was hoping you'd want to get the answers about Laurie Reddick as much as I did. But I guess not."

"All I want is for you to get out of this town as soon as possible."

"Chief Earnshaw, in all the time I've known you, that's the one thing you and I agree on."

When I got back to my car to drive over to see Maureen Wilcox, my phone rang. It was Alex. She was still in Groveton.

"They just got back to me with the sketch they put together after talking to Shirley Hunsaker of the mystery woman in the mall. I'm sending it to you."

"Great!"

"Prepare yourself."

"What do you mean?"

"You'll see."

A few seconds later the message from Alex with the drawing arrived on my phone. The sketch of what was supposed to be the woman at the mall who probably paid Laurie Reddick to pose as my sister and then maybe—very likely—was the one who killed her. I looked at the sketch of the face for a long time. It was eerie. Because she did look like me. Just like Shirley Hunsaker had said.

"It was like she could have been your sister," Shirley had told us.

And that's just what the woman in the sketch looked like.

ELEVEN

I had only come back to visit the house in Huntsdale where I grew up with my family twice since the time my mother sold it and moved away to another town.

The first time was with Billy Weller when I showed it to him, and we stood together on the front porch. The same front porch where I used to sit with my father a long time ago, listening to his police stories and playing detective games with him. I left that day with Billy very quickly because the memories were too powerful.

The second time was more recently. Just a few weeks ago. I stood on the front porch again that time, and the woman living in the house came out to talk with me. Maureen Wilcox. She was the one who had called after my last visit to tell me about the strange girl who showed up at her door claiming to be my sister Caitlin.

But I'd never been inside the house since I was young.

I had no idea what my reaction would be to that.

And I wasn't sure I wanted to find out.

I had no choice. I rang the bell, and Maureen Wilcox

answered. I hadn't called ahead to let her know I was coming. But I suppose she expected me to show up again after telling me the story about the strange girl claiming to be Caitlin at the house. Wilcox invited me in. I hesitated on the porch for a second or two, then walked through the door.

At first, I felt a sense of relief. Because it didn't seem like my old house at all. It was someone else's house now and everything looked and felt different.

"You probably don't even recognize the place," Wilcox was saying to me as she led me through the living room to a dining room table. "We've made a lot of changes, inside and out."

"How long have you lived here?"

"Let's see... I guess it's twelve years now."

"And your family?"

"My husband is an accountant. We have three children—two boys, eleven and twelve, and an eight-year-old girl. I used to work too; I was a nurse at Huntsdale Hospital. But taking care of the house and raising three kids is a full-time job in itself, I soon found that out."

I smiled and nodded. I was making small talk with this woman because I always found it was the best way to begin an interview with a friendly witness, helping to get them to relax and open up more to me. But I was also doing it to avoid dealing with the reality of being in this house and the questions about why the girl claiming to be my sister had shown up here after all these years.

"Do you want to see the rest of the house?"

"No, that's fine."

"C'mon, you must be curious. You grew up here, right? So let me give you the tour. That's gotta bring back some memories for you."

It sure did. And that's when the house stopped being the one where Maureen Wilcox and her family now lived, and it was suddenly the Cassidy family house all over again. As we walked through the rooms of my old house, I could see my mother in the kitchen cooking us dinner, and my father watching TV and smoking a pipe after coming home from work at the Huntsdale Police Station.

But the worst part was our bedrooms. The bedrooms that once belonged to me and Caitlin. We had separate bedrooms, side by side on the second floor of the house. Sometimes we ran back and forth between the two, talking and giggling to each other. Standing in my old bedroom—even though it was decorated completely differently now—brought back a flood of conflicting emotions.

Then, when I went into Caitlin's old bedroom, I felt something else.

An overwhelming sense of sadness and grief.

All the memories of how I felt that long-ago summer after Caitlin disappeared at the carnival and was later found murdered flooded through me.

Finally, I was able to convince Mrs. Wilcox to go back to the dining room to talk about the girl—Laurie Reddick—who had come to her door.

"Well, I was in the house, and I heard the doorbell ring. I opened the door and saw this young girl standing there. I figured she was selling magazine subscriptions or raising money for charity or something, like high-school kids do sometimes. She looked very ordinary, not threatening or anything like that. But then I saw she was crying."

"Crying?"

"Yes. Not obvious tears. Not at first. But her eyes were wet, and she looked like she was going through some sort of emotional crisis. I asked her what she wanted, and that's when she said she was Caitlin Cassidy and she used to live in this house."

"Did you recognize the name?"

"Of course I did. You were in the news the last time you visited. After you came here that last time, I heard all about you in the newspapers and on TV. About you and your sister. So I knew the name. But it made no sense."

"What exactly did the girl say to you?"

"I can't remember all of it. But it was something like: 'My name is Caitlin Cassidy. I used to live in this house. I want to come home again. Please let me in.' Well, at that point, I got a bit scared that she was a crazy, unbalanced person who was going to force her way into my house. I started to shut the door on her, and she tried to stop me. She kept yelling about how she was Caitlin Cassidy, and she was alive and back in Huntsdale again."

"What happened then?"

"I realized she could not be your sister Caitlin, even if Caitlin was alive. This girl was about the same age as your sister was when she died fifteen years ago. It would have been like time stood still for her. I told her that, and she started crying. Really crying now. Then she ran away. I went outside afterward and found the note she left on the front porch. And that's pretty much all there is to it. The whole thing probably only lasted for a few minutes."

I had seen the note, of course. And everything else she'd said had been pretty much what I already knew. I was hoping for more.

"Is there anything else at all you remember that the girl said to you that day on the porch?" I asked her.

"Let me see. I don't think so. Oh, wait, she did say something else, as I remember. When I was trying to close the door on her and she was crying, she said: 'Tell Nik I miss her.'"

I sat there stunned.

"Tell Nik I miss her," I repeated.

"That's right. I assumed she was talking about you. Your name is Nikki."

Everyone had always called me Nikki when I was growing up here, no one else called me Nik.

Except my sister did.

Caitlin always called me Nik, instead of Nikki.

She was the only one.

Until the girl at the door.

TWELVE

"What in the hell did you do in Columbus?" Dave Blanton said angrily to me over the phone. "You attacked a man in your hotel room?"

"I didn't attack anyone."

"A reporter named Brett Anson says you did."

"I was defending myself."

"Against a member of the media?"

"I found him hiding in my room."

"Was he a danger to you?"

"I thought so at the time."

"Is that why you used excessive force against the guy?"

"I didn't use excessive force, Chief. I subdued him. I controlled the situation. I did what I had to do. And I used the minimum amount of force necessary to do it. No more, no less. I overpowered him, got him on the floor, and handcuffed him until police arrived."

"He claims you held a gun to his head. Did you?"

"Briefly."

"Jeez, that doesn't sound like minimum force."

"Well, it wasn't maximum force either."

"What might have qualified as maximum force in your judgement?"

"I pull the trigger and blow the son of a bitch's head off. This guy was in my room. I found him hiding in my bathroom. And then he came running out toward me. I had no idea he was a reporter. I thought he might be the killer out to get me. I defended myself in that situation. I did what I had to do."

"And you neglected to mention any of this—including dealing with the local police on the matter—to me or anyone else in the bureau?"

"That was a mistake. I'm sorry. I got so caught up in following some leads on Laurie Reddick that I never got around to it. I should have informed you."

Which brought up another interesting question, now that I thought about it.

"How did you find out?" I asked Blanton.

"I read about it, the same way as the rest of the world. That's how I found out what my agent had done. Check out the *National Investigator* website."

I clicked on my laptop and found the site. It didn't take long to see what Blanton was talking about. I was their lead story. The headline said:

STAR WOMAN FBI AGENT ATTACKS OUR REPORTER

An out-of-control female FBI agent went ballistic and attacked National Investigator *reporter Brett Anson while he was covering a story in Columbus.*

Anson had gone to the hotel room of FBI agent Nikki Cassidy to attempt to interview her about the murder of a teenaged girl named Laurie Reddick that was being investigated there.

Instead of cooperating with the media like most law

enforcement officials routinely do, Cassidy assaulted the reporter.

She struck him physically, put him in handcuffs so tightly that his hands turned black and blue, and threatened him with a gun held to his head.

"This woman is out of control," Anson said afterward. "She's scary. Someone like that should not be carrying an FBI badge and a weapon."

I stopped reading at that point. I knew the rest of the post would be more of the same.

I saw that the article had conveniently left out the details of how this guy Anson wound up in my room—breaking in without my knowledge and then hiding in my bathroom when I walked in. I guess that would have messed up his story of being a victim of law enforcement brutality.

I told all that now to Blanton.

"And you identified yourself to him as an FBI agent?"

"I did."

There was a long silence on the other end of the line.

"You've put the bureau and you've put me in an awkward spot here, Agent Cassidy. Whether your actions were justified or not. It's still another black eye for law enforcement at a time when everyone is looking at us to find something wrong. Even worse, I had to find out about it by reading the *National Investigator*. By the way, you're being covered big-time on their TV show too. With all sorts of pictures and video from your previous cases and earlier controversies too. Somehow, you've managed to go viral all over again. But this time for the wrong reasons. I really should reassign you. Pull you out of there. Bring you back to Washington and put you behind a desk for the foreseeable future along with an official reprimand."

"I need to be here to work this case, Chief."

"There's other FBI agents we can use besides you."

"Not on this case."

Blanton knew I was right. Everything about the Laurie Reddick case revolved around me. She had gone to my old house. She was posing as my sister, and that presumably played a part in getting her killed afterward. And the note from the killer after the murder even brought up the roses from my sister's case. I was at the center of it all, whether Blanton liked that or not.

"Okay, you're still on the case. But for God's sakes, try and act more responsibly out there. Be careful what you do and what you say with any interaction you have with the media from now on."

"I promise not to handcuff or beat up or pull a gun on any member of the media from now on unless I have a good reason."

"Jesus, Agent Cassidy..."

"Don't worry, I'll be on my best behavior."

I got calls, emails and texts from a lot of other people about the *National Investigator* article. I didn't return most of them. But there was a message from one name I couldn't ignore. Jeffrey Galvin.

I'm just checking to make sure you're okay, Galvin texted. *I want you to know that Doris and I don't believe a word of the terrible things that article said about you. You're one of the good ones, Nikki. Don't ever forget that.*

Jeffrey Galvin and his wife reached out regularly like this to me. They had ever since their daughter Sara—a twenty-two-year-old college student—had been gunned down on the street in Los Angeles during a senseless murder. I guess it was some kind of therapy for them to do that. And they always asked me the same question.

Is there anything new about Sara's murder? he asked now. *Anything at all?*

Jeffrey Galvin was a big-time lawyer in Los Angeles. From what I understood, a very successful lawyer who almost always accomplished anything he set out to do in a case. Except for this one. He'd never been able to get the answers he was looking for about the death of his daughter by us catching the killer. I felt bad all over again now that I had never been able to provide that kind of closure for Jeffrey and Doris Galvin.

I wrote back to Galvin. *No. The trail is still cold. I wish I could tell you something better you want to hear. But we will catch him and make him pay for what he did to your daughter.*

You promised us that would happen. That the monster who murdered our Sara would be brought to justice, Galvin replied.

Yes, I'd made that promise to them.

A promise I hadn't been able to keep.

And a promise that had haunted me since then, just like my sister's death.

"You seem to always catch the killer," Bonnie Tatarko had said to me after we met.

"Not always," I told her. "Sometimes they still get away, no matter what you do."

But I pushed all those memories aside to concentrate on the job ahead of me.

I couldn't think about Sara Galvin.

Not right now.

Because I had another priority.

Laurie Reddick.

THIRTEEN

If Laurie Reddick had suddenly shown up at the doorstep of my old house like that, it meant she must have been in other places in Huntsdale too. I mean she couldn't have simply dropped down from the sky or anything. There must be a trail she left behind. All I had to do was find it.

There were only a few motels or hotels in the Huntsdale area. So I checked them first. No sighting of anyone who looked like Laurie Reddick. I wasn't surprised. She was sixteen years old, and a girl that age checking into a hotel somewhere on her own would likely set off alarm bells and come to light before this.

Unless she was with someone. Someone like the woman from the mall who seemed to be behind all this. But I had no idea if the woman had been still with her by the time Laurie got to Huntsdale.

I checked some of the fast-food restaurants, local stores and asked around at the city park in the middle of town—she might have slept there—to see if anyone remembered her. I showed Laurie Reddick's picture to plenty of people at all of these places. But it turned up nothing at all.

Maybe she really had just shown up out of nowhere at my old house and there was no trail at all of her coming or going.

Except I knew there was.

There had to be a trail.

It started in Groveton on the other side of Ohio with the woman she met in the mall. Shortly after that, she disappeared from her home and wasn't seen in Groveton again. After that, she came to the door of my old house in Huntsdale. And finally, the end of her brief life for Laurie Reddick happened at that restroom on the Ohio Turnpike outside Columbus.

So why hadn't anyone seen her? Hell, they probably did. But there was nothing memorable about her as a sixteen-year-old girl—nothing to set her apart from every other teenaged girl her age—until she wound up dead.

Meanwhile, I had Alex—who was driving now from Groveton to Huntsdale to meet up with me again—trying to follow Laurie's trail across the state. Driving along Route 70 from Groveton to Columbus, then Route 33 when she went from Columbus into Huntsdale. If Laurie had made the trip by car with someone else, or even if she'd hitchhiked or taken a bus, this would have been the way she most likely went.

As for me, once I'd failed on finding any sightings of her from people and places in Huntsdale, I turned to a standby of law enforcement investigation these days: social media.

I found accounts for what appeared to be the right Laurie Reddick on both Twitter and Instagram.

The last post on Instagram was from a few months ago and had been a picture—a selfie—taken in her backyard with four other children: identified as her three brothers and a sister. Looking at them in the photo, I wondered if Dave Blanton had heeded Alex's warning and done anything to try to protect them in that dysfunctional family environment.

I should probably check. But, sad as the Reddick family situation was, it was not my priority right now. My priority was finding out who killed Laurie Reddick and why and what the hell it had to do with my long-dead sister. Unfortunately, I hadn't made much progress on that front.

I decided to take a more proactive approach on social media.

I went onto my own Twitter account. I had a lot of followers these days—thousands of them—because of all the notoriety I'd achieved in the media with my recent cases. So I posted that I was looking for information about Laurie Reddick and asked anyone who might have seen her or knew anything about her to contact me online.

I figured I'd get the usual amount of weirdos.

But who knows, I might get lucky.

I was so desperate for answers I even turned to Chief Earnshaw for help. I phoned him to ask if he could have his officers show pictures around town of her—just like I did—to see if they could come up with any leads.

He agreed to do it, but reluctantly.

"I'm not here to do your job for you, Cassidy," he said.

"It's your job too."

"Like I told you before," Earnshaw said with a deep sigh, "there was no crime committed here in Huntsdale. All the girl did was knock on a door and say some strange stuff. Whatever happened after that was in someone else's jurisdiction. Not here in Huntsdale."

"You're a real inspiration as a law enforcement officer, Chief."

"I don't give a damn what you think of me."

"I'm just glad my father can't see how someone was now in the job he loved so much and was so good at."

"Oh, right... your father, the great police chief of Huntsdale past."

"Hey, he was a better police chief than you'll ever be."

"I'm not so sure about that."

"What do you mean?'

"From what I've been told, maybe he wasn't so good at all."

"Who told you that?"

"I hear things, Cassidy."

"What kind of things?"

"Oh, things he did—and things he neglected to do—when he was in this office. Maybe he wasn't such a great police chief at all. Goodbye, Agent Cassidy. Good luck on your case."

He hung up before I could say anything else.

"I mean you're just making friends and spreading good vibes wherever you go," Alex said to me when she arrived in Huntsdale after her drive from Groveton and I told her about my latest encounter with Earnshaw.

"Well, he started it, not me."

"My God, sometimes when I listen to you talk like that, I feel like my four-year-old has more mental maturity than you."

"What about the stuff he was saying about my father?"

"He was probably only trying to get you riled up. And he sure succeeded."

"I guess so."

Alex said she had come up empty on her questions during the trip to Huntsdale. I told her all the details about my visit to the crime scene and my conversation with Maureen Wilcox, including the stuff about the girl at the door calling me "Nik" instead of "Nikki."

"She must have heard it from someone," Alex said.

"But who? The only other people who knew she called me that were my mother and father. I never told anyone else about it. My father is dead, and my mother sure didn't tell her."

"Someone did, that's the only possible explanation."

"I guess."

"What do you think is going on here anyway? Any speculation?"

"Only that someone seems obsessed with me. The woman who looked like me. The girl sent to my old home. The line about roses in the note from the killer of Laurie Reddick—just like the roses connection for my dead sister. But why? Why would someone go to all these lengths to get at me?"

"Maybe someone who has a grudge against you."

"Like who?"

"Uh, from what I've seen, the list of people who could be mad at you, blame you for their troubles whatever they are, might be a pretty long one. You've crossed swords with a lot of people."

"Starting with Chief Earnshaw," I said.

"Do you really think Earnshaw could have something to do with it?"

"No, I guess not. I mean I suspected him last time we were here, and I was wrong about that."

"Then who?"

My phone rang. I looked down at the screen and saw the call was coming from Lt. Tatarko in Columbus. Maybe there'd been a break in her investigation. I answered the phone.

"There's been another murder here," Tatarko said.

"A murder connected to Laurie Reddick?"

"Same kind of place. A rest stop on the turnpike."

"And the victim is...?"

"Another teenaged girl."

FOURTEEN

The new victim was still unidentified.

All anyone knew about her was she was a teenaged girl—apparently about the same age as Laurie Reddick—and she'd been strangled in the same way in another turnpike rest stop about twenty-five miles north of the first one.

"This time the strangulation was done quickly, the medical examiner says," Tatarko told me when I got back to Columbus. "No evidence of prolonging it by stopping and then starting again, cutting her breath off, like with the Reddick girl. No staging of the body of any kind this time either. The girl was found lying on the floor inside one of the stalls. Presumably, that's where she was killed."

"And no one saw anything?" I asked.

"Nothing."

"Isn't that unusual? Wouldn't there normally be traffic in and out of the women's restroom?"

"They estimate the time of death during the early-morning hours. Same as Laurie Reddick. Not a lot of people use the restroom in the middle of the night. At least that's what we figure. The killer must have planned it that way."

"Still taking a big chance someone might walk in on them, even at that time."

"Maybe that was part of the thrill of it for whoever did this."

There wasn't much to see there at the crime scene. Yellow tape blocked the door, and we had to step through it to get inside. There were five stalls there. Tatarko pointed to the stall where the body was found. The only difference from the Laurie Reddick murder was that this time the body of the girl was left inside a bathroom stall, not prominently displayed on a sink as Laurie's body had been. Maybe the killer heard someone coming and needed to get out of there in a hurry.

"Who found the body?"

"A cleaning woman. She came in, screamed and ran off to tell everyone. But she didn't see anyone going in or out of this place. Believe me, the local cops and us questioned her thoroughly about it. No security video or anything that shows us any more. Just like at the other rest stop."

Tatarko grimaced and shook her head. Obviously, she was as frustrated by this case as I was.

"I guess we'll have to stake out every rest stop bathroom on this turnpike and hope the killer comes back to try for a third time. But that's not likely. Whoever is doing this is smart. They'll come up with something different next time," she said.

"Next time?"

"This killer has already murdered two teenaged girls. He's going to keep doing this until we stop him. Don't you agree, Cassidy?"

"Yeah, but I wasn't sure you thought that, too."

"Hey, I'm just a local state trooper—not a hotshot FBI agent from Washington like you—but even I can figure that out."

We drove next to the coroner's office where the dead girl's body was. I wasn't sure what I expected to find. But I wanted to see her.

"No handbag, no wallet, no ID of any kind on her," Tatarko said. "Her identity remains a mystery. We're checking missing girl reports to see if any likely candidates turn up there. Trying dental records and fingerprints too, although the fingerprint thing seems unlikely for anyone her age to have them on record. Right now, she's simply a Jane Doe."

The official police name for a female victim with no identity.

"What does she look like?"

"She looks like a teenaged girl." Tatarko shrugged.

"Does she look anything at all like me?"

I had to ask the question, as unlikely as it seemed.

"Well, she has red hair, and you don't. Different color eyes. And she was a teenager. So I'd say that's a 'hard no' to your question."

When we got to the coroner's office, we were met by the medical examiner who had carried out the autopsy on her. He was young, probably not even my age. Decent-looking, slim with an earring on one of his ears. I thought how different he was from the medical examiner I knew best, Michael Franze, back in Huntsdale. Or as everyone called him back in Huntsdale, Big Mickey.

This ME said his name was Ken Mullane. I wondered how a young guy like Mullane wound up in a job like this. Who grows up wanting to be a coroner as their life's work? I didn't ask him that question though. What the hell, not many young girls grow up wanting to be an FBI agent chasing after serial killers either.

He took us to the body.

"By the way," Mullane said to Tatarko. "No one has made arrangements to claim the body of the other girl yet. It's still here."

"Haven't Laurie Reddick's parents talked with you about bringing the body back to Groveton?" I asked.

"Not yet. We've contacted them numerous times. But we haven't heard back yet. Not sure about what they're doing."

I was pretty sure I knew what Carl and Helen Reddick were doing. Sitting in their house drinking instead of dealing with their dead daughter. There's a lot of bad people in this world, but not all of them are criminals that you can put in jail. I thought again about the other four kids living in that house, and decided Alex was right. We had to do something to save them before they wound up like Laurie.

There wasn't much to see when Mullane showed us the dead girl's body lying on a gurney.

Like Tatarko had said, she had red hair. There were some freckles on her face. Average size for her age—around five foot five and weighing a hundred and ten pounds, according to the ME's report.

Nothing unusual at all there.

Mullane pointed to ligature marks around her neck and explained that they appeared to be from a rope noose, the same as with the Reddick girl.

He said there was no sign of any other injuries, and the cause of death was apparent strangulation.

No surprises there either.

"There is one thing we noticed though," Mullane said. "Almost missed it at first because she was wearing a bracelet when the body was brought in here. But when the bracelet was removed, we noticed a mark on her wrist. A tattoo of some sort. Maybe it could help you to identify her."

He picked up the dead girl's wrist now and showed us the mark on it that he was talking about.

"It's a rose," Mullane said. "This girl had a tattoo of a rose."

FIFTEEN

There were forty-eight tattoo shops in the Greater Columbus area.

I had no idea tattoos were that popular. Even though I had noticed a lot of people—women especially—sporting them on their arms, chest, neck and God knows where else under their clothes.

Me, I've never gotten a tattoo. Never even considered getting one. I got freaked out just thinking about someone putting a needle into me in a doctor's office. But it certainly seemed to be a popular trend these days. Tattoos were every-where now. Which made it harder to track down whoever might have given the rose tattoo to the girl in the morgue.

I couldn't realistically check out all forty-eight of the tattoo places in Columbus, but I felt like I'd visited most of them before I was done. Some of them were in grubby parts of town; some in classy-looking buildings or houses; and I even found one in a shopping mall between a Starbucks and a Banana Republic.

Of course, Jane Doe—God, I hated having to refer to the girl that way—might have gotten her tattoo somewhere else long before she came to Columbus. But Ken Mullane in the coroner's office seemed to think from examining it that the tattoo was recent. Which made sense to me.

No reason a sixteen-year-old girl would coincidentally have a tattoo of a rose. It made more sense that someone—presumably the same woman seen talking to Laurie Reddick—had convinced her to get the rose tattoo because of me and my sister. But then the girl was killed for some still unknown reason at the turnpike rest stop.

I found out a lot about the tattoo business while I made the rounds of all these shops. I learned that your skin is pierced fifty to three thousand times per minute by a tattoo artist, which sounded pretty horrible—even though I was assured it wasn't. I learned that more women than men have tattoos. I learned that virtually all of the tattoo artists had multiple tattoos themselves. I learned that angels and hearts were the most popular motifs. I learned that the tattoo world almost collapsed when the stores were shut during the height of Covid, but the demand had surged again after that.

Yep, I learned a lot about tattoos at all these places.

What I did not learn for a long time during my tour of these places was where my Jane Doe got her tattoo.

No one specifically remembered working on the girl, even though I described her as best I could from the body I saw at the morgue.

"What's this all about?" one female tattoo artist asked me after I'd shown her my FBI credentials and asked her about the girl. The woman was about thirty, and very pretty with long black hair. She was wearing a short-sleeved shirt that showed tattoos on both of her arms. A lot of tattoos. I guess that was one of the tricks of the trade. If you give people tattoos for a living, you advertise your own too.

"The girl was murdered," I said.

"How did it happen?"

I told her.

"We're thinking that whoever might have convinced her to get the tattoo might also be the same person who murdered her. You don't remember any young girl who fit my description that was in here recently?"

The woman shook her head no.

"No, but then I usually don't spend too much time looking at faces. I'm focused on the part of the body where they're getting the tattoo."

"Do you get many young girls her age in here?"

"Tons."

"What about the rose tattoo. Is that unusual?"

"A lot of people ask for a rose. Sorry, but there's nothing unique about that."

I got the same reaction at plenty of other places. Nothing at all. But that's the way I work on a case. I keep plugging away, asking questions of everyone I can in the hopes of getting a lead.

And that's what finally happened here.

After I'd talked to what I felt like was every tattoo artist in Columbus, even though I knew I hadn't.

I found someone who remembered the girl.

"It was about a week ago," the owner of the place said. His name was Wayne Conte, and he was around fifty with tattoos all over his arms like the others I'd met. But otherwise he looked like a guy who could have been a salesman in a clothing store or a lawyer or anyone else you ran into. He was friendly and cooperative too, which I always liked.

"The girl was in here with a woman," Conte said to me. "The woman said she wanted a rose tattoo for the girl. She was very specific about that. The girl didn't say anything. I had a feeling she might be a little afraid about the needle. But I assured her everything was going to be fine, and we did it."

"Can you describe the woman?"

"Decent-looking, about forty I guess, she was dressed in a fancy-looking outfit. I got the feeling she had money. Anyway, she paid me in cash after the tattoo was done on the girl. That's about it."

I asked him more questions.

"Did the woman look like me?"

"Like you?'

"Yes, was there any resemblance?"

"Why would she look like you?"

"No reason." I sighed.

So was this the same woman who had looked like me at the Groveton mall? Or was there a second woman in the picture somehow? Or a woman who could change her appearance so that people had trouble identifying her from one time to another?

"Do you have any records about it that I could look at?" I asked him.

"Of course. We require every client to sign an agreement before the tattoo is done saying they chose to have this process done. My lawyer makes me do it. Standard business procedure."

"This girl signed her name to the agreement?" I said excitedly.

This might finally identify her for me.

"Can I see that document?" I asked, hoping against hope that he kept it filed here somewhere.

"Sure. Let me take a look."

A few minutes later, he came back and handed me a piece of paper.

The top was standard boilerplate language about volunteering for the tattoo and waiving any potential legal claims against the artist or the store.

The signature was at the bottom.

I read it.

I read it again.

And then I stared at it in amazement for a long time.
"Do you recognize the name?" Conte asked.
I sure did.
The signature on the paper said:
"Caitlin Cassidy."

SIXTEEN

I wanted to talk to two people next—the cleaning woman at the turnpike restroom and the mother with her daughter—who had discovered the bodies of the two girls in the two different Ohio Turnpike bathrooms at separate times. Neither of them saw anyone else in those bathrooms, just the dead girls, they both said afterward. But maybe they had seen something else before or after they found the bodies that might help me identify the mystery woman.

The cleaning woman's name was Kathleen Ayers. She was middle-aged, probably between fifty and sixty, and I found her on the job at the turnpike rest stop. She told me she'd been doing this work for two years. She said her husband had died and her children were grown up and out of the house, so she was looking for something to do. She said it really wasn't a bad job, no matter what people thought.

"Tell me exactly what happened that night?" I asked her.

"Oh, Lord, how terrible that was! I was just doing my job. I clean a lot of areas at this place, but obviously the bathrooms are paramount. We do it several times a day. But the easiest time is in the middle of the night like this was, since there isn't much traffic in and out of the bathroom at that time.

"Anyway, I brought my stuff in and started cleaning. At first, I didn't see anything unusual. But then I realized—or thought I did—that someone was in one of the stalls. I could see a shoe and a leg in the opening below the door. I kept cleaning, assuming the person would come out at some point. But no one did.

"Finally, I knocked on the door. There was no answer. I became concerned someone might be sick in there or something. So I pushed on the door. It wasn't locked, I opened it and that's when I saw that poor girl lying on the floor inside the stall."

"Did you see anyone else in the bathroom during the time you were there?" I asked her.

"No, it was completely empty."

"What about before?"

"Before what?"

"Before you went in. Anyone else outside the bathroom that you remember?"

"Not really."

"But presumably you did see other people walking around the places that were open at that hour in the rest stop."

"Oh, yes. There's always a few people there. Even at that hour. There's a Starbucks and a McDonald's that never close."

"Did anyone out there seem... unusual?"

"Unusual how?"

"I don't know... suspicious for some reason. Something about them seemed unusual. Do you remember anything at all like that?"

She shook her head. "No, nothing at all."

I took out the sketch of the mystery woman in the mall based on Shirley Hunsaker's description of her.

"Did you see anyone who looked like this?"

She stared at the picture.

Then back at me.

"She looks like you," Kathleen Ayers said.

"I know."

"But you weren't at the rest stop that night, were you?"

"No, but this woman who looks like me might have been. Does it ring any bells at all?"

"Sorry, but I never saw anyone who looks like this drawing until I met you."

The other woman, the one who found Laurie Reddick sprawled on the sink, was named Grace Hazlett.

She wasn't in the area anymore. She'd been driving with her daughter on the turnpike headed back to where they lived in Pittsburgh. But—after being interviewed by police from the local town nearest to the turnpike rest stop—she left a contact number with authorities investigating the case, and that's how I reached her on the phone. She agreed to talk with me. But, like the cleaning woman, she insisted she had already told everything she knew to the local police.

"Normally I would never have been out on the road—stopping at a turnpike rest stop—at that hour of the night. It was like three a.m., but my daughter Erica and I had been visiting my sister in Toledo, and we left for home late that night. I thought about us stopping off at a motel, but we were only a few hours away from getting back to Pittsburgh. So, I decided to drive on through. I'm sure you understand how much I wish now I would have stopped at a motel so Erica and I wouldn't have had to go through this ordeal."

I didn't really care about Grace Hazlett or her daughter's backstory or why they were there. I just wanted to know what they remembered from that rest stop. But I let her keep talking.

"We got some coffee there, and doughnuts too. We talked

about how nice a time we'd had in Toledo and about how much further we had to drive to Pittsburgh. Stuff like that. Then, before we left, we walked to the women's restroom. When we went inside, that's... that's when we saw her. The girl lying on top of the sink. At first, I thought she was drunk or asleep, but then I realized she was dead. My daughter—she's only fifteen—was hysterical. I was really shaken up too, of course, but I ran out and found someone to call the police. We waited for the police to arrive, we told them everything we knew—which wasn't much—and that's really all there is I can tell you."

I suppose that's what I expected from her. But I was disappointed. I always go back and talk to eyewitnesses in a case—even if it seems futile—to see if anything was missed. Sometimes it works. But now going back to Kathleen Ayers and Grace Hazlett just seemed like a waste of time.

I asked her if she'd seen anyone else outside the restroom that she could remember, specifically a woman.

I asked her if there was anyone else in the restroom she saw leaving before she and her daughter entered.

I asked her if she had seen anyone suspicious in the rest stop at all while they were having their coffee and doughnuts.

She said no to everything.

I asked her if she could put her daughter on the phone. I thought maybe the daughter might have remembered something the mother missed. But she said she didn't want to do that.

"Erica has been really traumatized by what she saw in that restroom," she said, apologizing for not letting me talk to her daughter. "She has nightmares about it, she says she can't get that sight out of her mind. That dead girl in the bathroom was just about the same age as my daughter, you know. I think she somehow sees herself in that girl's place, and it's left her terrified. I'm going to be taking her for some kind of counseling to deal with all this. She's my little girl, and I want to help her get through this emotional turmoil she's experienced since it all happened. I hope you understand. I want to cooperate with you. But I don't want Erica to talk about it right now. I don't want her to have to relive that all over again."

"Of course," I said.

Hell, I'd probably react the same way if I was a mother. She was protecting her child. It was the only thing she could think of to do in this situation. I thought again about the Reddick family back in Groveton, and how they didn't seem to care much at all about their daughter. Hopefully, there were more parents in the world like Grace Hazlett than Carl and Helen Reddick.

I walked out of Tatarko's office, where I'd been using the phone at the state police headquarters, and I headed for the front door to leave.

That's when I saw him.

And I forget all about Grace Hazlett and Kathleen Ayers.

It was Brett Anson, the reporter from the *National Investigator*.

"Hi, remember me?" he said.

SEVENTEEN

"Yeah, I remember you," I said. "You're the asshole I found hiding in my bathroom."

"I'm sorry about that."

"What in the hell were you doing there?"

"Just doing my job."

"Shouldn't you be hiding in the bathroom here and then jump out at me like you normally do?"

He smiled.

"I guess I deserved that."

"You deserve a lot more than that. You caused me a lot of problems with that story you posted. I know what happened in that hotel room, and so do you. But it bears no resemblance to the story that sleazy website of yours ran about it. Now get out of my way and go back to doing your job, whatever that is."

I started to walk away from him.

"Wait, I want to talk to you about that article."

"Why? So you can accuse me of police brutality again? Tell everyone more about how I beat you up and traumatized you with a gun. Maybe I should have done everything you said I did. What's the difference? You'll just make up another story for your website again, this time making me look even worse. Adding a bit more pizzazz to my out-of-control FBI agent image."

He smiled again. It was actually a nice smile. I realized now he wasn't a bad-looking guy either. Sandy curly hair; tall, probably over six foot; but he had a trim body. I didn't notice any of this when I was pinning the guy down and handcuffing him. If I'd met him under some other circumstances, I might have been interested in having more of a conversation with him. But it wasn't here.

"I didn't want to do that article," he said now. "I know what happened in that room. I told my bosses at the *Investigator* the truth about that. But they wanted a sensational story. They thought it would bring us a lot of web traffic. And it did. But that wasn't my idea. I complained to my bosses and asked them not to do it. But no one cared. They wouldn't listen to me. They went ahead and posted that story on the *National Investigator* site without getting my approval."

"And you just let that happen?"

"I had to."

"Why?"

"Look, I was in trouble because I got arrested. I could have lost my job over that. So, in the end, I went along with whatever they decided to do. Which was the story that you had attacked me for no reason in your hotel room when I simply went there to ask you for a comment."

"So you compromised your integrity to hold onto your job, huh? That's pretty pathetic."

"I need my job," Anson said.

"You can't find some other kind of work than the *National Investigator*? More respectable work?"

"I like my job. I know that the *National Investigator* does some things that I'm not proud of. But it's a stepping stone for me in journalism. If I make a name for myself here, I can move up the media ladder. To a big newspaper or a TV station or a cable news network."

"It's all about ambition," I said. "Your ambition."

"There's nothing wrong with ambition. You're ambitious, too. I've read all the publicity you get for chasing after criminals in big cases. The Singles Slayer a few years ago and a bunch of other big cases like that; your sister and father's killer; the rogue FBI agent who was secretly a serial killer. You're a media star, Cassidy. You don't get that without enjoying the limelight yourself. Okay, this thing with me was not good publicity for you. But it was still publicity that put you out there in the public eye. As someone once said, any publicity is good publicity."

"I think we're done here," I said, and started to walk away again.

"What's going on with the cases of Laurie Reddick and the Jane Doe in the morgue?" he called out after me. "Have you made any progress on either of those murders?"

I whirled around.

"You've got to be kidding, right?"

"What?"

"Do you really expect me to tell you about my active cases?"

"That's part of your job, to cooperate with the media."

"The legitimate media, yes. But not you."

"C'mon, I'm not a bad guy. I said I was sorry. I need something—anything—from the star serial killer chaser, Nikki Cassidy. Give me a quote. Just one quote.'

"Okay, here's my quote," I told him. "No comment."

"No comment," he repeated.

"You want me to repeat it for you?"

Anson wasn't giving up though.

"How about you and me go somewhere for a drink?" he asked.

"Why would I want to have a drink with you?"

"Maybe it will relax you. Loosen you up a bit. So you don't

have to play the role of the tight-ass, the tough-as-nails FBI agent for a while. There must be a nicer side to you, Agent Cassidy."

"You'll never know," I said.

I started to walk away again, and this time I kept going.

"I'm following you," he called out after me.

"I can handcuff you and beat you up again too.'

"C'mon, you'd really do that? After all we've meant to each other. I mean we have a sort of relationship here now... you and me."

I kept walking.

"Where are you going next?" he asked.

"Back to Washington."

"Huh?"

"I'm done with this case. Laurie Reddick and Jane Doe are both going to be handled by local authorities going forward. Good luck to you with them. Me, I'm on my way back to D.C. right away.'

It was a lie, of course.

But it was the only way I could think of to keep this guy from following me around while I worked here.

"Will I see you again?" he asked.

"Not if I can help it."

I looked around at him one more time before I walked out the front door of the state trooper building.

He wasn't smiling anymore.

I just hoped he bought my story.

EIGHTEEN

I set up a whiteboard with everything we knew so far at the state trooper location in Columbus.

It's a technique I use when I'm on a big case. Especially a complex big case like this one. Three locations to investigate in Groveton, Huntsdale and Columbus. Law enforcement to deal with in each place. And, so far anyway, a ton of confusing facts that we needed to try and somehow sort out.

I wrote everything down on the whiteboard. About Laurie Reddick and her disappearance from Groveton. About the dead Jane Doe in the morgue. What we knew about each one. The woman in the mall. Laurie Reddick showing up at my family's old house in Huntsdale and claiming to be my dead sister Caitlin. The Jane Doe getting a rose tattoo on her wrist before she was murdered, like the roses in other cases I'd been involved with in the past—including my sister.

I stared at all this information on the board for a long time, hoping to find some clues or lead that I had missed. But I saw nothing. So I called a meeting in the hopes that someone else might do better than me.

Alex and Lt. Tatarko were there, of course. I set up a Zoom

call with Dave Blanton, my boss back in Washington; the local police chief in Groveton; and even my old pal Chief Frank Earnshaw in Huntsdale. Earnshaw wasn't too happy about participating in any meeting I called—he still insisted the case had virtually nothing to do with him or Huntsdale—but he showed up on the Zoom call anyway.

Tatarko's superior, the head of the state trooper barracks in Columbus, was here, too. His name was Dale Kovach and he seemed friendly and cooperative and even happy to have the FBI involved in trying to solve the cases.

I pointed to the drawing of the mystery woman from the mall that I had posted on the whiteboard.

"Let's start with the elephant in the room," I said. "We're looking for a woman—very likely a murderer—who looks like me. But obviously she is not me. Any ideas?"

"It's a coincidence," Tatarko said. "People look like other people sometimes. Maybe that's all there is to it. It's possible, right?'

"Possible, but unlikely," I said.

"The woman could be trying to look like you deliberately," Alex said. "To get your attention. The same as with the rose reference in the note we got and the rose tattoo on the second victim. That makes the most sense."

"How do you make someone look like someone else?" Blanton asked.

"Could it be someone you're related to, Agent Cassidy?" Dale Kovach, the state police chief, wanted to know. "Someone from your family. I know you don't want to hear this, but it does seem like it could be someone you're related to, like a twin sister or—"

"I only had one sister," I snapped. "And she's dead!"

But I realized it was a reasonable question. Especially given all the references to Caitlin from the dead girl at my old house and the signature of Caitlin Cassidy the other used when she got her tattoo.

"The facts are very clear," I said. "My sister died fifteen years ago after being abducted from a carnival and then murdered. Roses were left on her body as a sign from the killer. She is buried in Huntsdale. Whoever is doing these new murders is using the memory of my sister to taunt me for some reason. These are clearly thrill murders that are being carried out. Just like my sister died from a thrill killer. This new killer could very well be this woman we have a drawing of. I understand all of that. What I don't understand is how she looks so much like me."

"Maybe it is you," Earnshaw said now.

"What?"

"Yeah, you're so hungry for publicity you create some phony female character who looks like you and act like they're involved in these murders. All to get more attention for yourself in the media. You love that media attention, Cassidy. I know that, you know that, everyone knows that."

I used all my willpower to not lash back at Earnshaw in a fit of anger. Instead, I just ignored him and tried to continue on with the meeting.

"Does anyone have any reasonable suggestion that can contribute to the investigation?" I asked.

Dale Kovach had one.

"Let's assume that someone is trying to look like Cassidy," he said. "How would they accomplish that? There are two obvious ways. Someone with theatrical experience who knows how to use makeup or other techniques to change their appearance. Or else plastic surgery. We need to start checking out theater groups and plastic surgeons to see if anyone knows about a woman doing something like this."

"Good idea," I said. "Let's make that happen."

Everyone agreed.

Even Earnshaw.

I guess I'd shaken up enough to keep him under control for the rest of the meeting.

"What about our Jane Doe in the morgue?" I asked.

"No fingerprints on file," Alex said. "But then we didn't figure there would be for a girl that age. We can't compare dental records until we have a potential name to check. And so far none of the names of missing girls from this area—or even nearby states—seem to fit the Jane Doe."

I wasn't surprised. I knew that identifying a body like that can be difficult, sometimes impossible.

In the end, we decided to simply keep digging and also to check out all those scenarios from Kovach about a theater person or someone who might have undergone plastic surgery for some strange reason to look more like me.

"We'll figure this out," I assured everyone. "We always do."

"Let's hope it happens before the next one," Kovach said. "Before we find the next victim."

The same fear Tatarko had brought up earlier.

"Do you really think that this killer is going to strike here again soon?" I asked Kovach. "Murder another teenaged girl?"

"Yeah, I don't think this is finished yet, do you?"

"No," I said. "I think this is just getting started."

NINETEEN

I drove back to Huntsdale the next day. It was only about an hour's drive. I didn't really have any reason to go back there, I suppose. Except I did. My mother was there. And the graves of my sister Caitlin and my father.

I made the rounds of stores and businesses and people on the street throughout downtown Huntsdale again, showing them the picture of Laurie Reddick and the drawing of the woman who looked like me and even asking if anyone knew anything about a girl resembling our Jane Doe.

I got a lot of negative responses.

A few "that woman looks sort of like you" comments.

And people who made it clear to me that they were too busy to stop and answer questions on the street, even if the questions were coming from an FBI agent about a murder investigation.

But my tactic of asking as many questions as I could of as many people as possible finally paid off when I stopped in a women's clothing store in downtown Huntsdale. One I'd missed on my first round of store checks.

"Yes, I remember that girl," the woman behind the sales counter told me when I showed her the picture of Laurie

Reddick. "Hard not to remember her. She bought a lot of clothes. Blouses, jeans, slacks, even a summer jacket."

"How did she pay for it all?"

"In cash. She had a whole wad of money with her. I thought it was unusual a girl that age would have so much money. But I figured it was none of my business. She really went on a buying spree though."

"And she was alone?" I asked.

I figured I knew what the answer was going to be before I even asked the question.

But I was wrong.

"Someone was waiting for her. By the door. I saw them leaving together."

"Another teenager?"

"No, an adult."

"Did the person with her look like this?" I asked, showing her the drawing of the mystery woman Laurie Reddick had been with at the Groveton mall.

"Not like that at all."

"What did the woman look like?"

"It wasn't a woman, it was a man."

A man?

"Did you get a good look at him?"

"Nah, I only saw him for a second or two when he met the girl at the door."

"Anything at all?"

She shrugged.

"Average height. Average weight. Average looking in every way. That's really all I can tell you."

"And you're certain it was a man, not a woman, the girl was with that day?"

"I know it's getting hard to tell the difference these days, but yes, I'm certain that this person was a man."

"Any idea where they went after they left the store?"

"I-I saw them get into a car parked outside on the street."

"What kind of car?"

"It was big. An SUV, I guess. A white SUV."

"You didn't by any chance get the license plate number on the SUV, did you?"

Hey, it never hurts to ask.

"No, I just glanced at it."

"Are you sure you don't remember any letters or numbers?"

"There was no reason to pay that much attention."

"Do you maybe remember what state the license plate on the SUV was from?"

She shook her head. "Sorry."

"But you definitely saw the girl get into the SUV with this man?"

"Yes. She took all the stuff she had bought, put it in the car —and they both got in. Then they drove away. That's all I can tell you. Does it help at all?"

It did.

I now had a man connected to Laurie Reddick—as well as a woman—in one of the sightings before her murder.

And I had a vehicle too.

A white SUV.

Sure, there were a lot of SUVs on the highways these days, and plenty of them were white ones too.

Still, it was something.

Laurie Reddick was accompanied by a man driving a white SUV.

It was a clue.

I finally had a clue.

It wasn't much of a clue, but it was better than nothing.

TWENTY

My mother and me have had a troubled relationship ever since my sister—and then my father—died.

I guess on some level she blamed me for Caitlin's death. Because I was the one responsible for bringing my little sister with me to the carnival where she was kidnapped and later murdered. I've had to live with that guilt ever since then.

A few weeks later, my father was dead too.

Instead of embracing me, her daughter who was still alive, I seemed to be a reminder to her of everything she had lost. "Your sister died because of you," she had screamed at me on more than one occasion.

Maybe she was right. But I had responded by trying to make up for my youthful indiscretion that had resulted in my sister's death. I joined the FBI, asked to be assigned to the Violence Against Children unit—where I brought a lot of teenaged girls home safely and put dangerous predators in prison. It didn't assuage all of my guilt on Caitlin. But I felt like I was at least making a positive contribution and doing the best I could in remembrance of my sister. Not like my mother who was still living in the past.

The last time I'd seen her had been especially bad.

I'd brought up Caitlin that time too, like I needed to do now. Even though I'd solved her murder a short time earlier I still had questions about Caitlin—and about some of the things my father did in the investigation of her murder—that I asked her. She got very upset over that, and it opened up a lot of old emotional wounds between us.

I was expecting more of the same now.

But she surprised me by greeting me warmly at the door.

"Nikki, it's good to see you," she said. "I heard you were back in town, and I was hoping you'd be here soon. Come on in."

She actually seemed happy that I was there this time.

And she even talked to me like a normal mother might talk to her daughter after not seeing her for a while.

Except my mother and I had not had a normal relationship for a very long time, if ever.

I didn't bring up Caitlin right away or the reason that I'd come back again to see her.

Instead, we talked about a lot of mother-daughter things. She even asked me about the details of my love life. I went through it all with her.

About the ending of my engagement to Greg Ellroy who I was supposed to marry in the fall. About Billy Weller, the Huntsdale cop who died in my arms. And about Connor Nolan, the police chief of Dorchester, Pa. who I had a passionate relationship with on my last case, but hadn't heard from since then.

"I'm not sure I understand exactly what happened with Greg Ellroy," she said.

"I'm not sure I do either."

"He seems like a wonderful man."

"He is."

"And you say he really loved you?"

"He sure did. Almost too much sometimes."

"What do you mean?"

"I felt smothered by him."

"Well, he sure sounds like the perfect man to me."

"He is perfect. Or almost perfect."

"Then why...?"

"Greg's perfect for someone else, not me."

I never had any regrets about calling off my engagement with Greg Ellroy. I had plenty of regrets about my doomed relationship with Billy Weller. The same with Connor Nolan. If I'd just done some things differently with both Billy and Connor, maybe things could have turned out better. But we don't get second chances in life very often to make things right again after we've screwed them up.

I knew that all too well from what I did—and what I didn't do—at the summer carnival on that long-ago day when I lost my sister forever.

Which brought me to the reason for my visit to my mother.

To talk about Caitlin.

Again.

"Someone is using Caitlin to get my attention while carrying out new murders," I pretty much blurted out when I'd run out of other things to say to her.

I told my mother all about the woman who bore a striking resemblance to me, or what Caitlin might look like today if she was alive. About the visit to our old house in Huntsdale by the girl claiming to be Caitlin, and the bizarre note the girl left behind. About the rose tattoo found on one of the victims. And about the dead girl who signed Caitlin's name to the tattoo form before her death.

I explained that I was still looking into unanswered questions I had about Caitlin's long-ago murder to see if there was any reason the killer might be using her name and memory now in these new cases. When I was finished, I waited to see if she would get mad at me again like she had last time I talked about unanswered questions involving Caitlin. But that didn't happen this time.

"I saw her too, you know," my mother told me.

"Who?"

"Caitlin."

"You saw the Reddick girl claiming to be Caitlin, too?"

I hadn't thought about that possibility before, but it seemed likely whoever sent Laurie Reddick to the old house in Huntsdale might easily have done the same thing here with my mother.

"No, this was no young girl. It was a woman. A grown woman. She looked a lot like Caitlin might have looked. A lot like you too, Nikki. I knew it wasn't you. But she looked so much like... well, like I've imagined Caitlin might look today."

Was this the same woman from the mall in Groveton?

"Did you talk to the woman?"

"No. I saw her on the porch. Or at least I thought I did. I mean, at first I assumed it had to be my imagination, right? But she seemed so real. Except by the time I opened the door where the woman was standing, she was gone. If she was ever really there."

She shook her head.

"Maybe I'm just an old woman living in the past who sees things that aren't there."

After I left my mother, I drove to the cemetery where Caitlin and my father were buried.

I liked visiting their graves, even though that might sound strange. It somehow made me feel close to them again, even in death after all these years since they've been gone. It brought back a lot of good memories.

I did not like visiting my mother. That only brought back

bad memories for me.

The last time I'd been here at the cemetery I was involved in a shoot-out that nearly cost me my life. But I wasn't thinking about that now. I was thinking about Caitlin and my father.

Their graves were side by side under a row of oak trees, and next to a pond that usually had ducks swimming by.

Luke Cassidy—the former police chief of Huntsdale for a lot of years. He was a great police chief, people said, and I knew he was an even better dad. I still miss him so much.

Standing there at his grave, I remembered again the games we used to play growing up. Crime detection games. Like Clue or something, but even more interesting. He would give me clues about a case, and then I had to solve it. If I couldn't, he would give me one more clue—and then another and another— until I figured it out.

"I wish you could give me a clue right now," I said out loud to myself. "I sure could use one. Who is the mystery woman who looks like me and Caitlin? Is there anyone else involved? Why is there this obsession with Caitlin by someone playing this game with me? Did Mom really see the same woman—or was she simply imagining Caitlin there?"

There was no answer, of course.

Just the wind blowing gently through the leaves of the oak trees.

And the sounds of the ducks on the pond.

I "talked" to Caitlin too.

"Someone is pretending to be you. I only wish it were true. No matter how or why it is happening, I wish you were really still alive out there somewhere. Except that can't be possible, can it, Caitlin?"

But Caitlin couldn't answer me, any more than my father could.

Both of them were dead and buried.

I'd lost them a long time ago.

TWENTY-ONE

There were two different local cops from separate police forces that had shown up from the two towns when the bodies of the two girls were found in restrooms along the Ohio Turnpike in the Columbus area.

I went with Bonnie Tatarko to talk to both of them.

It was a thirty-minute ride from Columbus for Bonnie and me back to the cops in Brockton who found the Jane Doe victim. Which turned into a one-hour trip because of jammed-up traffic heading out of Columbus. It turned out not to be too bad though because it gave me a chance to find out more about Bonnie Tatarko. She was an interesting woman.

"How long have you been a state trooper?" I asked.

"Nine years."

"Do you like it?"

"It's fine. Not as glamorous as your career with the FBI though."

I laughed.

"I don't usually get these kinds of big cases here in Columbus," she said. "This is the biggest one I've been involved with. But you're the one who gets all the publicity from it, whether you solve it or not. You're the star. Don't get me wrong, I don't begrudge you all your fame, Nikki. You deserve it. I just wish that I could get a little more attention like that sometimes."

"Are you married?" I asked Tatarko. I realized she hadn't told me anything about her personal life. "Children?"

"Neither. Oh, I've thought about all that. But it's not easy meeting the right man in a job like this. Mostly, all I meet are a bunch of other cops. They're usually married, drunk too much and don't really make my heart sing. How about you?"

"Uh, I was engaged."

"And now?"

"I'm not engaged."

"Do you think we'll ever solve this case?" Tatarko asked me at one point.

"Of course, we will."

"You're pretty confident of that, huh?"

"I'm always confident I can solve every case."

"And you always do, don't you?"

"Not always."

"Which one couldn't you solve?"

"The Singles Slayer case. It was a while ago."

"Oh, I remember hearing about that one."

I remembered it too. Oh, I remembered it all too well. It happened relatively early in my career with the bureau. I somehow got thrust into a prominent role investigating a series of murders across the country carried out by a psychopathic killer the media dubbed The Singles Slayer.

Like a latter-day Son of Sam or Ted Bundy, The Singles Slayer had waited for and stalked young women outside singles bars and clubs, then shot them to death for no apparent reason other than the sexual thrill of it. At least twelve women died during his murderous spree.

Me, I became the face of the investigation. Appearing at press conferences, talking to the media on TV, giving updates about whatever we knew. Why did I get that assignment? I think it was because it was such a thankless job becoming a target for all the frustration from the media and the public in general because we couldn't stop him. I lived with The Singles Slayer case for months, day and night. So, no, I could never forget it. Even now.

"What happened?" Tatarko asked.

"We never found him."

"And the murders?"

"They just stopped at one point."

"You figure he died or something?"

"Well, since serial killers don't usually retire... yes, I think something bad probably happened to him. Hopefully, something very, very bad. Anyway, he just disappeared completely after that. But we never found a definite answer."

I thought about Jeffrey and Doris Galvin still looking for that answer about their daughter Sara's murder. She had been one of The Singles Slayer's victims. But I had no answers for them about Sara. Or for any of the families or loved ones of the other Singles Slayer victims either."

"Maybe some time you'll find out for sure," Tatarko said.

"In the meantime, let's concentrate on the case we're dealing with here."

The guy who found the Jane Doe from the Brockton police force was named Gene Braxton. He was a slightly built African American cop who said he'd been on the force for five years. But he'd never seen a murder victim before. The only dead body he ever had to deal with was a traffic accident victim, he told me. Until he came onto Jane Doe.

"The cleaning woman was the first person I talked to there," he said, recalling the details of that night. "She was very upset, which was understandable. She took me into the bathroom and I saw the girl's body lying in that stall. I called for backup, medical people and anyone I could think of. I guess I was pretty rattled, too."

"What about other people in the rest area?"

"After the body was secured, I questioned as many people as I could. Not a lot of people there at that hour. And, to be honest, it seemed unlikely any of them could have been involved. The killer would have made sure he got out of there right away before the police arrived, right?"

"Not necessarily," I said. "Sometimes the killer—especially a high-profile killer like this one seems to be who seeks attention —might stay around to observe the results of what he did."

"You mean like an arsonist who turns up at a fire he set to watch the building burn?"

"Exactly. Or a murderer who attends his victim's funeral. That's an old law enforcement ploy that catches a number of killers. Look at the crowd of mourners, and then try to pick out someone who seems suspicious. Did any of the people in the rest stop area that night seem suspicious to you?"

"Not really. No one stood out for any reason. And no one knew anything about the girl in the bathroom."

"Do you remember a woman there at all?"

"There were a couple of women."

"Anyone who looked to be about my age? Maybe she even looked a bit like me?"

"Nah. The only women there were a lot older. One was heavy-set too and looked nothing like that. The other one was with her family. Nobody that looks like the person you described."

"Anyone else there suspicious in any way?"

He thought for a second.

"There was this one guy. He was standing off to the side while I was talking to the women. I was going to question him next. But when I turned around to start walking over to him, he was gone. Just like that. He disappeared. I never saw him again.

I doubt that he had anything to do with the girl's murder. I figured he didn't want to get involved."

"What did this man look like?"

Braxton shrugged. "Nothing special I remember. Just a guy, not too young and not too old. I didn't really pay much attention to him because there was so much else going on there. Sorry."

He was right, the guy probably had nothing to do with the murder.

Still, there was a guy seen at the clothing store in Huntsdale earlier with Laurie Reddick.

Was there a man involved in this?

Along with the woman at the mall and possibly another woman who had been at the tattoo parlor?

The second officer I talked to was Walt Springer. He was from the town which covered the area of the turnpike where Laurie Reddick had been found. Springer was a big, red-headed cop who had only been on the force for six months. He'd never encountered a dead body before, he said, and certainly nothing like the scene with Laurie Reddick found sprawled dramatically over the sink in the turnpike rest stop.

He told basically the same story I already knew. Grace Hazlett and her daughter went into the restroom, saw the body and screamed for help. Once the paramedics and other police arrived on the scene, he questioned anyone in the rest area who might have seen something or been a possible suspect themselves. But, just like in the other case, nothing turned up.

The only real witnesses were Grace Hazlett and her daughter, and they hadn't really seen anything except for the body. There wasn't much else they could tell him, Springer recalled.

"Wow, they were so upset too. Especially the daughter. She kept crying and holding onto her mother. She was almost hysterical. I guess a girl that age—she was probably about the same age as the Reddick girl—can easily get traumatized by seeing something so horrible. We questioned them both as best we could. They said they were driving to Pittsburgh. But they promised to stay in touch if we needed any more from them. I can give you the contact number for them, if you want."

"No, I already have it," I said.

"I heard another girl was killed too," Springer said.

"Yes, about twenty-five miles away in another turnpike rest area a few days later. Don't you know about that?"

He shrugged. "I'm just a rookie street cop. They never tell me anything. All I did was show up at the crime scene and turn it over to the detectives. Nothing else for me to do. Not my job anymore."

Jeez, another murder of a teenaged girl in another nearby town—and this guy barely knew about it. I didn't figure that Walt Springer was going to have a long, successful career as a cop. Or maybe he could hang around for thirty years until his pension and never care much more about any case. I've seen it before.

"What happened to the other girl?" he asked finally.

"Same kind of murder as the one you found. Strangulation. Body found in a bathroom at the rest stop too."

"So you figure they're connected?"

"They must be."

"Who is the second girl?"

"We don't know. She's still a Jane Doe."

I took out a picture of the dead girl from the morgue and showed it to Springer.

He looked at the picture casually at first.

Then more carefully.

Finally, he let out an excited shout: "That's her!" he said.

"Who?"

"She's the girl at the rest stop. The daughter of the woman who found the body. The girl who was so upset."

And now she was dead too.

TWENTY-TWO

"Her name is Rebecca Burgess," Alex said. "She's fifteen years old—or rather she was fifteen—and she's from Portland, Oregon."

"Oregon. How the hell did she wind up in Ohio?"

"Her parents said she'd been missing for three months. Ran away from home. Left a note saying she wanted to experience the world outside Portland. That's the last time they heard anything about her. Until this."

We'd been checking anew into the girl's identity since I found out she was the girl in the restroom where Laurie Reddick had been found.

It turned out we got lucky. After going through a lot of missing girl reports, we checked out Rebecca Burgess from Portland. We compared the dental records of our Jane Doe to the one Rebecca's parents provided. Rebecca had some dental work done before she went missing. It matched our dental records for the Jane Doe. After that, her parents identified our Jane Doe as their Rebecca from a picture in the morgue. They were on their way to Columbus now to claim the body. It was tragic, but at least we knew who the girl was.

"What about Erica Hazlett, the girl we thought found the body?" I asked. I was back at the state police headquarters with Alex and Lt. Tatarko.

"From what we can tell, Erica Hazlett never existed," Tatarko said. "It was Rebecca Burgess all the time."

"And the mother? Grace Hazlett?"

"Gone. In the wind. That phone number she gave us doesn't exist anymore. It's been disconnected. We checked out the address we had for her, too. It's a vacant lot somewhere in Pittsburgh."

"So she was probably the killer," Alex said.

"It makes sense," I told them. "She killed Laurie Reddick, but then she posed as a concerned mother with the other girl with her. Talked about how upset the girl was after seeing the body. Maybe the girl—who we now know was Rebecca—was really upset. Maybe she feared she would be next. She was right. But probably too scared to do anything but play along with the woman.

"This woman—whoever she really might be—is very smart and very cunning. Instead of fleeing the scene after killing the girl, she stays around. Pretends to have just found the body with her 'daughter.' If you think about it, that's a perfect way to avoid being thought of as a possible suspect. Don't look suspicious, don't run away—you just stay around and pretend to be an innocent witness.

"Then she played the rest even better. She came across as a really concerned mother because the girl with her had seen the body. It was a wonderful performance. Then she carried out the whole charade all over again—posing as the non-existent Grace Hazlett—with me on the phone. And I bought it. I never suspected she was making up the whole thing about how worried she was about her daughter. I thought she seemed like a good, responsible mother. How could I have been so stupid? God, that pisses me off!"

Tatarko looked at me quizzically.

"I get your theory about why she stayed around at the crime scene," she said. "That part makes sense. But why talk to you on the phone about all this stuff afterward? What did she have to gain from that?"

"She was playing a game with Nikki," Alex said. "With all of us."

I nodded.

"Alex is right. She's been playing some kind of sick game with us since the beginning. Especially playing a game with me. All the references to my sister. The roses stuff, like the roses in my sister's murder. The letters she's sent. This is all a game for her, whoever she is. A deadly game."

"Well, she's gone again now." Tatarko sighed. "We have no idea who she is or where she went."

"Or who else she might be working with," I added.

"You mean the man we've heard about?" Alex asked.

"Uh, huh. Or another woman. Or maybe another teenaged girl is with her too. She recruited Laurie Reddick and Rebecca Burgess. No reason she can't go after another mixed-up girl on the run from home like that. Who knows how she does it? But she must offer them something to make the girls feel safe. Until it's too late."

"Jesus!" Alex said. "That is scary."

Tatarko looked worried too. I figured she'd been around long enough to be involved in some other murder investigations. But I believed she'd never come across anyone like this before.

"Did the woman—the one who posed as this person, Grace Hazlett—look anything like me?" I asked. "Have you checked?"

"We did, and it's hard to say," Tatarko replied.

"What do you mean?"

"She was about your age. And maybe she had some resemblance to you, or the woman—that was seen before. But no one could say for sure. It sure wasn't exactly the same as that woman."

Which made think again that the woman might have some kind of theatrical background. An actress who could change her appearance at different times, depending on the situation she was in.

Or else, there was more than one woman involved in this.

I was heading for my car in the parking lot afterwards when I heard footsteps behind me. I turned around, figuring it was Alex or Tatarko coming to tell me something else they'd forgotten about while we were in the barracks.

But it wasn't Alex or Tatarko.

Instead, it was the last person that I expected—or wanted—to see again during my lifetime.

Brett Anson.

"I hear there's been a big development in the case," Anson said.

"Who told you that?"

"I have my sources."

"So go talk to them, not me."

"You're still mad at me?"

"Just stay away from me," I said, getting in my car and locking the door in case he kept trying to get to me.

When I pulled away, I saw him still standing there watching me.

TWENTY-THREE

I stopped off at the bar in my hotel when I got back there after leaving the state police place. It had been a long day. I needed a drink. I needed something to eat. I needed a lot of things right now. But a drink would do for a start.

I'm one of those people who drink sometimes because it makes me feel better. I sure am not an alcoholic; I can't remember the last time that I was even close to being drunk. But alcohol relaxes me and helps me deal with stress. The kind of stress I always feel when I'm searching for answers on a big case. Especially this one.

The bartender brought me a vodka and tonic, my favorite drink these days. The bar area where I was sitting was pretty much empty, which was good. I wanted some quiet time alone to think.

I took a sip of the vodka and thought about all the questions swirling around in my head.

There were a lot of them.

Who was the mystery woman from the Groveton mall?

What about the one in the Columbus tattoo shop?

Was there a man involved—the man waiting for Laurie at the clothing store, or maybe even the man who disappeared quickly at the rest stop after Rebecca Burgess' body was found?

Was there any motive to the murders of Laurie Reddick and Rebecca Burgess—or were they just thrill killings?

Why was there such an obsession with my sister Caitlin?

And why—given all the Caitlin stuff—was there such an obsession about getting my attention to work on this case?

Lots of unanswered questions for a hotshot investigator like you, Cassidy, I thought to myself. You have no real clues, no real leads, no real ideas on this one. Have you lost your crimefighting instincts or something? Will this turn out like The Singles Slayer case? The one case you were never able to break? A case that would haunt me for the rest of my life. And like Caitlin's murder would.

Which brought up the one other question that was still out there.

The one unthinkable question.

But I thought about it anyway.

Was there any possibility that Caitlin was still alive and somehow involved in all this?

Of course, that was impossible. My sister was murdered fifteen years ago and buried in Huntsdale Cemetery. My own father investigated the case. And I caught the person that killed her, who confessed to the murder before he died. Those are all cold, hard facts.

Still, a lot of strange things had happened recently. The woman at my mother's house. The woman who looked so much like me. The references to "Nik" instead of "Nikki" from the girl at Maureen Wilcox's house in Huntsdale. All of these things... well, they all made a lot more sense if Caitlin was still alive.

I finished off my drink and was working on a second one

now. Maybe I was getting drunk, after all. I mean why else would I have all these crazy thoughts running through my mind.

There was something else too. Ever since I had solved my sister's murder, I still had questions about what really happened to her. I was never sure I really had uncovered the whole truth. Especially when I found out that someone—presumably my father before he died—had removed several pages from the official police report on her death. What were on those missing pages? Why did my father not want anyone to see them? Could this possibly have some sort of significance for the case I was working on now, no matter how crazy that might seem?

I was deep in thought about all this when I heard someone slip onto the barstool next to me.

"Can I buy you another drink?" a man's voice said.

Great, I thought to myself. Some local Romeo who wants to hit on me. I whirled around to face him. And saw it wasn't simply someone trying to make a pass at me.

"What are you doing here?" I asked.

"It's a bar. I wanted a drink. Imagine meeting you here," Brett Anson said.

"You followed me."

"Okay, I followed you."

"I didn't see anyone following me."

"That's because I'm very good at it."

"Following women into bars and hiding in their bathrooms, those are your specialties, huh? Pretty creepy, Anson."

He shrugged and ordered a beer from the bartender. He didn't seem like a guy who insulted easily.

"What do you want from me?"

"I just want to talk."

"About the case, right?"

"Well, that would be nice."

"You said you had sources on it. Go talk to them."

"Ah, but you are the ultimate source."

"What exactly is it you expect me to tell you?"

"Hey, I know there's been a big development in the case. From what I understand, the woman who discovered the Reddick girl wasn't who she said she was. She very likely was the killer. And I also know that you've got an ID on the second girl. Rebecca Burgess. Who just happens to be the same girl that was with the woman claiming to be her mother when Laurie Reddick's body was found."

He took a sip of his beer and smiled.

"How am I doing so far?"

I sat there pretty stunned. How did he find out about all this? But I tried to keep my best poker face on to make sure he didn't see he'd gotten to me.

"I have no idea what you're talking about," I said.

"Sure you do. I'm only looking for some kind of confirmation from you before I go with the story."

"I'm not confirming anything for you."

"Okay, how about we do it like they did in the Watergate movie with Dustin Hoffman and Robert Redford. *All the President's Men.* You don't have to answer me, just give me some sort of sign. If I'm right, you order another drink and we sit here talking some more. That's all you have to do. How about it?"

I finished the rest of the drink in front of me quickly, called for the bartender and asked for my check. I paid it, then got up to leave.

"Have a nice night, Agent Cassidy," Anson called out after me.

"It'll be a lot nicer once I get away from you," I told him over my shoulder.

I kept walking out of the bar and through the hotel lobby.

When I got there, I waited and watched to see if Anson would follow me.

He didn't. He just went out the front door of the hotel, walked into the parking lot, got into a car and drove off.

It was a white SUV.

Of course, there are lots of white SUVs on the streets these days.

But I didn't believe in coincidences...

TWENTY-FOUR

"You've got a leak," I told Bonnie Tatarko.

"What are you saying?"

"A reporter confronted me last night with almost everything we've found out and know. He had it all, chapter and verse. The woman at the Laurie Reddick crime scene who wasn't who we thought she was. The fact that her supposed daughter turned out to be the second victim, as a Jane Doe for a long time. He even knew her name now as Rebecca Burgess. We haven't released any of this stuff to anyone yet. But this son of a bitch had it all down."

We were sitting around a table in a small, private conference room at the state police headquarters the next morning. Just me, Tatarko and Alex. I wasn't comfortable talking around anyone else in this building right now. At least until we found out who the news leak had come from.

"You think the leak came from here?" Tatarko asked.

"Well, it sure didn't come from Alex or me."

"It's kind of hard for me to believe someone here would actually leak confidential information like that to the public."

"Believe it. It happened."

She shook her head in frustration.

"I don't know. I'm still not sure the leak came from here. I mean nothing like this has ever happened before."

"You never had a case this big before either, did you?" Alex asked.

"No, I guess not. Who's the reporter?"

"His name is Brett Anson," I said. "The same guy from the *National Investigator*. That website is sleazy and sensational. But it does get a lot of traffic and it makes a lot of headline news."

"Has he put the story up yet?"

"It wasn't there this morning when I checked. But I expect him to go with it soon. He said he was looking for confirmation from me. But I don't expect him to hold off too long. That's the kind of journalist Brett Anson is. This isn't the *New York Times* we're talking about here."

Tatarko said she'd launch an investigation into all of her people to try and find out who talked to Anson about the case. I agreed, it was the obvious thing to do. But I didn't hold out a lot of hope she would be successful with the search. Plugging a leak like that in a law enforcement agency when someone is secretly giving stuff to the media has always been a tough task to accomplish.

Alex said we needed to keep all the information we gathered on a need-to-know basis, going forward. Only the three of us. Plus any officer involved in a specific aspect of the investigation. But that was all. At least for now. Until we knew who we could trust in this place.

"I just had a crazy thought," Alex said.

"I'm very into crazy at the moment. Tell me."

"What if it's Brett Anson?"

"Huh?"

"What if he's the killer?"

"We've basically been looking for a woman. Or maybe two women."

"We don't know that. We've had a man sighted at some of these places, too. Maybe he's behind it. Maybe he's using the woman or women the same way they used those two teenaged girls."

"Anson's a reporter, Alex. Not a murderer."

"It's happened before. A reporter seemingly just covering the story turns out to be the bad guy. That was the way it was on a murder case I worked on several years ago—before you joined the bureau—in Florida. The reporter was very ambitious, and he decided to make his own sensational news. Then he'd break the big story to further his own career. So he killed someone, and then covered the story himself."

"That seems pretty far-fetched."

"But you said this Brett Anson guy was ambitious too. This could be his big break to be a star in the media, Maybe catapult him to a big job at a network or a cable news outfit. How far would someone like Anson go for something like that? Far enough to commit murder?"

I thought about Anson and what I knew about him. Following me, hiding in my bathroom and all that kind of stuff. Even the fact he drove a white SUV, like the man seen picking up Laurie Reddick in Huntsdale. Sure, Anson would do almost anything for a story like this. But was he a murderer just setting up his own story to cover and become famous?

"I don't think so, Alex. I can't see it."

Alex shrugged.

"I told you it was a crazy idea."

Still, it might not be a bad idea to find out more about Brett Anson.

His background covering other big stories, any controversies in his past, everything at all we could round up about him. It would be good information to have, even if it wound up leading us nowhere on the case.

I told that now to Alex and Tatarko.

"Do you really think doing something like that is going to help us?" Tatarko asked skeptically.

"It can't hurt," Alex answered.

"She's right," I said. "It's worth the effort, whether we turn up anything significant or not. I am curious about him. There is definitely something 'wrong' about Brett Anson. We should find out how 'wrong' a guy he really is."

My phone rang. I looked down at it, and I saw the name of Shirley Hunsaker.

The girl who had been with Laurie Reddick back in Groveton when she met the mysterious woman who looked so much like me—and maybe Caitlin too—at a mall right before Laurie disappeared.

"Hello, Shirley," I said. "What's up?"

"You asked me to call you if I saw or remembered anything else."

"Of course. Did you?"

"I saw her again."

"Who?"

"The woman."

"The woman you met at the mall with Laurie?"

"Yes, I'm sure it was the same woman."

"Where did you see her, Shirley?"

"TV. I saw her on television."

TWENTY-FIVE

Her name was Susan Stratton.

That was her show business name anyway, the one she used as an actress. Her real name was Erica Golanski. She'd changed it because she thought the name Susan Stratton sounded more like a famous actress, which she wanted to be. She said in an interview I read that she did it to emulate Susan Seaforth, a longtime soap opera star she used to watch growing up in Peoria, Illinois.

The show Shirley Hunsaker had seen her on was a cable TV series called *Pick Your Partner*. It was about a group of young men and women living together in an apartment in New York City. The idea was everyone kept changing romantic partners, dating someone else—at times people in the same apartment—every week.

There were eight of them living together. Susan Stratton wasn't part of the main cast. Instead, she played a smaller role as a neighbor who dropped in regularly—usually once a week for the show—to exchange quips with the cast.

It was a lesser part, and it must have been pure chance that Shirley Hunsaker happened to see her while watching the show. And then recognized her as the woman she'd seen in the Groveton mall talking with Laurie Reddick before she disappeared.

The most interesting thing I found out about Susan Stratton was that her character had a gimmick on the show: every time she appeared, she would look different. Almost like a different character. The idea was that the neighbor had this look to her that kept changing every time anyone saw her on screen.

It was supposed to be a funny, recurring bit—changing her appearance to look like different people.

And I suppose maybe it was.

But it wasn't funny at all to me.

Not if one of the people she tried to look like was me.

I stared at a picture of Susan Stratton/Erica Golanski I'd called up on my computer screen from the show's website. She didn't look quite like me in the picture. Not exactly. But there were similarities. Same approximate age. Some of the same facial features. I could see how someone—especially someone with expertise in theatrical or TV experience in changing their appearance for a role in the way that she had—could alter their look to resemble me in a number of ways.

"Okay, she does different roles on screen," Alex said when I told her about it. "But could she really change her appearance that much?"

"Look at this," I said.

I showed her a series of pictures of Susan Stratton from the show. Different times when she made her appearance as the ever-changing next-door neighbor. Blonde, brunette, redhead, or sometimes something in between. A stern, businesswoman look. Then a scantily dressed, over the top glamor girl. A frumpy look in a tattered bathrobe with her hair in curlers. And on and on.

"She's like a chameleon," Alex said.

"Exactly."

"But wouldn't she need some kind of plastic surgery to

change her face enough to pull off that much of a resemblance to you?"

"Not necessarily. I did some research on this. There's a lot of different ways a person can change their appearance besides plastic surgery. Especially someone who is a professional actress who plays a variety of different looking roles like she does on a TV program. None of this stuff is permanent like plastic surgery is. But it can be used to dramatically change a person's appearance. It's all temporary. Just like the changing woman character she played on the *Pick Your Partner* show every week. I think she's the one, Alex. I think she really is the woman Shirley Hunsaker saw that day with Laurie."

"But why?" Alex asked. "Why would she do something like that? Go to all that trouble to look like you? And presumably to be involved in some way with the murder of a young girl like Laurie Reddick. And maybe the other girl too? It just doesn't make any sense to me. Why, Nikki, why do it?"

"That, my fellow crime stopper, is the question we need to find out the answer to right now."

We did some more research into Susan Stratton/Erica Golanski and found out she had been trying to make it big in show business for nearly ten years. The role on *Pick Your Partner* was her first big break. Before that, she had done a series of bit roles with TV shows and even a few small movie roles.

She also was a stand-up comedian at times. Playing at small clubs in New York and Los Angeles and elsewhere around the country. One of the facets of her comedic act was damn interesting to me. She would imitate a lot of famous people, from Kim Kardashian to Lady Gaga to Hillary Clinton and more.

"It wasn't an actual change in appearance when she did the imitations," I said to Alex. "But she could alter her facial expression and the way she moved and a lot of other things to remarkably resemble the different women, according to the accounts I've read. She's made a career out of changing into other people,

Alex. That's how she got the job on *Pick Your Partner* as the ever-changing neighbor. So it's not really that much of a stretch that she could make herself look and act a lot like me."

Alex said she still had trouble believing that.

"Is the Hunsaker girl absolutely sure that the woman she saw on TV was the same one she saw with Laurie Reddick that day in the mall?"

"She's... well, she's pretty sure."

"What if she's wrong?"

"What if she's right?'

"So what are you going to do?"

I'd thought about that ever since my conversation with Shirley Hunsaker. The *Pick Your Partner* show was shooting at a location in New York City, I found out. A sound stage in Astoria, Queens—where they shot a lot of TV shows. They were about to begin work on some new episodes right now.

"I'm going to go to New York, try to talk to Susan Stratton or Erica Golanski or whoever she calls herself—and find out why she was in a Groveton shopping mall talking with Laurie Reddick."

TWENTY-SIX

"Can you tell me where to find Susan Stratton?" I asked the director of the *Pick Your Partner* TV show.

"I wish I could find her myself."

"What do you mean?"

"She's missing."

"Since when?"

"Yesterday. I talked with her during an afternoon rehearsal. But she didn't show up for work today. Left me a message that she wasn't coming back to work here."

"Did she say anything during that conversation that might be a reason for her leaving so suddenly?"

"No, not then."

"What did you talk about?"

"I told her an FBI agent was coming to interview her today."

The director's name was Eric Flaherty. I had called him from Ohio the previous day to set up an interview on the set with Stratton. I didn't tell him why, of course. Just indicated it was part of a routine investigation. Then I'd flown to New York City in the morning. It was only an hour flight from Columbus, so I figured it would be easy for me to talk directly with her in person, rather than getting her on a phone or Zoom call.

But I realized now I shouldn't have given her any warning that I was coming.

I should have just shown up unannounced. But it was too late for that.

"Why are you looking for her?" Flaherty asked me.

"I can't really talk about it."

"It's about those dead girls, right?"

I was surprised.

"How do you know about that?"

"I saw stuff about you investigating those cases on TV news. But what does Susan Stratton have to do with any of it?"

"That's what I'm trying to find out."

I asked him some questions about Susan Stratton. He said she'd shown up on the set a few months earlier, looking to try out for a part on *Pick Your Partner*. At first, he said, they were only interested in her for a bit, walk-on part with no specific lines to say or anything like that at all.

"But then we discovered she had this real ability to change her appearance. To look different from one show to another, if she wanted. It was really pretty unusual and amazing. She'd be glamorous, then plain, then dowdy and so forth. Different hair color and styles, different looks completely. At first, it was going to just be a quick gimmick. A laugh or two from it, then she'd be gone. But then we got the idea to incorporate her talent for this into the show on a more regular basis. Have her pop in every week for an appearance as the strange neighbor who always looked completely different. It was a small role. Only a minute or so in each show. But a great gimmick that she could do that so easily. It's the kind of unusual talent that can really help a show."

Or useful in murdering young girls, I thought to myself.

"Do you know any more about her background before

coming to your show? Do you have contact information for her?"

"I can look up that stuff for you."

"And what about a dressing room? Did she have one? Or an area where she changed into her different looks. She must have makeup, wigs, a variety of clothes and other things there to do what she did on the show."

"Let me show you what's there."

Susan Stratton's "dressing room" turned out to be a small alcove off to the side of where the *Pick Your Partner* leading stars got ready for the show. Clearly, she was not a leading star. Still, it was a TV role, and she'd apparently been willing to give it up in order to avoid talking with me.

That seemed pretty significant.

There was a dresser in the area. I looked through the drawers. There were scripts in there, various kinds of makeup and wigs that she must have used for her appearances. But, when I kept looking, I found something else too. A picture of her. Dressed in what looked like a judo outfit and standing in a fighting pose.

"She was into judo?" I asked Flaherty.

"In a big way. She took classes in it. She was really strong too. Some guy—another actor—tried to hit on her here one day, and she punched him so hard she knocked him unconscious. We were afraid at first she'd killed him. He was okay. But, believe me, no one messed with Stratton after that."

She knew judo and she had a lot of strength. Enough physical ability to strangle the life out of those girls?

Or was there someone else working with her—someone with comparable or even greater physical skills—who carried out a series of murders with her?

One way or another, Susan Stratton was involved in the deaths of those girls.

I was pretty sure of that at this point.

But I was even more certain a few minutes later when I found another picture in her belongings.

I stared at the picture for a long time.

In surprise.

In shock.

And with a bit of trepidation too.

Because it was a picture of me.

There was only one possible explanation I could think of for that.

She was using the picture to make herself look like me.

"Do you have that contact information for Stratton I asked about before?"

"Sure."

He gave me a phone number and an address in Lower Manhattan that he said came from her personnel records. There wasn't much else in her personnel file that was useful to me. I found a list of several minor acting roles in her past, some acting courses she'd taken in New York. But a lot of it was left blank. No family members or schools she'd attended.

Flaherty said the filling out of the personnel records was really a formality for the production company's HR department, and no one really checked to see if they had been completed. I wished they had. It would have made my search for Susan Stratton a whole lot easier.

Flaherty told me, too, that he didn't think the phone number or address on file would do me much good.

"We tried to reach her this morning when she didn't show up for work. The phone goes right to voice mail, we left a ton of messages without getting any response. Hell, we even sent someone to her address on file here. We thought maybe she was sick or something bad might have happened to her. But the super of the building told us she didn't live there anymore. You can try the building and the phone again, if you want, I suppose."

I said I would, even though I was certain I wouldn't fare any better with either one than the people from *Pick Your Partner* did.

I thanked Flaherty for his help and gave him my card. I asked him to call me if he heard from Stratton or found out any more about her.

"Do you really think she had something to do with your murder investigation?" he asked.

"It's possible."

He nodded.

"You don't seem surprised," I said.

"I always thought there was something off, something strange, something... well, scary about her."

He looked down at the card I'd given him, and then back at me.

"What are you going to do next?" he asked.

"I'm going to do whatever it takes to find Susan Stratton."

"Well, if you do, give her a message from me: tell her she's fired!"

TWENTY-SEVEN

"We've finally got a break in the case," I said to Alex. "We have a name. We have a person that we're looking for. Susan Stratton. Or Erica Golanski, if you prefer. We're not just chasing an unknown killer anymore. All we have to do is find this Stratton woman."

"How do we do that?"

"She's a well-known TV personality. Or at least she's semi well-known. She can't simply disappear from sight the way other people might do. Someone is going to recognize her from the show. We just have to keep looking until that happens."

"But you did say she's an expert at changing her appearance. If she changes it again now, well... that's going to make it hard to find her, Nikki."

"We'll find her," I said determinedly.

Alex had picked me up at the Columbus Airport to give me a ride after my return from New York City and the *Pick Your Partner* TV show. I was driving the car now—a rented 2022 Honda Accord we'd gotten when we first arrived in Ohio— while Alex sat alongside me in the passenger seat.

I reached into my handbag as I was driving and handed her

a picture from Stratton's actress profile that I'd gotten from people at the show.

"This is a good starting point for us. This is the real Susan Stratton, no matter how much she tries to change her appearance."

"How about one of the different characters she played on the show? Her different looks on air. Do we have them too?"

"I'm in the process of getting a file of them all from the show. There's maybe twenty different looks. But I doubt if she'd change herself to one of those looks. She'd want to pick some-thing completely different if she was on the run. Something that no one would remember from TV."

"Probably," Alex agreed.

"We'll put this stuff out everywhere," I said. "The authori-ties in New York City. Cops and our FBI bureaus around the country. We can talk to SAG and other TV industry groups too that might have information on her. It's going to be an all-points search for her. She can't hide from us forever."

"The whole thing still doesn't make a lot of sense, does it?"

"What do you mean?"

"I mean she's a professional actress. She's on a TV show. Maybe she's not a big-time TV star, but she's still a TV star of some kind. What would make her want to be involved in murdering young girls? Why try to look like you? Or like your sister Caitlin might look if she was alive today?"

"Let's make sure to ask Susan Stratton that exact question as soon as we find her."

Then there was still the question too of who Susan Stratton might be working with on all of this.

There had likely been at least two women so far—the woman at the Groveton mall with Laurie Reddick and the one on the Ohio Turnpike who claimed to have found Laurie's body with her "daughter" inside a restroom. There was a woman at the tattoo shop too. And then there was the report of a man—

maybe at the Turnpike rest stop and definitely seen at the Huntsdale clothing shop with Laurie before she was killed.

Were we looking for a team of murderers?

Working in unison to murder young girls for some reason.

But why?

Why were they killing these girls, what possible motive could two women and a man have to do this? Why make it all up about me and my dead sister Caitlin? Why was any of this happening?

I talked about it with Alex now.

"Maybe there is no reason," she said. "No motive at all. Someone is murdering these young girls for the thrill of doing it, that's the only reason. Hey, you know as well as me—there's been serial killer cases like that before."

She was right.

"Yes," I said. "Son of Sam. Ted Bundy. They weren't about money or even really about sex or anything like that. They were simply about cold-blooded murder. No reason. No logical reason at all for all of those victims of theirs to die. It was just for the goddamned thrill of it for David Berkowitz—the one they called Son of Sam—and for Bundy."

"And those are the toughest cases to solve, right? The ones with no discernible motive for anyone to chase after."

"Definitely. It took a year and a half for the cops in New York to catch Son of Sam. Years to nab Ted Bundy, not until he'd killed more than thirty women—maybe a lot more. Because the authorities had no real motive, that made it so hard to find them. It's the same thing that happened to me with the big Singles Slayer case. Some guy's killing women outside singles gathering spots for no reason anyone was ever able to determine. And we never caught him either. Just like Son of Sam and Bundy stayed on the lam for a long time. But this time is differ- ent, Alex. Like I said, we have a break here now. A real lead. This woman Susan Stratton is the key for us. All we have to do is find Stratton and hopefully the pieces to this will begin to fall into place."

Alex looked down again at the picture of Susan Stratton—the headshot from the show—that I'd given her.

"Where are you, Susan Stratton?" she asked out loud.

Suddenly, my phone began to ring.

Alex's phone beeped with a text message arriving.

Both at the same time.

Someone was trying to get us in a hurry.

"It's Dave Blanton," she said.

"You take it," I told her, handing her my phone.

She did.

Alex answered, listened to Blanton on the other end of the line for a few seconds, and then she let out a loud groan.

"There's a new post that just went up on the *National Investigator* website," she said to me. "All about Susan Stratton and her disappearance from the *Pick Your Partner* TV set and her potential involvement in both the Laurie Reddick and Rebecca Burgess murders. That son of a bitch has it all."

Damn.

It had happened again.

Another big scoop for Brett Anson.

TWENTY-EIGHT

The headline on the *National Investigator* site said:

STAR FBI AGENT NOW ON TRAIL OF MISSING TV STAR

Wacky Neighbor on *Pick Your Partner* Eyed as Suspect in Murders

I really didn't want to read Brett Anson's article, but I knew I had no choice. I plunged into it:

There has been a stunning new twist in the story of two teenaged girls found slain in separate incidents in Ohio, the National Investigator *learned today.*

FBI Agent Nikki Cassidy, notorious to Investigator *followers for her unorthodox, yet highly successful tactics in solving high-profile cases, showed up on the set of the hit TV show* Pick Your Partner *this week in an effort to question cast member Susan Stratton about the murders.*

But Stratton had fled, apparently after learning that Agent Cassidy was coming to see her.

A source close to the investigation told the National Investigator *that authorities believe Stratton—known for her ability to change her appearance from week to week in the popular show—may have used that same technique to look like Cassidy, or even to show a possible resemblance to what Cassidy's sister Caitlin—murdered fifteen years ago—might look like if she was alive today, in connection with the murders.*

It is not clear to Cassidy or other authorities why Stratton might have done this, according to the source.

But the name of the dead Caitlin Cassidy has consistently come up in these current murder cases.

I read the piece all the way through to the end.

It was a very long article, and it didn't get any better, at least as far as I was concerned.

Then I went back and read it again.

"How in the hell does this guy Brett Anson know so much?" I said out loud after I was done.

"I think we need to call a press conference," Dave Blanton said on a Zoom call after we'd filled him in on the *National Investigator* article and more about Brett Anson's constant exclusives.

"God, I hate to call a press conference," Alex said.

"Me too," agreed Tatarko who was on the call with us.

"Let's call a press conference," I said.

"Seriously."

"It's the only choice we have at this point."

We had tried to keep many of the sensational details about this case under the radar as much as we could so far by not going public with all the leads and links we'd uncovered. Just putting out press releases about an ongoing investigation with results expected soon, blah, blah, blah.

But now Anson had forced our hand. There was nothing we

could do about that. Our only option was to beat him at his own game by being totally transparent with the public. Tell them everything.

"Do you want to hold the press conference back there with you in Washington, Chief?" I asked.

"No, I think it has to be done in Ohio."

"Here?"

"Yes, that's the site of the murders. Do it there."

"Uh, do it?"

"That's right."

"What exactly—and who—do you mean by 'do it?'"

"You, Agent Cassidy."

"Me?"

"Yes, you should run the press conference."

"Uh, why me?"

"Because you're the face of all this. Alex and the state police and local people should be there too. But you're the one who should stand up in front of the media, tell them exactly what we've been doing and then answer any of their questions. I know it's not going to be easy. But, as you say, this is something that has to be done. And, if it has to be done, you should be the one doing it."

He didn't say this was your mess, Agent Cassidy, with this guy Anson—so you clean it up.

But he might as well have.

I looked over at Alex and Tatarko.

"He's right," Alex said. "You should be the one doing the press conference. No question about it."

"Yeah, it's gotta be you," Tatarko said.

"Okay, we're all agreed then," Blanton said. "Nikki, you'll do the press conference."

I sighed.

"Lucky me."

TWENTY-NINE

The press conference itself was tense, confrontational and put me pretty much on the defensive the whole time.

I figured that was what would happen.

But it turned out to be even worse than I expected.

I did my best to answer the onslaught of questions that were hurled at me.

"Are you close to catching the killer?"

"Is there more than one killer?"

"Do you have any leads at all?"

"Do you fear that more young girls are in danger?"

There was a lot of media there.

TV stations, cable news channels, newspapers and, of course, the internet journalists of today like Brett Anson.

Anson sat in the front row of the press section, smirking at me the whole time I talked and answered questions.

He was clearly enjoying being in the spotlight as the reporter who had forced us to call the press conference after all of his exclusive stories breaking news about the cases and our investigation.

Anson stood up now to ask a question.

"Brett Anson, the *National Investigator*," he announced.

"I know who you are."

"I'm sure you do."

"Do you have a question, Mr. Anson?"

"How did you let Susan Stratton just get away like that, Agent Cassidy?" Anson asked then.

"She didn't just 'get away.' She left the set of the *Pick Your Partner* show on her own before I arrived."

"After she found out from her director on the show that you were coming to the set to question her about the murders?"

"That's right."

"Don't you think it was a mistake—a lapse in judgement on your part—to announce to a suspect that you were investigating her?"

"She wasn't a suspect at the time."

"And now?"

"She's a suspect."

"Who is free at the moment because you gave her advance warning of your arrival, allowing her time to flee before that happened."

Anson was right about that.

I had screwed up by giving Susan Stratton that advance notice.

I knew that myself, but I wasn't going to discuss it with him or the rest of the reporters at this press conference.

"We are conducting a massive nationwide search for Susan Stratton, who we believe is connected in some way with the murders of these two young girls—Laurie Reddick and Rebecca Burgess. We are confident we will be able to apprehend her very soon and question her about anything she knows about the deaths."

Another reporter brought up the issue of the fake Grace Hazlett who claimed to have found Laurie Reddick's body along with her supposed daughter, who turned out to be Rebecca Burgess—a later murder victim.

"This woman—whoever she is—was the killer of the Reddick girl, right?"

"We believe that is the most likely possibility."

"And she simply walked away from that restroom on the Ohio Turnpike after talking to authorities?"

"That's correct."

"No one suspected she was the killer?"

"Not at that time."

"And isn't it true that you yourself later talked to the woman called Grace Hazlett on the phone, and continued to believe her story about being an innocent witness to the crime?"

"We did not find out the truth until later."

"Until after another girl, Rebecca Burgess, was strangled to death. Do you feel responsible for her death at all, Agent Cassidy? Do you admit that you and the FBI's actions—or lack of action—on this fake Grace Hazlett woman might have cost the second young girl her life?"

There was no good way to answer that question.

So I just responded with the best stock reply I could think of.

"We are conducting an extensive search for the woman who identified herself as Grace Hazlett," I said. "We expect to get more answers when she is apprehended."

"Just like you expect to catch and get more answers from Susan Stratton, huh?" someone yelled out sarcastically.

"We are pursuing the investigation actively on all fronts."

The whole event brought back memories for me of being peppered with questions like this that I couldn't answer about the FBI's activities during The Singles Slayer case. But I was younger then, and I guess it didn't bother me as much. Now, I was angry with Blanton that he'd put me out there as a punching bag for the media like this. At the same time, I realized someone had to do it. And that someone turned out to be me. It was just a part of the job, I told myself.

I continued to answer questions as best I could.

They came fast and furious.

The toughest question though came from Brett Anson at the end.

"One of the strangest things about this case has been the inclusion of your sister Caitlin—slain fifteen years ago—in various aspects of these murders," Anson said. "Why do you think this is happening?"

There it was.

Caitlin.

I knew it was coming, and I knew it would likely come from Anson himself.

"I don't know," I said.

"Do you think that whoever is behind this is trying to get your attention—specifically, not the rest of law enforcement— by bringing in all of these things about your dead sister Caitlin?"

"I don't know."

"Can you at least give us a theory about what's going on here with your sister?"

"I don't know."

"Okay, how about this? Have you ever considered the possibility that your sister is still out there somewhere? That your sister—unbelievable as this might sound—is still alive? And somehow involved in all of these murders? And that's why she keeps turning up as a part of all of them? Have you thought about that? In other words, are you absolutely certain your sister Caitlin is dead, Agent Cassidy?"

There were several logical ways for me to answer that question.

I could have said that I was "absolutely certain" Caitlin was dead.

I could have called him out and tried to embarrass him for asking such a ridiculous question.

But I didn't do either of those things.

"No comment," I said, and then ended the press conference.

THIRTY

On the night after the press conference, Anson reached out and asked me if I'd meet him for a drink that night at my hotel bar.

I was about to say no, but then I reconsidered.

I wanted to find out more about Brett Anson. Maybe this was a way to accomplish that. And so I agreed to have a drink with him. Just one drink, I said, one drink only. He said that was fine.

"I'm not going to talk to you about anything involving this case," I told Anson as soon as we sat down.

"Okay."

"And I'm not going to answer any more questions from you about my sister Caitlin either."

"Well, then, I guess I shouldn't even be wasting my time with you."

He smiled when he said it. A big smile that I'm certain he thought was charming. I had the feeling he'd used it on a lot of other women to get what he wanted from them. Either a big story or a roll in bed. Maybe sometimes even both. But charming smiles didn't work on me. I'd seen a lot of them from men in my time who didn't turn out to be so charming. No, I was definitely immune at this point to a guy who tried to win me over with his charming smile.

"I'm serious," I said.

"I understand, we won't talk about the case or my story or any of that stuff."

"Then why are you here?'

"To talk. Just you and me. Have a real conversation with each other. No press conference, no police—only the two of us. Talking with each other."

"Will you tell me who the source is feeding you information about the case?" I asked him.

"I'm afraid I can't do that."

"Well, if we can't talk about the case or about your stories on the case, what in the world are you and I going to talk about?"

"Anything you want. Politics. Music. Books. Your favorite TV shows. I'd love to know more about you, Agent Cassidy—"

He stopped in mid-sentence.

"Agent Cassidy sounds so formal," he said.

"It's who I am."

"How about I call you Nikki instead?"

"How about we keep it at Agent Cassidy?"

He smiled again. I guess he figured he could win me over with that smile, sooner or later.

"Look, Agent Cassidy," he said, "I think we got off on the wrong foot, you and me."

"We sure did. You broke into my hotel room. I found you hiding in my bathroom. You practically ran me over trying to get away. I subdued you, and I put you in custody. Did I leave anything out about that first meeting of ours?"

"It was not my finest moment, I admit."

"And your story about what happened between you and me which was total fiction—or at least your website's story, even though you claim it wasn't your idea—made me look bad to the public and to my boss back in Washington."

"Guilty on all counts," he said.

"So once again—why are we here?"

"Like I said, I'd love to get to know you better. And let you get to know me a bit too. Maybe I can help you realize I'm not as bad a guy as you think I am."

I'd ordered a beer, and so had he. I figured a quick beer was the way to go with him. I'd finish that off, and then be on my way. Until then, I wanted to get Anson talking about himself, instead of him asking about me. So I started peppering him with questions.

"How long have you been a reporter?" I asked.

"Oh, awhile. Officially. But it was only just recently that I got my shot at the *National Investigator*. I'm trying to turn this into something even bigger. Okay, maybe I do try too hard sometimes, but haven't you ever done that in your job to get people to notice you? This is what I always wanted to do. Be a journalist. Be a reporter. Break big exclusive stories. It's what I've aspired to ever since I grew up watching *All the President's Men* and a lot of other journalistic stuff."

"And you imagined yourself as one of those reporters?"

"That's right."

"Which one—Woodward or Bernstein?"

"Woodward." He smiled.

"The Robert Redford character."

"Right. I have friends who tell me I even look a lot like Robert Redford."

I chuckled at that.

"Hold onto those friends, Anson, people like that are hard to find."

He didn't tell me anything about his personal life, and I didn't ask. I sure didn't want to go down that road with him. But then he didn't ask me anything about my personal life either. Instead, he started talking about my career.

"You're quite the superstar at the FBI," he said. "I knew

about you before all this, but I've also done some more research since then. Your most famous case—at least until this Caitlin business happened here in Ohio—was you chasing down a child molester in Denver and saving the life of a thirteen-year-old girl named Julie Mathieu he was holding. She'd been missing for six weeks. You saved her life when everyone else thought she was already dead.

"Most of the cases you've handled have involved young people, especially teenaged girls. But you've been a part of a lot of other big successful FBI investigations too. There was The Highway Killer who shot a half dozen girls at random in passing cars on highways through several states until you found him. Or The Psychic, where you figured out someone was using astrology charts and palm reading to target young women as his victims. And then there was The Greenfield Rapist who terrorized a lot of women until you caught him.

"It's a damn impressive record you've got there, Agent Cassidy. That's why you're such a media star."

I asked Anson what he was working on. Did he have another big story in the works?

"I was hoping I'd get one from you."

"Well, we know now that's not going to happen."

"Bummer."

"Haven't you found out anything else except whatever I know about?" I asked him, just for something to say.

"Actually, I have. I'm following up a big lead right now. I hope to break another exclusive very soon."

"Really?"

"You heard it here first."

"What's the story?"

"I'm sorry, but I don't talk about my stories. Just like you don't talk about your cases. Wasn't that our arrangement for tonight?"

THIRTY-ONE

If we didn't catch the killer—or killers—very soon, there was very likely to be another murder. I was pretty sure of that. So was Alex. And Bonnie Tatarko.

And yet, when the new death happened, it was still more shocking and unexpected than any of us could ever imagine.

Tatarko again was the one who broke the news to us.

"My God, there's been another murder!" she said. "Another young girl found dead. Strangled to death just like the last two."

"Who is she?"

"Unidentified as yet."

"Where?"

"It's back in your hometown, Nikki. Huntsdale."

I was driving as Alex and I raced back to Huntsdale from Columbus. Alex sat in the passenger seat texting and receiving messages with the latest updates on the murdered girl.

"We've got a positive ID now," she said. "Jeez, Nikki, she was even younger than the others. Only twelve years old."

The same age as my sister, I thought to myself.

"Her name is Linda Grasso. Found strangled in bed. Ligature marks on her neck. They indicate someone put a noose or rope of some kind around her neck, then tightened it and loosened it until she finally suffocated. Just like happened with Laurie Reddick and Rebecca Burgess. She was a sixth grader at some school about seventy-five miles away from here. Scheduled to go to middle school or junior high, whatever they call it now, this fall. Had blue eyes, blonde hair, pretty girl—everyone says she was really adorable. Oops, here she is... I just got a picture of her."

Alex turned the phone toward me so I could see it. I looked at the picture of Linda Grasso as best I could quickly, not wanting to take my eyes off the road for too long. But even a quick glance was all I needed to confirm what Alex was saying. Linda Grasso had been an adorable little girl. Like Laurie Reddick and Rebecca Burgess.

Seeing the pictures of young girls who had died violently like this always affected me deeply, no matter how long I'd been doing this job and no matter how many of these pictures of young victims that I had seen.

There was a haunting quality to the face of Linda Grasso—just like with all of them—even in the brief time I'd looked at it. So full of energy and hope and life in this picture. With no idea that her life was about to be cut tragically short by someone who was pure evil. Linda Grasso would never grow up to be a woman, follow a career path, get married, have children, or even grow old. Instead, her life was over in only twelve short years.

Again, the same age as my sister Caitlin.

Maybe that's why this death shook me up so much. The girl was the same age as Caitlin; she was murdered in the same town; she even looked a little like Caitlin.

"The case is being handled by your old friend Chief Frank Earnshaw and the Huntsdale Police Department. They're all over the crime scene—the house where the body was found—right now, turning the place upside down. Searching the area for a possible suspect. But it seems likely whoever did this is long gone. Like the cases from Columbus."

Alex looked down at the screen on her phone and read some more information that was coming in.

"Nothing from the house, nothing from the neighborhood, nothing anywhere so far, according to what we're getting from the Huntsdale police."

"The Keystone cops at work," I grunted.

"You don't think they're capable of handling this on their own?"

"With Chief Frank Earnshaw in charge? I do not."

"I don't imagine Earnshaw will be too happy to see us back in town. Even if he can't make any headway on the case, he's not going to want any help from the FBI."

"Especially from me, huh?"

"Yeah, he hates you, Nikki."

I sighed.

"What can I say? I think you've summed up my relationship —or my non-relationship—with Frank Earnshaw pretty damn well. And the feeling is mutual."

"Why does he bother you so much?"

"He's incompetent."

"You've worked with incompetent law enforcement people before."

"He's a pain in the ass to deal with."

"You've worked with pain in the asses in the past too. But there's something different with Earnshaw. Something besides him being incompetent or a pain in the ass that sticks in your craw. What is it?"

Alex was right about that.

"He's not my father," I said.

"That's what bothers you about him?"

"My father was a top-flight lawman. He was a decent human being. He did a great job when he was the police chief. I guess it's just difficult for me to see someone like Earnshaw in the job my father was so proud of and did so well."

We were on the outskirts of Huntsdale now. Passing by buildings and landmarks and other places that I knew so well growing up. Ever since Caitlin's death, I'd spent my entire adult life trying to stay as far away as possible from Huntsdale. But now something—or someone—kept pulling me back here to deal with the same kind of evil that had taken my sister's life away a long time ago.

Why?

Why was this so much about me?

"Do you want to go to the Huntsdale station house first?" Alex asked.

"Let's go directly to the crime scene. Where is it?"

Alex studied some information on her phone.

"This says it's near the First Presbyterian Church. All we have to do is find that, and we'll see all the police cars on the street."

"The First Presbyterian Church? That's right in my old neighborhood."

"Okay, the address we're looking for—the exact place the girl died—is 611 Stockton Road. Do you know where that is?"

I let go of the steering wheel in shock, almost driving the car off the road, before I regained control.

"Jesus, Nikki," Alex yelled at me. "What's going on?"

"611 Stockton Road?"

"Yes, do you know that address?"

Oh, I knew that address all right.

I knew it all too well.

That was the address of the house where I grew up.

THIRTY-TWO

My old house at 611 Stockton Road looked the same on the outside as I remembered from when I'd been here not long ago to talk to Maureen Wilcox, the woman who lived here now. The same house I remembered as a young girl growing up in Huntsdale. But I knew it wasn't the same house anymore. It would never be the same house for me. A girl had been murdered inside this house now, the house where I grew up and had so many fond memories of from that time.

And no matter how many different ways I tried to look at it, I couldn't get away from the fact that this twelve-year-old girl had died because of me. I was the reason she was murdered here. I had to be the reason.

There were police cars all over the street in front. Cops inside and outside the house too. Chief Frank Earnshaw was there with them, leading the investigation for the Huntsdale Police Department. He met me at the front door when I walked up onto the front porch where I used to sit with my father a long, long time ago.

"This is your old house," he said to me when he saw Alex and me. "You used to live here."

But he said it more like he was talking to himself—out of confusion or surprise or desperation—rather than talking to me."

"I know."

"Do you have any idea why a girl would be murdered here in your old house?" he asked.

"No, not really."

"Well, there has to be some reason. A connection to you or to your family."

"I think..." I wasn't quite sure how to say it. "I think it was done as a message."

"What kind of message?"

"A message to me."

"My God, who takes an innocent young girl's life just to send some sort of a sick message?"

"The same kind of person who takes the lives of two innocent girls at rest stops to send their message, Chief."

It was the first time in quite a while that I called him chief. Maybe out of a sign of some sort of respect since he was heading up the investigation here, whether I liked it or not. But there was something else too. Earnshaw was less confrontational with me this time. Not exactly friendly, but at least professionally courteous.

I really think this new murder—and the circumstances behind it—had truly shocked him. He wanted answers, and he wasn't sure how to get them. Maybe for once he was happy, or at least relieved, to have the expertise of a couple of FBI agents on the scene to help him in the investigation. Even if one of those FBI agents was me.

"Who found the body?" I asked.

"Maureen Wilcox. The owner of the house. She came into the house, saw someone had been there, searched to see if anything was missing—it wasn't—and that's when she found Linda Grasso dead."

"Linda wasn't one of her own children?" Alex asked.

"No, she'd never seen the girl before."

I'd been hoping the victim wasn't from Maureen Wilcox's family. She'd told me during our earlier conversation she had three children, and one of them was a girl. The different name made me think Linda Grasso wasn't her child, although I wondered at first if the name could be different because of a divorce or something.

"Where is Mrs. Wilcox now?" I asked Earnshaw.

"At the station. They're trying to talk to her about anything she might know or remember that could help us solve this thing. So far, they haven't had much success. She's crying and distraught and pretty much an emotional mess, I've been told. Which is understandable after what she just experienced."

"And no one else is dead or missing or anything?" I asked, wondering about her three children.

"No, just Linda Grasso."

"Does anyone have any idea how the girl got into the house?" Alex wanted to know.

"Sure. There's a glass pane shattered in the back where an intruder must have entered. It could have been the Grasso girl on her own, I guess, although that doesn't make a lot of sense. Under that scenario, someone came into the house afterward and murdered her. Not likely. It makes more sense that someone came in with her, and that person murdered her after they were inside the house."

"Or killed her somewhere else and brought the body in here for some reason?"

"That's possible too, I guess."

"And she was strangled?"

"That's what it looks like."

"Just like the girls in Columbus."

"This girl was from the Columbus area, too," Earnshaw said. "A little town south of there called Circleville. No one in

Huntsdale knew her as far as we know, or has any idea why she wound up here."

"Had she been missing—run away from home or something —like the other two girls were?"

"No, she was at home and at school for the past few days. And then suddenly she turns up here. It makes no sense. None of this makes any goddamned sense at all.'

"Where is the body right now?" Alex asked.

"At the coroner's office. The ME did an autopsy, and the girl's family is on the way now to claim the body. But we probably won't be able to release the body to them until the investigation is further along."

We were standing in the living room now where I had sat that day with Maureen Wilcox. Like that day, a lot of memories came rushing back to me. My father sitting in his easy chair. My sister running through the house. My mother cooking in the kitchen. The furniture was different now though, the wallpaper different... everything was different.

"Where exactly was the body found?" Alex asked Earnshaw.

"Upstairs. I'll show you."

We walked up the stairs. The same stairs I'd been up and down so many times as a kid. There were three bedrooms up there. One had been for my mother and father; another belonged to Caitlin; and the third one—the one in the corner— used to be mine.

I looked in there first, thinking that might have been the best way to deliver the message to me, leaving the girl's dead body in the same room where I used to sleep.

But that room was empty. No crime scene ribbons, no evidence markers, nothing at all.

"The body was found in the next bedroom," Earnshaw said. "The one down the hall."

Caitlin's bedroom.
The same room where my little sister had grown up.
Until she was murdered.
And now another girl had died in there.

THIRTY-THREE

I needed to maintain control. I needed to keep my emotions in check. I needed to make sure I didn't make this too personal, even though I knew whoever killed this girl had tried to make it as personal as they could for me.

But I knew, if I succumbed to that emotion, I'd simply be playing along with the killer's game. That was the reason for all of this. The sightings of the Caitlin/Nikki look-alike. The roses stuff, reminding me of the roses found on my sister's body. And now the body of another murdered young girl, twelve years old just like Caitlin, in my sister's old bedroom.

No, what I had to do right now was remain professional.

Do my job as an FBI investigator, not act like the sister of Caitlin or like a person who saw Caitlin's face on all of these dead girls' bodies.

That wasn't going to be easy, but the best thing I could do for all of these girls—including the memory of Caitlin—was catch the sick son of a bitch who was doing all this.

"Are you okay?" Alex asked as we stood next to the bed where Linda Grasso's body had been found.

"I'm fine."

"You don't look fine."

"Let's get to work. Check out this room. See if there's any possible clues or evidence the killer left behind."

"I imagine the Huntsdale police already did this."

"Maybe they missed something."

I put on a pair of evidence gloves and began examining things in the bedroom. The first thing I noticed was that this didn't seem to be a child's bedroom anymore. There were clothes in the drawers and the closet, but they belonged to a grown woman—not a teenaged girl or any other young person.

I wondered how the house was set up now. Where did the three kids sleep? All together in one room? That seemed odd, even though it didn't seemingly have anything to do with what happened in this room. Still, I made a mental note to check that afterward.

On the bed in the room—which was still made with a pink, floral-covered bedspread on top—you could still see the imprint of where the Grasso girl's body had lain. I took a picture of that with my iPhone.

Alex and I went through the rest of the room without finding anything relevant. Other than the woman's clothes, there wasn't much in here at all. It seemed like it hadn't been used much, just as an extra room for storing things or for an overnight guest to the house maybe.

"Where are Maureen Wilcox's three children?" I asked Alex.

"Not here."

"Why not?"

"All I know is that Earnshaw said there was no one else in the house when the Wilcox woman came home and found the girl's body."

I made another mental note to ask Maureen Wilcox about the whereabouts of her children when I talked with her again. I wanted to make sure they were safe and sound. There were too many dead children already.

We got a break before we left the house. At least it seemed like it could be a break. Maureen Wilcox had a video security system set up to protect the house.

"Covers front and back," Earnshaw told us. "It's supposed to have an alarm too if there's an intruder. None of the neighbors heard anything. Maybe the intruder disarmed it somehow once he got in the house. But the video—which was still working—hopefully caught someone entering the house. We're just going to look at it now. We downloaded it onto this laptop. So let's watch what's on the video."

Ah, the wonders of technology.

It used to be that accessing a security video like this was a lot more difficult and time consuming.

Now you could do it with the push of a button or two.

The footage at the front of the house showed nothing at all. No one there, no one trying the door or windows, no sign of any forced entry of any kind.

But the video in the back was more likely to show something. That's where we found the shattered window that had apparently been used to gain entry. So we watched more video from there. Lots of video. From all that day before Maureen Wilcox came home and found the body. Then from the night before. A small meter at the bottom of the screen clicked off the time as we scrolled through. It was at 2:14 a.m. when we finally saw something. A figure moving in the dark.

"Smashing the window in," Earnshaw said as we watched the scene.

"We can't see the face," I said. "It's just a figure in the dark."

"Only one person?" Alex asked.

"That's all I see," Earnshaw replied.

"Where's the girl?" I said.

We got our answer—or what we assumed to be the answer—

a minute or so later. The figure moved back outside the house, stepped out of camera range briefly and then returned holding a long object. It looked like a plastic bag.

"Do you think that's the girl?" Alex asked.

"Has to be," I said. "It looks like she was killed somewhere else, and then the killer came here to leave the body,"

"Can we get any kind of a better close-up of the figure in the video, maybe make out something from the face?" Alex asked Earnshaw.

"We can try to get a better view once we take it back to the station and use some of the equipment we have there."

"It won't do any good." I sighed. "Whoever did this knew there was a security camera there. Knew they'd be caught on it. Knew we would be looking at this. They weren't going to be stupid enough to reveal their face to the camera."

We went back to the Huntsdale Police Station afterward to talk more with Maureen Wilcox, who was still there. I was eager to do that. She'd already been helpful the first few times we met. Maybe she could tell us something else now that she knew or remembered leading up to this.

"Where is she?" I asked Earnshaw once we were inside the building.

"Waiting in a conference room over there," he said, pointing to a door off the main entrance to the station.

"How is she doing?"

"Pretty upset."

"I can imagine."

"We've tried to go slow—being as sensitive as we can—in questioning her. I hope you will do the same, Cassidy."

"Of course."

We walked over to the door, Earnshaw pushed it open and the three of us—me, Alex and Earnshaw—went inside. There was a woman sitting at a table there drinking from a cup of coffee. She looked up at us when we came into the room. Her hair was white, she looked old with plenty of wrinkles and I figured her age to be at least in the sixties.

"Who is this?" I asked Earnshaw.

"Maureen Wilcox."

"This isn't Maureen Wilcox. I met her. She's around forty, with dark hair, she looks nothing like this woman, whoever she is."

"She says she's Maureen Wilcox," Earnshaw said.

"Of course, I'm Maureen Wilcox," the woman at the table said to me now. "Who are you?"

I told her and showed her my FBI badge. Then I asked for some identification from her. She gave me a driver's license, a Social Security card and several credit cards. All of them identified her as Maureen Wilcox.

"Do you believe me now?" she asked.

I believed her.

This was Maureen Wilcox.

But then who in the hell was the woman I talked to living in my old house?

THIRTY-FOUR

We spent a long time questioning Maureen Wilcox and trying to get some answers from her about what was going on here.

We got a lot of answers from the woman.

They just weren't the answers we wanted to hear.

Among the things we learned from her were:

- She had not lived in that house for more than a year. She had moved to a condo on the outskirts of town. She had left all the furniture and some of her belongings there to help attract potential renters.
- She had two children, not three like the woman in the house had told me. Both of them were grown now and hadn't lived in the house with her for a number of years. Her husband was dead, and she had lived in the house alone until the move to the condo.
- She had rented the house out to someone after she left it. That sounded like a promising lead until I found out more about it. It turned out to be elderly couple—even older than Maureen Wilcox—who

were just staying there until their retirement home in Florida was ready so they could be close to their daughter and grandchildren in Sarasota. No, it didn't seem very likely they were the people we were looking for.

- Maureen Wilcox had been on a lengthy world cruise—something she decided to treat herself to, she said—and hadn't visited the house for quite a while until she went there and found the body.

"I got a call that something was wrong at the house," she told us. "I had just gotten back from the cruise recently and hadn't been to the house. I went to check and that's... that's when I found that poor girl."

"And you never saw the girl before?" Alex asked.

"No, I had—I still have—no idea who she was."

"Her name was Linda Grasso, and she was from a little town called Circleville, near Columbus," I said. "Does that mean anything at all to you?"

Maureen Wilcox—the real Maureen Wilcox—shook her head.

"No. What would she be doing in my house?"

"I think it had more to do with the fact that I once lived in that same house a long time ago."

She looked at me more closely now, and I could see a sign of recognition on her face. "Of course, you're Luke Cassidy's daughter. I heard you and your family lived in that house before me. But what in the world could your living there have to do with this girl's body I found?"

"That's what we're trying to figure out," Alex said. "Tell us more about the call you got telling you something was wrong at the house."

"Not much to say. They just told me that and hung up."

"Was it a man or a woman?"

"Um, it was a man. I think. Or maybe it was a woman. It's hard to say."

"What do you mean?" I asked.

"Well, the voice sounded strange. Not normal. Almost like it was... I don't know."

"Disguised?"

"Yes, that's right. It seemed like whoever was on the other end of the line didn't want me to recognize their voice for some reason."

"What do you think?" I asked Alex and Tatarko afterward. Tatarko had joined Alex and me back here in Huntsdale after the discovery of the dead girl in my old house. It was a bit out of her jurisdiction, but I think she felt she was a part of this case working with us on it. I remembered her telling me how she wanted to be part of a big, high-profile investigation instead of the usual routine kind of cases she handled in Columbus. Well, now she had one. Me, I was glad to have her there.

I didn't include Earnshaw in this conversation. Even though he'd been better toward me since I returned to Huntsdale this time, I still wanted to spend as little time with him as possible. I preferred working with Tatarko.

"Someone finds out that the Wilcox woman is on a long ocean cruise and not in town. And that the people she rented the house to have moved out. So they—or at least the woman you met there earlier—live there themselves. But why?"

"Because I used to live there."

"That doesn't make any sense."

"Nothing about this case makes any sense."

"Here's another question," Alex asked. "If someone was living in that house like this—and they really were the killer, pretending to be Maureen Wilcox—why break in that back window to get the girl's body inside? Why not just go in the front door, like they must have done so many times before?"

"Wait a minute!" I said. "What you just said about going in and out the door, Alex. That means there must be a record of them on the video security system. All we have to do is go back far enough on the video to see the woman or anyone else living in the house after the renters. They'll be a picture of the woman I met. Maybe we can use that picture to compare it with someone else in our files. Maybe someone will know her."

"Sorry, but I already checked with Earnshaw and his people on that," Alex said. "There is no earlier video. Someone disabled it. It wasn't working from the time the renters moved out until the night we saw the intruder with the body breaking in."

I nodded.

I understood now what had happened.

I understood it all too well.

"That's why the video was suddenly working again."

"Huh?" Tatarko said. "If it had been disabled, why did it start working again that night?"

"Because whoever disabled the video started it up again."

"Why would they do that?"

"To make sure we saw them. To make sure we knew who it was without actually revealing their identity. Letting us see that video was deliberate. A kind of symbolic 'Fuck You' to all of us."

"Jesus." Tatarko sighed.

"Well, at least we know more about everything going on than we did before," Alex said. "We know that someone connected with this was living in that house for quite a while. The woman you met, Nikki."

"Maybe if we dust the place for fingerprints something will turn up," Tatarko suggested. "I mean it seems like the woman was living there all that time. Ask the local police to check the place for prints or anything else that might trace her. We can give Earnshaw some of our crime lab people to help too."

"It won't do any good," I told her. "Yes, you're right. We should go look for fingerprints or any other evidence of the woman that might be there. But I'm pretty sure we won't find anything. Whoever is doing this is too smart for that. They would have cleaned up the place very thoroughly before they left."

"Always one step ahead of us," Alex muttered.

"And we better catch up in a hurry," I said, "before someone else dies."

THIRTY-FIVE

One of the things I always did when I came back to Huntsdale was to go to my favorite diner. It was on Main Street in the center of town. I'd gone there regularly when I was growing up here—first with my father and mother and little sister, then with friends from high school before I moved away.

I still liked to go back there.

This diner always felt like home and brought back some good memories of my time in Huntsdale.

I could use some good memories of Huntsdale right now.

So I went back there again, this time with Bonnie Tatarko.

I ordered the same thing I always used to order whenever I came here—a tuna fish triple decker sandwich, with French fries on the side. Bonnie was working on a cheddar cheese omelet, with hashed brown potatoes.

"What the hell is going on here?" Tatarko asked between bites of her omelet.

"I don't understand it either."

"Leaving that girl's body in the house where you used to live. Even putting it in your sister's bedroom. And the woman living there—the phony Maureen Wilcox you met—she must have been in that house for weeks to pull all of that off. Why go to all that kind of trouble?"

"To get to me."

"But it's those girls the killer targeted—the ones that are dead."

"They're not the ultimate target, Bonnie. I am. He's using them to get to me. I'm convinced of that. What I don't understand is who he is or why he's doing this."

"He?"

"Or she. It was just a figure of speech."

"Yes, we still don't know for sure whether this is a man or a woman doing this. Or a man and a woman working together. Or —more likely—at least two women are involved. We don't know any of that."

"We don't know very much," I said.

I took a big bite of my tuna fish triple decker. Amazingly enough, it tasted as good as I remembered it used to taste. The last time I'd been here had been with Billy Weller. Before he died. I had a quick flashback in my mind to that moment with Billy, but quickly dismissed it. I needed to focus on the problem in front of me.

Most of all, I needed to figure out about Caitlin.

Why was she suddenly such a big part of this case, even though she had been dead and buried for fifteen years?

"Being back in Caitlin's old room like that really rattled me," I said. "It was tough enough going back to that house the first time I was there. But now—to have a body of a young girl, a girl close to Caitlin's age found lying dead there on the bed—it's almost too much for me to take. If whoever did this was trying to get to me, to play on my grief for Caitlin, they certainly accomplished that purpose."

I took another bite of my tuna fish, then pushed the plate

away. Suddenly it didn't taste so great. Comfort food like that can only be comforting for so long.

"Being back there in Caitlin's bedroom like that... well, a lot of thoughts came rushing back to me about the last time Caitlin and I were in that room together," I said.

"When was that?"

"The night before she died."

"Jeez."

"Yeah, I'll never forget that. I'd gone into Caitlin's room late that night—long after she was supposed to be asleep—and we talked and giggled for a long time there. God, I remember that conversation so well. It was about boys. I was excited about maybe meeting some boys at the carnival that had come to town. And Caitlin, well, she had just discovered boys—at the age of twelve—and she was sweet on this boy in her sixth-grade class. I hadn't thought about all that in years. I guess I must have just pushed it out of my mind after Caitlin was gone. But all of it—that last conversation we had about boys—came rushing back to me standing in that bedroom again."

Tatarko nodded sympathetically.

"Whoever is behind this thing to keep you remembering Caitlin, to make her such a big part of this, to even pretend she is still alive—they're doing a very cruel thing to you, Nikki."

"What if she is?" I suddenly blurted out.

"What if she is what?"

"Alive."

"Caitlin?"

"Yes, Caitlin."

"What are you saying?"

"I know that sounds crazy."

"It sounds insane."

"But there's been a lot of crazy, insane things that have happened about her since this all started. None of them seem to make any sense to us. Not if Caitlin is dead. But if she were somehow alive... well, then a lot of this falls into place."

"Nikki, do you realize what you're saying? If your sister was alive and really involved in this, that could mean she was helping carry out these killings in some way."

"I understand that."

"How would that make you feel?"

"If it was true, I would feel bad about what Caitlin had become. But I would feel good too. Good to know..."

My voice trailed off at even the wild thought of it all being possible.

"She would be alive," Tatarko said.

"Yes."

"Listen, we both know that's not possible. She was dead and buried fifteen years ago. You've talked about visiting her grave. You almost died in that shoot-out recently at your sister's gravesite."

"What if that's not her down there?"

I had just said out loud something I had been thinking about in the deepest recesses of my mind, something I was afraid to admit even to myself was a possibility.

"What if that's not her down there in that grave?"

"An empty grave?"

"I don't know. Maybe there's another body, of another young girl, buried there."

I told her now about all the strange things I'd encountered surrounding Caitlin's death, including the missing pages from my father's official police report on the case.

"It still sounds crazy," Tatarko said.

"I know that."

"But you're thinking about it anyway."

"I can't get it out of my mind."

"Is there anyone here you can ask about this? Anyone you

can trust? Anyone who can at least put your mind to rest about Caitlin?"

"There is one person."

"Who?"

"Michael Franze. He was the Medical Examiner back then when Caitlin was murdered. He still is. I've known him for a long time. He was a friend of my father's."

"Then go talk to him," Tatarko said.

THIRTY-SIX

We had a long history, Michael (Big Mickey) Franze and me. Going all the way back to when he was a close friend of my father. He'd been the Medical Examiner in Huntsdale during those years my father was the police chief. And he was still here doing the job now. It was a pretty remarkable record of longevity.

He was more than just the Medical Examiner in Huntsdale though. The man was a force, a presence around town. Everyone called him Big Mickey because he stood well over six foot and must have weighed somewhere around three hundred pounds. He showed up everywhere in Huntsdale too—drinking coffee at a diner every morning; in the stands at Huntsdale High football and basketball games; he was even grand marshal for the annual Fourth of July parade through downtown Huntsdale.

As someone once said about him—for a guy who dealt in death for his job, he sure brought a lot of life to the town.

He was the only person who I thought I might be able to talk to candidly about Caitlin.

To tell everything I was thinking right now about my sister, no matter how crazy or outlandish or impossible it might seem.

I couldn't really do that with my mother.

So here I was in Big Mickey Franze's office trying to make some sort of sense out of everything that had happened.

"It certainly is strange," he said. "I mean that body being found in your old house. And in your sister's bedroom, too. I'm sure all of these things keep bringing up some terrible memories for you, Nikki."

"And they never seem to stop happening either, do they?"

First, there had been The Nowhere Men, a group of sexually sick men who abducted teenaged girls, then filmed their murders for their own perverted enjoyment. I caught the man in the group who confessed to killing my sister before he died—who amazingly turned out to be a respected man in Huntsdale, the District Attorney.

You never know about the evil that is hiding in some people.

After that, there were more murders connected to my sister's death, with the killer leaving behind roses just like the roses that were on my sister's body when she was found. Taunting me with the memory of Caitlin again. That killer turned out to be another FBI agent who had been going through the motions of working with me on the case, while secretly carrying out a series of murders on young girls.

First the DA, then an FBI agent. People I thought I could trust. As a result, I trust very few people these days, except—I suppose—my partner, Alex. You always have to trust your partner. And I trusted Franze because my father had trusted him.

"What do *you* think's going on?" he asked me.

"Obviously someone has targeted me—and the memory of Caitlin too—in some sort of crazy, deadly game that they're playing. The woman who's the look-alike for me and maybe my sister. The note claiming to be from Caitlin. And now the girl dying in Caitlin's old bedroom. But I have no idea who or why or how they are doing this."

"I wish I had an answer for you," he said, "but I'm completely baffled by all of this, too."

"And there's even more. The woman at the house—the woman who pretended to be Maureen Wilcox, who must be involved in all this—used the name 'Nik' for me. No one has ever called me 'Nik,' always 'Nikki.' Except Caitlin. I was always 'Nik' to Caitlin."

"That is mysterious. But there has to be some sort of an explanation. Some logical, normal answer for all this."

"What if there isn't?"

"Huh?"

"What if the explanation for what's been happening isn't logical or rational or even seemingly possible at all?"

"What are you talking about, Nikki?"

I told him the same thing I'd told Bonnie Tatarko.

"What if it really is Caitlin still out there somewhere?" I asked him.

Franze looked stunned.

"My God, Nikki," he said.

"No, listen to me. That would explain so much, wouldn't it? The woman who looks so much like me or like what Caitlin might look like today. The note that sounds so much like her. And calling me 'Nik,' her pet name for me. If Caitlin was really alive somehow, this would all make so much more sense."

"You're not serious, are you?" he asked.

The stunned expression on his face had been replaced with a look of concern for me. Like I was crazy or something. Maybe I was. But I kept talking about it.

I brought up the missing pages of my father's official police report on Caitlin's murder. I asked him how or why that could have happened. He said yes, the pages were missing for some reason. But he insisted there was no real significance to that, as far as he knew.

"Your sister Caitlin is dead and buried in Huntsdale Cemetery," he told me. "That is a fact."

"And you did the autopsy?"

"Of course, I did. You know that."

"Did you bury her?"

"No, that was the funeral director who put her body into the coffin and then down into the ground."

"Then how can you be sure it's really her down there?"

He shook his head sadly. "Whatever else you might imagine—whatever crazy ideas you have because of how traumatic this is to you—it is simply not possible. Caitlin is dead. She's been dead for fifteen years. The answers you're looking for have to come from somewhere else."

He was right, of course. I realized that too. And I already regretted bringing up the bizarre notion to him. I hoped he didn't tell anyone else about our conversation. I didn't want anyone else to know about this crazy, impossible stuff I was thinking. If it ever got back to Dave Blanton in Washington, he'd probably take me off the case. Maybe put me on some kind of medical leave. No way I was going to let that happen.

But I also knew that I could not let it drop.

Not entirely.

Not yet anyway.

"That police report from my father," I said. "The one with the missing pages. My father kept a lot of records like that at home. Some of them are still there, I've seen the boxes my mother keeps stored away. Maybe there's something in one of them—some clue from my father—that I've missed. I've got to go back there, look through it all and find out for sure."

"So you're going to go through all your father's old records looking for something about Caitlin. Fifteen years after they both died, Caitlin and him?"

"I've got to go back to Columbus for a meeting later—and I'll probably be there for a day or two. But when I get back, yes, I'm going to do exactly that."

"Nikki, I gotta tell you, that sounds..."

"Crazy, huh?" I smiled.

THIRTY-SEVEN

Alex and I had just started driving back to Columbus from Huntsdale that night when my phone rang. I looked down and saw a number I didn't recognize. Normally, like most people these days, I ignore unknown numbers like that—figuring they're simply some kind of spam call. But there was always a chance it could be something important about the case. I answered it.

"Is this Nikki Cassidy?" a woman's voice on the other end of the line said.

I didn't recognize the voice.

"Yes, it is," I said cautiously.

"The FBI agent?"

"That's right."

"I saw you on TV. You asked anyone in the public to call in if they see something suspicious. Well, I think something suspicious is going on in the house near me. Just like that house in Huntsdale where a strange woman had moved in before the girl's body was found. The case you're involved in. That's why I'm calling you instead of the local police. I thought you'd want to check it out yourself."

"What did you see?"

"Well, my neighbor hasn't been here for a few weeks. The family has been on vacation. But tonight I saw lights going off and on in the house. So, after that, I started paying attention to what was going on over there."

"Maybe your neighbors came home unexpectedly," I suggested.

"No, it's not them. Someone else is in the house."

"How can you be sure?"

"Because I heard a scream too."

"A scream?"

"Yes, a loud, high-pitched scream. It was a woman's scream."

"Did she say anything? Could you make out any words?"

"No, but she sounded like she needed some kind of help. I'm afraid to go over there myself. I live alone here. That's when I remembered you on TV, talking about how someone had moved into your old house and then murdered that girl there."

"Did you call the police?"

"No, just you. Did I do the right thing?"

"Where are you? Where is this house?"

She gave me an address for a location that was about fifteen miles outside of Huntsdale. I wasn't sure who the local police were for that area, so—after I hung up from the woman—I called the Huntsdale station instead. I told them to get some police—either them or someone else—out to the address she had given me.

They checked first with Earnshaw, I found out after I was on hold for a bit, and he wasn't happy about deploying manpower in what he said was most likely going to be a wild goose chase.

But he said he'd send a squad car out to investigate.

We were closer to the address than the squad car coming from Huntsdale though. I looked over at Alex who was driving, and she nodded. She turned the car around in that direction so we could check it out ourselves.

Alex sped down the road we were on as fast as she could, while I put the specific address for it into the GPS. It said we were five minutes away. Alex heard that, then stomped on the accelerator even more. Before long, we were doing over eighty mph on some rural Ohio roads. Fortunately, there was no other traffic.

The house—an old-fashioned, farmhouse-looking place—sat alone at the end of a long, gravel driveway. There were no other houses in sight. No neighbors who could have seen or heard anything from the house. Alex pulled up in front of the lonely house.

"What do you think?" I asked her.

"Something's not right here. I don't see any sign of anyone else living around here. How could that woman who called know about what was or what wasn't happening in this place?"

"Maybe we've got the wrong address."

There was a mailbox out front with an address on it. I checked that with the address the woman had given me. It was the same. This was the place she had been talking about.

"Or the woman got confused," Alex said.

"Perhaps she was just trying to play some kind of practical joke or something on us," I said.

"Maybe."

"Only one way to find out," I said.

We got out of the car and checked out the house a little closer. There was no sign of life anywhere. No lights. No noise. No activity of any kind. Just a lonely house situated in the middle of nowhere.

"I don't like this," Alex said.

"Me either."

"We should wait for backup from Earnshaw's people before we do anything else," she said.

"How far away are they?"

Alex checked on her phone to get the location of the police squad car on the way to meet us here.

"Only five minutes away," she said.

Normally, my instinct was to be aggressive in a situation like this. We could go knock on the front door, check the place out more—without waiting for the Huntsdale police. That's what I wanted to do. But then I realized Alex was right.

"Let's wait for the backup," I said to Alex.

That was the smart approach.

The by-the-book way to handle this.

The local police would be here soon, and then all of us—them, Alex and me, and anyone who might be inside that house could figure out together what the hell was going on here.

Yep, that was definitely the way to play it.

But then everything changed.

Suddenly and without warning, we heard a scream coming from the house.

A high-pitched, frightened scream—just like the woman on the phone had described—that sounded like someone was in grave danger.

Alex and I took out our weapons and headed for the house.

THIRTY-EIGHT

We decided to split up. Alex took the back of the house, I stayed in front. I stood on the front porch for a few seconds, listening for any sign of life or activity inside.

There was nothing.

Finally, I pounded on the door.

"FBI!" I said in a loud voice. "If there's anyone in there, please open up this door right away!"

Still nothing.

I heard Alex screaming at me from behind the house. "I don't see anything through the back door here or the windows. What about you?"

Suddenly, there was another scream coming from inside the house.

"I'm going in," I shouted to Alex, and I then used my foot to try and smash the door down. It didn't take much effort. The door was old and worn and opened up very quickly for me.

"FBI!" I yelled again inside the house. "We're coming in. We are armed. Whoever is in here, you need to show yourself right now."

More silence.

I made my way from the doorway to the living room. It was dark. I took out a flashlight and shined the beam around the room. Everything—the furniture, the carpets, even the wallpaper—looked very old. There was no indication or sign of anyone living in this house recently.

I tried to turn on the lights, but nothing happened when I clicked the switch.

"The living room is pitch black," I yelled to Alex, assuming she'd come in through the back by now and was close enough inside to hear my voice.

She was.

"Same with the kitchen," Alex said. "All dark, no one here. Looks like there's been no one here for a long time. No food, no garbage, no nothing. And no electricity. Does anyone live here, you think?"

"Well, someone screamed," I yelled out as I kept going further into the house.

The place was big. Bigger than I expected. I walked down a hallway off the living room and saw a series of doors. Presumably for different bedrooms. There could also be an attic and a cellar. No way of knowing where the screams had come from. Not without checking out every part of the house.

I pushed open the first door in the hallway. It was a bedroom. Like the rest of the house, it appeared as if no one had been it for a while. There were no clothes or personal belongings anywhere.

I tried the light switch here too. But nothing happened. Same as in the living room and kitchen. There was no electricity in this house. Just another sign that it was uninhabited.

Then who was screaming in here?

I made my way back out of the bedroom and started down the hall again. My flashlight beam shined on the other doors, and I was ready to go through each of them one by one with

Alex, if we had to. After that, we'd check for an attic and a cellar.

"Alex, I'm in the hallway," I yelled to her in the kitchen. "Come meet me out here. We'll divide up the rest of the house."

"Okay, I'm on my way now and then—"

Suddenly, her voice cut off.

There was nothing but silence for a few seconds.

And then a gunshot rang out.

"Alex, what's going on?"

I started running toward the kitchen. Hoping against hope, it was Alex who had fired the shot at someone else, not the other way around. But I never made it there. When I pushed open the kitchen door, gun in hand, someone yanked the gun away from me and it dropped to the floor.

Then a hand grabbed me from behind by the throat, putting me into a choke hold I couldn't break away from no matter how hard I struggled. I felt a rag being pulled over my face and mouth so I couldn't speak.

The rag had a strong, medicinal odor, and I realized it was some kind of a disabling drug to knock me unconscious or at least to immobilize me.

I kept trying to fight back, but it was no use.

The combination of the person holding onto my neck and the drugged rag on my mouth were too much for me to overcome.

Then I felt something—it felt like a rope—squeezing tighter around my neck.

Tighter and tighter.

I had to fight to breathe.

Just like Laurie Reddick and Rebecca Burgess and Linda Grasso must have fought until it was too late for them.

I thought about that as I began to lose consciousness.

Was I going to meet the same fate?

Then, as suddenly as it started, the pressure on my neck and throat subsided. I could breathe again. I took in several big gasps of air.

"See how that feels," a voice behind me said. I couldn't make out more about the voice. Not even if it was a man or a woman. I was pretty sure that the speaker was disguising it.

"I could do that for hours with you. Take you to the brink of death—make you feel like each breath is your last, leave you desperate for just a little breath of air in your lungs, and then let you live or die whenever I felt like it. Right now, I'm going to let you live, Cassidy. But I wanted you to see what it feels like. I wanted you to know that I'm in control. I wanted you to know that you can't beat me. No matter how hard you try, you can never beat me.

"We'll meet again, Agent Cassidy. And next time I'll just keep squeezing until every breath of life is out of you. Just like I did with those stupid girls. Think about that. Think about the fate you have waiting for you out there. I want you to have nightmares about it. I want the anticipation of death for you to be so horrible that maybe it will be a relief when I finally finish the job with you.

"Until we meet again…"

He squeezed my throat again and pushed the rag into my mouth.

That's all I remembered.

Everything went black after that.

I'm not sure how long I was out for. When I regained consciousness, the kitchen was empty. I took a quick look around with my flashlight in the dark. No sign of the person who did this to me. No sign of Alex either.

Then my flashlight beam picked up something on the floor.

It was red.

Blood.

There was a trail of it leading out the back door. That's

when I saw it. A body lying in the backyard just outside the door. I ran out there.

It was Alex.

She'd been shot.

But she was still alive.

"Officer down! Officer down!" I screamed into my phone after punching in an emergency number and giving my location. "This is FBI Agent Nikki Cassidy. We have a wounded FBI agent here."

It seemed like an eternity of waiting, but then I heard sirens coming.

First, the Huntsdale police.

Then an ambulance with medical personnel.

"Hang in there, partner," I said to Alex. "You're gonna make it."

THIRTY-NINE

"It was an ambush," Alex said from her hospital bed.

"Yeah, and we walked right into it."

"Didn't really have much choice, did we, Nikki? Once we heard that scream. We had to go in and check it out, even before the backup arrived."

"Whoever was in that house knew that, and they played it that way."

Alex was sitting up in her hospital bed, with a large bandage and a sling on her left arm. The doctors said the gunshot wound —despite all the blood I'd seen at the house—was not as serious as everyone, including me, first feared. They expected her to be released from the hospital in a day or two.

Me, I was okay too. Just some bruising around my neck where the assailant had squeezed on my windpipe. There was no rope left behind, but they found the rag used on me at the scene. It contained traces of chloroform, which apparently had been what knocked me out temporarily. But the doctors said I was all right, just like Alex.

"We were both pretty damn lucky," Alex said.

"I don't think it was luck."

"What do you mean?"

"I could have been strangled to death. You could have been shot more seriously. But whoever did this was careful about that. Just applied enough pressure to immobilize me, not kill me. And shot you in a place that he knew would incapacitate you, but you could recover. He didn't want to kill us, Alex. He wanted to scare us."

"He?"

"Okay, or maybe she."

I told her about the warning to me that I was going to die of strangulation like that at some point in the future, and how this taste of that was supposed to terrify me. And about how strong the grip of the rope or whatever it was around my neck had been.

"Was it a man or a woman?"

"I think it was a man, but I don't know for sure."

There was something else bothering me. The phone call that lured us to the house. It came to my cell phone. How did the person on the other end—whoever that was—know my cell phone number?

"Didn't you give out a number asking people to call you if they saw anything suspicious, like this caller claimed?"

"Yes, but that was a hotline number. Not my personal number.'

"Who else knows that number?"

"A number of people, I guess. But no one who would want to do something like this. As far as I know anyway."

"Another mystery," Alex said.

"We've got a lot of them to figure out, Alex."

I told her what we'd found out about the house where it had all occurred.

"The house has been empty for months. The owner died, and no one has been in it since then, except for a housing inspector who ruled it structurally unsound. And there's not another neighbor within a mile of the place. No one who could have seen lights there or heard a scream from inside. So that was a total fabrication. Someone simply found an empty house, moved in there and pulled off something like this."

"Just like someone did with your old house in Huntsdale," Alex said.

"It worked both times."

Lt. Tatarko called while I was there with Alex. She'd heard about what happened. We put it on speakerphone, so we could both talk to her at the same time. I told her Alex was in good shape, and then Alex talked to her, too.

"I'm just glad it didn't turn out any worse," Tatarko said when we were finished.

"Me too," I said.

"Me three," Alex chimed in.

"So what happens now with Alex wounded, Nikki?" Tatarko asked. "Will Washington send you a new partner to work with?"

"Yes, I suppose so."

"No!" Alex said emphatically.

I looked over at her sitting up in the bed. She had a belligerent look on her face. I'd seen that look before. I'd never been able to change her mind about anything when she gave me that look.

"I'm staying," she said. "The doctors say I should be able to use my arm in a few days. Besides, it's my left shoulder and arm. I'm right-handed. I can still use my gun or do anything else I have to do on the job."

"Alex, you've been shot.'

"That's why I need to be here working this case with you, Nikki. Somebody did shoot me. And I can't leave here without us catching the person who did it."

As I was leaving the hospital, my phone rang again. I looked down to see who the call was from. Brett Anson. Terrific. The last person in the world I wanted to talk to right now. But I answered anyway.

"I just heard about it," Anson said. "An FBI agent shot, another assaulted and almost choked to death. That's a helluva story. What can you tell me about it?"

"Alex and I are both fine, thanks for asking."

"Sorry. I mean that's good to hear. Now about my story—"

"There's going to be a press statement later," I told him. "At that time, the media will be briefed on whatever we can reveal about the investigation."

"C'mon, Nikki."

"Agent Cassidy."

"Okay, Agent Cassidy. Give me something here."

I was about to hang up on him when I thought about something. The number. He'd called me on my cell phone number. My personal cell phone number. The same number someone called to lure Alex and me to that abandoned house.

"How did you get this number?" I asked him.

"Uh, you must have given it to me. The night we had the drink together."

"No, I didn't."

"Are you sure?"

"Where did you get my number, Anson?"

"Oh, I have my sources," he said and laughed.

After I hung up, I thought about what Alex had once said about Brett Anson. Talking about how he might be the kind of journalist—desperate for a story—who not only covered it, but carried out the crime too.

Was it conceivable that a journalist—someone like Brett Anson—could carry out a series of murders the same way?

Of course not, I told myself.

That was an absurd idea.

There were lots of ways Anson could have gotten my phone number, like the person who used it to lure Alex and I to the house.

I was just being paranoid, I thought.

I almost convinced myself of that too.

Almost.

FORTY

"Here's where we are at the moment," I said to everyone. "What we know. And, even more importantly, what we don't know."

I was back in Columbus at the state trooper barracks. Lt. Tatarko was there, along with her boss Dale Kovach. Alex was back too, her arm in a sling but insisting on staying with the investigation. Dave Blanton was on a Zoom call from back in Washington, along with Ray Terlop—our main tech/computer man. Even Frank Earnshaw was on the Zoom, looking as sullen as usual on the screen in front of me.

I walked over to the whiteboard I'd put up on the wall. On it were pictures of the three victims—Laurie Reddick, Rebecca Burgess and Linda Grasso. Also, Susan Stratton, which was taken from her actress portfolio for the TV show. And the drawing of the woman at the Groveton mall who looked like me —or possibly an older version of Caitlin—as described by Shirley Hunsaker. Plus, another drawing—this one based on my description of the woman I'd met living in my old house who pretended to be Maureen Wilcox.

"This is the one person whose identity we know about for

sure," I said, pointing to the picture of Susan Stratton. "We have to assume that she's involved in these murders. She fled the set of *Pick Your Partner* as soon as she learned I was coming there to question her. She's an expert in changing her appearance, and she very well may be the woman who the Hunsaker girl saw at the mall. Oh yes, she's very strong and physically fit too, an expert in judo. So she could have strangled all the girls."

I moved on to the drawing of the woman living in my old house. "We know this woman is a part of all this as well. But we don't know yet who she is or where she is at the moment. Chief Earnshaw, have you been able to find out any additional information in Huntsdale about this woman?"

"Nothing yet," Earnshaw said. "We've been through the house, dusted for fingerprints and everything—but it's all clear. This woman left no trail that we've been able to find. She must have really cleaned up the place before she left. No evidence she was even there. This woman definitely knew what she was doing and how to disappear suddenly and easily."

"What about groceries, food deliveries?" I asked. "She had to have been living in that house for weeks, I saw her the last time I was here. She had to eat, she must have gone outside, there has to be some sort of interaction with neighbors during that time. Didn't anyone see her and ask what she was doing living in the Wilcox woman's house?"

"We're looking at all that too. But there were no food deliveries or anything like that we can find. A few of the neighbors remember seeing her and wondering who she was. But they simply assumed Maureen Wilcox had someone housesitting for her. There were never any conversations with her, the neighbors we spoke to said she rarely left the house. One neighbor said she rang the bell to introduce herself, but no one answered the door. She thought the woman was in there, but assumed she wasn't very social."

"Yeah, she probably didn't want to make herself known to anybody but Nikki," Alex said.

"Let's keep checking out stores and neighbors anyway," I told Earnshaw, "and let me know if you do find out anything significant."

"Yes, ma'am," Earnshaw said, in a sarcastic tone that made clear his disdain at having to take any kind of orders from me.

I looked back at the whiteboard. At the pictures and the drawings of the victims and the suspects.

"There's even more potential players in this that we don't know anything about," I said. "One of them is a mystery man. He was seen at the clothing store waiting for Laurie Reddick, and they probably—most likely—left together in a white SUV. Also, this man may well have been present at the rest stop when Rebecca Burgess' body was found. But we don't have any real description of him."

There was something else I wanted to talk about with all this. I wasn't quite sure how to bring it up. But I did want to talk about it. So I just went ahead with it. I took out another picture and put it up on the whiteboard next to the suspects I already had there.

It was a photo of Brett Anson.

"The newspaper reporter?" Kovach said.

"What's he got to do with this?" Blanton asked.

"Yeah, he's the one that did that piece about you that made you look so bad, wasn't he, Cassidy?" Earnshaw chuckled.

I ignored him and kept going.

"There's something not right about Brett Anson," I said. "Starting with the way he broke into my hotel room. He seems to know a lot about all of these murders. More than he should know. How does he know so much? Is it only him having good sources with someone in law enforcement? Or maybe he knows so much about the murders because he's personally involved in this case."

"You're saying the newspaper reporter could be the killer we're looking for?" Earnshaw said incredulously.

"It's possible."

"Are you sure you're not overreacting because he embarrassed you?"

"He had my personal phone number," I told them. "Whoever lured Alex and me to that house for the ambush had my personal phone number too. I'm only saying we should take a hard look at this guy."

I said that I'd tried to find out more about Anson and his background, but I hadn't been very successful. Ray Terlop said he'd run some computer checks to try to find out more if he could.

"Can you also check to see if you can find any similar cases to these three out there in the past?" I asked him.

"You want me to look for teenaged girls who got strangled? There's going to be a lot of them."

"Maybe. But look for similar circumstances with them. Found in restrooms. Being in houses that they didn't live in. Disappearing from home for a while before they turned up dead."

This case had begun with the visit to my old house by Laurie Reddick, claiming to be my sister—or had it? Was that just smoke and mirrors fed to me by the bogus Maureen Wilcox? But the murders followed that. Maybe that's all there was. But a killer like that—a serial killer of young girls—doesn't just start up out of nowhere for no reason. There might well be a trail of previous cases like this that had gone under the radar.

I'd had a lot of nasty surprises for me in recent days, and I hoped there were no more surprises for me today.

But there was one more surprise waiting for me when I left later.

Not a nasty surprise though.

This was a good one.

There was someone waiting for me at the front door of the state trooper complex.

Someone I hadn't seen for too long.

The last person in the world I expected to see here now.

It was Connor Nolan.

FORTY-ONE

"What are you doing here?" I asked him.

"I heard about what happened."

"Yeah, I'm pretty big news these days."

"Nikki, you almost got killed."

"I know. I was there, remember?"

We were having coffee at a place near the hotel where I was staying. Me and Connor. Just like old times back in Dorchester on my last big case where he was the police chief. Well, not quite the same. But it was still nice to see him. And for him to care enough about me to make the trip here.

"Actually, I don't think my life was truly in danger. Not then. Whoever did that could have killed both Alex and me, but didn't. Alex suffered a mostly superficial wound in her shoulder which immobilized her enough so she couldn't help me. And with me, it was a message, a warning, a threat. Or all of them."

"So you don't think that the person who attacked you really wants to kill you?"

"Oh, they do. But not quickly. The person in the house that night made it very clear to me—my death was very much on their agenda, just not right away."

"My God!"

"I know. Pretty crazy stuff, But, if you think about it, it's sort of the same as it was with Phil Girard. He could have killed me easily the first time we were in Huntsdale together, but instead he saved my life. Then the last time we were there he did try to kill me. Only…"

"Only I saved your life in time."

"Ah, yes." I smiled. "That was you, wasn't it?"

We drank some more coffee as I filled him in on the girls' murders and what I'd been doing and all the rest of it, especially the parts about Caitlin.

"Do you think Girard could be involved here again?" he asked.

Phil Girard had been a fellow FBI agent working on the last murder case with me, until it turned out he was the murderer. When Girard attempted to kill me, Connor had shot and seriously wounded him. Girard escaped, but his body was later found in a burned-out car at the bottom of a river. Except the body was so badly damaged from the fall that not everybody was sure it was really Phil Girard in that car. There was still the possibility—remote as it was—that he somehow escaped.

"I don't think it was him," I told Connor. "Phil Girard was pretty badly hurt, he'd lost a lot of blood. Even if he did somehow get away, he wouldn't be in any condition to kill again like this for a while. All of these deaths were by manual strangulation. Girard wouldn't have been strong enough to do it, given everything that had happened to him. At least, that's the way I see it. No, Phil Girard was a homicidal psychopath, no question about it. But this is another homicidal psychopath we're dealing with here."

I talked about the Caitlin part too. All my questions about my little sister, all my speculation, all my deepest fears.

"I just can't get the thought out of my head that Caitlin could still be out there and somehow involved in this."

"That is crazy, Nikki."

"Everybody keeps telling me that."

"Do you really think that's even remotely possible?"

"That Caitlin could still be alive somewhere or that she might be involved—maybe unwittingly, maybe not—in these killings?"

"Either of those two things."

"I suppose not."

"Makes no sense at all. I mean you've told me how your father was the police chief who investigated your sister's murder. If there was anything wrong, any chance that she wasn't dead fifteen years ago—wouldn't your father have been the first person to know that? Wouldn't he have told you and your mother about it? This was your father, Nikki."

"The thing is my father was the one who identified my sister's body," I said. "I've been thinking about that a lot recently. It was him who said it was Caitlin that was dead. She'd been missing for days, then her body was found in a wooded area near Huntsdale. I never doubted then the body was Caitlin's. Nobody did. I mean my father said it was Caitlin. Why would he lie about something like that?"

"Not that I'm believing any of this, but the only possible reason could be that he made a mistake about the ID."

"A mistake about knowing his own daughter?"

"Seems pretty unlikely, huh?"

"Sure does. I don't really think that's what happened. Which takes us to theory B. My father knew it wasn't Caitlin lying dead in those woods, but deliberately didn't tell anyone that. He let people believe it was Caitlin who was dead."

"Why?"

"I have no idea."

"And you have absolutely no suggestion that anything like that happened."

"Actually, I do."

I told him about the missing pages in my father's police report. The pages missing from the official report and also from the copy of his report I'd found at my mother's house. I said I was still going to go back to my mother's house as soon as I could to look for any of the missing evidence my father might have left behind there.

"I think you need to forget about this," Connor said when I was finished. "Just concentrate on finding this killer out there now. That's all you should be focused on."

"Except this killer is the one who won't let me forget Caitlin. She keeps coming up everywhere I turn. Reminders of her, reminders about her."

"The killer is doing this to keep you distracted, Nikki. To get to you. To upset you so you're not thinking clearly about this case."

"Well, if that's what it is, he's doing a pretty good job of it," I said.

A waitress came and refilled our coffee cups. This was like my fifth cup of coffee of the day. But that was okay. I needed all the caffeine buzz I could get. That—plus the appearance of Connor Nolan—had snapped me out of the funk I'd been in.

"So tell me about you," I said. "How did you suddenly wind up here?"

"I drove."

"That's not exactly what I meant."

"Hey, I woke up early this morning, got on the Pennsylvania Turnpike, then drove the six hours from Dorchester to Ohio. It wasn't easy. Don't underestimate the effort it took for me to get here and be with you."

I smiled. It was good to see Connor Nolan again. Real good.

"Look," he said, "I heard about what happened on the TV news. I was going to call you to make sure you were all right. But then I decided to do this in person. I told everyone in

Dorchester I needed the day off to take care of an urgent matter. After that, I got in my car and now... well, here I am."

"Here you are," I said.

FORTY-TWO

Connor and I made love that night in my hotel room.

It was even better than I remembered it being between us back in Dorchester. There's always something special about having sex with someone you are so familiar with in bed—you know their likes, you know their moves, you know what they are thinking. It's comfortable, it's natural and it's pretty damn exciting.

I've never been much interested in one-night stands with the men I met. I'm looking for someone I care about, someone I want to spend a lot of time with—someone I guess I hope one day I might love. I wasn't sure if it was love between Connor and me. But whatever this was, it would do until the real thing came along for me.

Afterward, we lay there in each other's arms and enjoyed the moment. This was just what I needed, I thought to myself as Connor gently hugged me and squeezed my hand. For now, for a few hours anyway, I was able to stop obsessing about Caitlin, about the dead girls, about the killer out there waiting for me somewhere.

"You are something else, Nikki," Connor said to me after we'd lain there in silence for a while.

"Right back at you, big guy."

"I've really missed you."

"I'm glad."

"Did you miss me?"

"Not a bit." I laughed.

"Is that the truth?"

"Would I lie to you?"

"How about we put you on a lie detector to check it out?"

"I'd flunk that lie detector test. Flunk it big time."

He leaned over and kissed me.

"So where do we go from here?" he asked.

"How about breakfast in the morning?"

"You know what I'm asking you about."

"I do, and I don't have any answer to that question, Connor, any more than you."

The facts of the matter hadn't changed for us. Connor still lived in Dorchester, Pa. near Philadelphia, where he was the police chief. I worked basically out of Washington.

"Maybe you could get transferred to an FBI office in Philadelphia," he said.

"Maybe you could quit as police chief and find a job in Washington."

"I don't think that would work out for me."

"Philadelphia for me either."

I leaned over and rubbed his back as we talked. This was an important decision. Even though I knew where it would all wind up in the end. I think we both did.

"Look, Connor, I was engaged not long ago to a man who wanted to try and fit me into his life. Wanted me to play the role of his wife in Washington while he worked as a big-time lawyer. That's not a good role for me. Helping someone else to do what they want to do. I want to live my own life. And my life—at least right now—is being in Washington and doing my job with the FBI."

"You'd like Dorchester, Nikki. It's a nice place."

"And you'd probably like Washington, too."

"But it's not going to happen, either way, is it?"

"No, at least for now."

"Maybe in the future."

"Things change, Connor. All I know is I want to be with you here right now. Can't we just leave it at that?"

"Sounds like a plan."

"An excellent plan," I said, and we began kissing again.

But the truth was there was more than simply geography keeping Connor and I apart. Each of us had a lot of past baggage to deal with. For him, it was the loss of his wife Lauren —well, his ex-wife—in a house fire. She was an alcoholic and a heavy smoker, and she fell asleep drunk with a burning cigarette. Connor was in the house and managed to escape. But he wasn't able to save her.

"I guess the lack of any kind of closure with Lauren is what I find the most difficult to deal with," he said now when I asked him again about her. "She had a lot of problems, and those problems had broken up our marriage. But I still cared about her deeply. I never got a chance to tell her that before... well, before she was gone."

In some ways it was the same thing for me—a lack of closure —that haunted me about Billy Weller. Billy and I had never been intimate together, in fact the first time I kissed him had been when he was dying in my arms. But there was something special between us. Something that could have easily turned into love. Except that ended for us in a horrible moment without any kind of real closure, just like with Connor and his wife.

Neither of us had ever gotten over that kind of sudden loss.

Maybe we never would.

"Any other men in your life since the last time we were together?" he asked me.

"Nope."

"C'mon, there must have been some guy who tried to put the make on someone as desirable as you."

"Oh, men have tried." I laughed.

"Anyone special?"

I hesitated, then told him about Brett Anson.

"Are you jealous?"

"Maybe. A little."

"Don't be. He's a jerk."

We'd made a pact before we started not to talk about the case anymore once we got into bed. I wanted a crime-free experience, at least for one night. But I brought up now my concerns that Anson could be involved in these murders somehow, as well as covering them.

"Do you really think so?"

"Probably not."

"But you still don't trust this guy."

"Nope."

Sometime later, after we'd drifted off to sleep, I was woken up by a loud noise. A pounding noise. Someone was pounding on my hotel room door. I rolled over and looked at the clock on the table next to the bed. 4:30 a.m. Who in the hell was pounding on my door at 4:30 in the morning?

It turned out to be Bonnie Tatarko.

"Why aren't you answering your phone?" she asked.

"I never heard it ring."

Then I remembered. I'd turned my phone off before Connor and I got into bed together. I didn't want us to be interrupted for any reason. I meant to turn it back on afterward, but I never had.

"What's so important?" I asked.

"We've got another body, Nikki. It's Shirley Hunsaker, the friend of Laurie Reddick's from Groveton!"

FORTY-THREE

"What happened here?" I asked the local police when we got to Groveton.

"Teenaged girl found dead in ladies' room at a department store in the Groveton mall," said Ed Roman, the Groveton Police Chief.

"Shirley Hunsaker?"

"Yes."

"She's been positively identified?"

"Right. Did you know her?"

"I knew Shirley."

"Poor kid."

"How was she killed?"

"It looks like she was strangled to death."

Ed Roman was a nondescript-looking guy who seemed to be in his fifties. Grey hair, a bit of a paunch hanging out over his gun belt, wearing a brown Groveton police uniform. He looked rattled. I figured him to be a guy who'd been on the job in Groveton for a long time, but never came across a murder like this one.

Obviously, I thought it was no coincidence that she had died in the same mall where she had gone with Laurie Reddick.

What was she doing here?

I asked Roman that question.

"There was an email printout in her handbag," he said. "It was from the department store here. The one where this restroom is located. The email said she'd been chosen as the winner of a hundred dollars' worth of free clothes and other merchandise. That's apparently why she was here. To claim her prize. Only problem is we checked with the department store and—"

"There was no email sent by them to Shirley Hunsaker about free merchandise."

"They knew nothing about it."

Bonnie Tatarko was with me. We'd raced to Groveton as soon as she told me the news. Alex stayed behind in Groveton. She wanted to come too, but I finally convinced her she'd be more useful staying there and trying to work the phones and the internet to get some idea of what happened to Susan Stratton.

Tatarko and I went into the ladies' restroom now with Chief Roman. Roman said that Shirley Hunsaker's body had been found sprawled on the sink in an awkward, artificial-looking pose—even in death. Like Laurie Reddick's body had been discovered earlier in another restroom on the Ohio Turnpike.

"The killer is staging these crime scenes, isn't he?" Tatarko said. "Laurie Reddick and this girl lying across the sinks. Rebecca Burgess inside the stall. Linda Grasso in the same bedroom where your sister once lived. It's all meticulously planned out. But why? Why go to all this trouble?"

"To put on a show for us. A performance. This is all a big game to whoever is doing this."

"But why this girl? Why pick her as a victim?"

I knew the answer to that one. Shirley Hunsaker had been

selected because of me. I'd talked with her. She'd told me about being here at this mall with Laurie Reddick right before Laurie disappeared. About Laurie having all this money to spend on clothes that she'd somehow gotten from someone. About the mysterious woman who looked like me she'd met with Laurie at the mall.

That was why she was dead now.

There was no other possible reason.

I was going to have to live with this feeling of guilt for a long time. Shirley Hunsaker was dead because of me, just like Caitlin had died because of me. There was no other way to look at this.

"Who found the body?" Tatarko asked.

"A woman who came into the restroom."

A woman?

Could this be the same woman who had discovered Laurie Reddick's body, accompanied by another young girl who later turned up dead?

But that turned out to not be the case.

"She's seventy-nine, and she's in a wheelchair," Roman said. "We wound up having to take her to a hospital afterward, she was so traumatized by what she saw. The doctors said she has a bad heart, and this sent it into a potentially dangerous situation. They're monitoring her now. They say she should be okay. But let's just say that this woman is definitely not any kind of a suspect for us."

Roman had people from his department dusting for fingerprints and looking for any other kind of potential evidence at the crime scene. I didn't figure they would find anything though. We hadn't been successful doing that at any of the earlier crime scenes. No reason to think whoever did this was going to suddenly slip up now and leave behind some kind of an obvious clue.

I'd talked to Shirley Hunsaker just a few days ago. And now

—probably because she had talked to me—she was dead. Sometimes I really hated my job.

But, at the same time, I knew if I didn't do it, even more girls like Shirley and Laurie Reddick and Rebecca Burgess and Linda Grasso might die. There were no easy answers for me here.

"My men just found something else," Roman said to me now. "It was stuffed inside one of the paper towel dispensers. Like someone had hid it there. But not hid it too well. Like they wanted us to find it eventually at the crime scene."

He held it up for me to see.

It was an envelope.

A manila envelope that had been folded over several times in order to fit into the paper towel dispenser.

"What's inside?" I asked.

"We haven't opened it yet."

"Why not?"

"Because it's addressed to you."

FORTY-FOUR

Hello, Nikki Cassidy:

Another day, another victim for you.

This takes us to four and counting.

Why did Shirley Hunsaker need to die? Why not? Hey, it just seemed appropriate to me. She was Laurie Reddick's friend. She knew about all the money Laurie had suddenly come into. She was there for Laurie's encounter that you know about in that mall. And—most of all, I guess—Shirley told you about all these things. She talked to you... so I decided it was time to shut her up.

Don't shed too many tears for poor Shirley though. She wasn't really worth that kind of grief on your part. Neither was Laurie Reddick, for that matter. None of them were truly worth my time and attention. Not like you. No, all these girls were just a means of getting your attention. You, Nikki Cassidy, I felt was a worthy adversary for me. I've had my eye on you for a while now.

I must say though that you've disappointed me so far in this battle of wits between us. Because that's really what it is.

You don't seem to have made much progress at all on this case. I mean you still don't know whether I'm a man or a woman. You still don't know how many of us there are out here. You still don't know how to find me. You still don't know why I'm doing this. And, maybe most importantly of all, you still don't know how Caitlin fits into all this.

Ah, sweet Caitlin. Let's talk about Caitlin. You see, I know the truth about Caitlin, Agent Cassidy. The truth you want to know so badly. A truth you could never even imagine. And I'm prepared to share this truth about your sister with you. Honestly, I promise that you and I will do that.

Just before you die.

Yes, I'm coming for you. But you already knew that, didn't you? And I'll tell you everything about Caitlin in those precious few minutes you have left as you gasp for your last breath.

Meanwhile, just remember this: "A rose is a rose is a rose," as Gertrude Stein once famously said. Just like the roses found with your dead sister. Or is she really dead? Oh, I know the whole story. But there's only one way to get it.

You have to catch up with me.

Before I catch up with you.

Until we meet again...

"You're his ultimate target, Nikki," Tatarko said. "That's a pretty scary thing."

"I already knew that," I said. "He pretty much told me the same thing that night he lured me to the house where Alex got shot. He made it clear that this was just a preliminary to the main thing he had planned. Finishing me off as the grand finale for this crazy, sick game that he's playing."

I looked again at the note. It was unsigned. No surprise there. Typed on plain white computer paper. I knew trying to get a match on the computer it came from or any fingerprints from the paper or the envelope would be futile. But we'd try anyway.

The killer had said a lot of disturbing things in the note.

But one thing he said was even more disturbing to me than all the rest—about killing Shirley because she had talked to me.

This girl was dead because of me.

I knew that for a fact now.

"She talked to you," the note said. "So I decided it was time to shut her up."

"You can't beat yourself up over this, Nikki," Tatarko said. "You were only doing your job."

"My job got the girl killed."

"My God, you can't stop questioning people."

"I know."

"So you really have to stop feeling guilty."

I knew that too. But I did feel guilty. With my sister, and now Shirley Hunsaker. And I still had all these questions about my sister and how she could possibly be connected with all this too. It was a lot to deal with.

But I had no choice.

We were back at the Groveton Police Station later. Going over everything with Chief Roman and people from his force when my phone rang. It was Alex calling.

"You're not going to believe this," she said. "Check out the link I just sent you."

I looked down at my phone. It was a link to the *National Investigator*. I clicked onto the site. There was a big headline on the top which said:

NEW TEEN GIRL FOUND SLAIN IN OHIO TOWN:
SERIAL KILLER LEFT NOTE FOR STAR FBI AGENT.

I started to read the article. It had Shirley Hunsaker's name. The fact that she was strangled to death. The way her body had been "staged" over the restroom sink, just like Laurie Reddick had been earlier. And, of course, that the killer had left behind a note at the scene addressed to—and taunting—me.

The byline on the piece belonged to Brett Anson.

No one had released anything about the murder to the media yet, as far as I knew.

"How in the hell did he get all of this information so quickly?" I asked Alex.

"He must have a good police source somewhere."

"I hope that's all it is."

"Do you really think this guy could be behind all this? Killing these girls and then writing exclusive stories about it to score big points in the media? I know I was the first to bring it up. But is it really possible, Nikki?"

"Anything's possible with this guy."

FORTY-FIVE

I went looking for Brett Anson. I wanted to have a confrontation with him about all this. He was smart, sure. But maybe he'd slip up and tell me something that could help me determine if I was off base or on target in my suspicions about him.

It didn't take me long to find Anson.

I learned that he was staying at the same hotel I was in Columbus. No doubt to stay close to me. Only this time I was going to be switching things around. I was going after him.

I knocked on his hotel room door.

He answered, with a look of surprise on his face as he saw me standing there.

But he swiftly changed back into his Joe Cool act.

"Well, well, well," he said, flashing me a big smile. "This is an unexpected pleasure."

"I figured it would be."

"What's the reason for your visit? Have you thought about expanding our relationship from a professional one to... well, something more personal?"

"Can I come in?" I said.

"Of course," he said, smiling again like he was right in his assessment of the reason for my sudden appearance at his door.

"I don't have a warrant or anything."

"Why would you need a warrant?"

"You'll see."

I walked into the hotel room. There were clothes scattered around the bed and more on a chair. Empty food containers and several empty beer and soda bottles were on a nightstand next to the bed.

"Sorry for the mess," he said, when he saw me looking around at it all. "I don't let housekeeping in here. A lot of what I'm working on is secret, confidential stuff. I don't want to take a chance on any of it leaking out to any of my competition in the media."

There was a desk in the room, too. His laptop was on top of it. I could see the screen from across the room. There was a picture on it. A picture of me.

"You seem awfully obsessed with me, Anson," I said, pointing to the image on the screen.

"The whole country will be obsessed with you before I'm finished."

"Why am I so interesting to you?"

"You just are. On many levels. Now that we're alone here, maybe we can explore some of those other levels."

He smiled once again. A big, confident smile this time. No question about it he was a good-looking guy with a gift of the gab who probably used his looks and his charm successfully on a lot of women. But not this woman. I still needed to find out if he was only a nosy reporter or maybe a killer.

"Where were you when Rebecca Burgess, Laurie Reddick, Linda Grasso and Shirley Hunsaker were murdered?" I asked him.

He looked confused now. "What's this all about?"

"Do you have an alibi for any of the murders?"

"Why would I need an alibi?"

"I take that as a 'no' to my alibi question?"

"Nikki—"

"Agent Cassidy."

"Okay, Agent Cassidy. I have no idea what this is about. I covered those crimes as a journalist. I was just doing my job as a reporter, no matter how much you don't like what it is I do. That's all. Why are you asking me about alibis?"

"Let's try this scenario, Anson. A hypothetical one, I admit. But still based on some hard facts."

I laid out for him my suspicions about how he'd managed to turn up at every one of the crime scenes. How he was there before any other member of the media. How he knew so much about each case. How maybe he knew so much about these murders because he was the one who did them—then wrote about it all afterward as a hotshot reporter for the *National Investigator*.

I wasn't sure exactly how I expected him to react.

Maybe not confess, but at least be rattled a bit.

Instead, he began to laugh loudly.

"My God, you really are pretty desperate, aren't you, Nikki... uh, I mean, Agent Cassidy. I'm the only thing you can come up with as a potential suspect?"

"Where were you when those girls were killed?" I asked him again. "Can you account for your whereabouts at the time of their deaths?"

"I don't have to answer that."

"No, you don't. Not here right now."

"C'mon, you don't have the kind of authority at all that could compel me to answer your questions."

"I can get a warrant, if you want."

"A warrant for what?"

"To question you."

He laughed.

"I'm a reporter, Cassidy. I know enough about the law to be aware that a warrant doesn't allow you to question anyone. Maybe search through their stuff or belongings where they are. But, if you want to question me, you'll have to arrest me for something. And you don't have any evidence to do that."

"Okay, then I'll get a warrant to search your computer," I said, looking over at the screen which still had a picture of me on there.

I was bluffing, of course, and Anson knew it.

"You're going to ask a court for a warrant to search a reporter's notes? The FBI tries to violate the First Amendment and the rights to a free press? I don't think so. And, if you try, that would be an even better story for us at the *National Investigator*. You'd really look silly then, Agent Cassidy."

Anson shook his head sadly.

"I've got an alibi for the murders. For all of those murders. If I have to—for some reason—I can prove that to you or any other authorities. But why should I have to? I'm a reporter. A very aggressive reporter. But for God's sake, I'm not a killer."

I still wasn't sure about that, but there was no way to pursue it at the moment.

"Now maybe that we've got this issue out of the way, we can get back to talking about you and me," he said.

"There is no you and me."

"There could be."

"There's still a possibility you could be a murderer," I said. "And I don't date murderers. It makes breaking up so hard to do."

He laughed again. Nothing I said seemed to bother this guy.

"Look, I get my information from a source. My business is all about sources. And I have a good one. That's how I know so much about you and about everything you've been doing. It's simple as that."

"Who's your source?" I asked him again, even though I knew it was a futile question.

"C'mon, no way I'm gonna tell you that."

"It has to be someone in law enforcement."

"No comment."

I looked over at the picture of myself that was still on the screen of his laptop.

"Well, I wish you'd stop writing so much about me. Why me?"

"Like I said, you're interesting copy. So much drama and colorful acts and, yes, tragedy too in your life. The murder of your sister at the carnival when you were a teenager. The guilt you've carried around about bringing her there that day. The tracking down and apprehension years later of the man who really killed her. The way you still remember that last night with your sister. Talking about boys you hoped to meet the next day at the carnival and some boy she was interested in. Sitting there late at night with the sister who would be gone the next day. And it happened in the same bedroom of the house where the Grasso girl's body was found. That must have brought back some real emotional flashbacks for you. The way your sister's name keeps popping up in this case now. All of this makes you fascinating for me to keep writing about."

He kept talking like this for a long time.

But I'd stopped listening.

Because he'd already told me one of the things I'd hoped to find out from him.

I knew who his source was.

FORTY-SIX

"Have you been talking to Brett Anson?" I asked Bonnie Tatarko.

"Who?"

"Anson, you know who he is."

"Oh, the journalist."

"He's hardly a real journalist, but yes, that's who we're talking about."

"Why would I have been talking to him?"

"You tell me."

"Nikki, this is crazy. Why are you asking me these questions?"

"I think you know exactly why I'm asking them."

We were sitting in the war room I'd set up at the state trooper barracks. Just her and me. I'd made sure of that before I started the conversation. I didn't want this to go any further than Bonnie Tatarko and me. At least for now. But I wanted her to know that I knew what she was doing.

"Someone in law enforcement has clearly been feeding information about the investigation to Anson," I said. "That's the only way he could know all these things he's writing about and getting it out there so quickly. His source has to be someone within the police."

"There's a lot of police involved in these cases. It could be anyone."

"It could be anyone, but it isn't. It's you, Bonnie."

"Why are you accusing me? Why not that Earnshaw guy back in Huntsdale who has it in for you. You always say what an asshole and a jerk Earnshaw is. So maybe he fed information to Anson that he thought could make you look bad."

"You're right, Earnshaw is an asshole and a jerk. But he's not the jerk and asshole who did this. He's not smart enough to think about doing it. You are."

She continued to deny everything for a few minutes. I'd seen suspects I was questioning for crimes do that too. Just keep denying, denying in the hope I'd eventually get tired of asking them the same question over and over. But that wasn't going to work here for Tatarko. I sat there silently, staring at her across the table where we were sitting, until she finally finished all her denials.

"Why?" is all I said when she was done.

"Why what?"

"Why did you do it?"

"I didn't—"

"I know for a fact it was you, Bonnie. There's no question about that. What I want to hear from you is what motivated you to sell me out like this. Not to mention selling out a lot of other good law enforcement people working on this case, too."

Tatarko started to make another denial. But then she stopped. I guess she realized her protestations of innocence were over. We both did.

"How did you find out?" she asked me.

"I talked again to Anson."

"He gave me up?"

"No, he never mentioned your name. But he didn't have to.

Instead, he mentioned a story about me from my past. The story about how Caitlin and I had stayed up late the night before the carnival talking about boys. How I told her about hoping to meet some cool boys there. And her telling me about a boy in school she liked, her first schoolgirl crush. We talked for a long time about boys that night, my sister and me. It was the first time we had ever done that. Because she was twelve years old, and just discovered an interest in boys. It was a special moment for us. The last special moment I ever had with Caitlin. So special that I never told anyone about it."

Tatarko's face tensed up now. She knew what was coming next.

"Until I told you. After we found the body in Caitlin's old bedroom. The same bedroom where Caitlin and I had talked that last night. It really shook me up. And so I shared that moment with you. Then you shared it with Brett Anson. It had to be you, Bonnie. No one else knew about that except you."

Someone from the state trooper force came into the room briefly to find a file they'd left in there. I waited until they were gone before continuing the conversation. Then I leaned over close to Bonnie Tatarko to make sure no one else passing by could hear us.

"So tell me why you did it?"

"You must know, you must have figured that out too."

"No, I didn't."

"Because I wanted to be like you," she blurted out.

Bonnie Tatarko sighed deeply.

"Look, I told you how I've been working here for nine years as a state trooper. It's okay, and, yes, I made lieutenant—the highest rank of any woman ever here at this barracks. But I'm still stuck in a career going nowhere. And a life the same way. I've got no husband, no kids and I wished I had a better job. Then you come along. A big-time FBI agent with all sorts of publicity and a big career and a reputation as a rising star in the media. I wanted that too. Anson promised he'd help me do that. He'd play me up in the media as the big star while he was covering these murders. That's right, he promised he'd make me a big star with the stuff he wrote. Maybe even a bigger star than you."

It was difficult for me to comprehend. I've spent most of my career—and my life—trying to stay out of the limelight, even though things hadn't worked out like that for me. Tatarko was the exact opposite. She was desperate for people to know her. No matter what she had to do in order to get that attention.

I felt sorry for her.

Angry at her, but still sorry for her too.

"Are you still telling him things about the investigation?" I asked quietly.

"No, I stopped. Ever since the Hunsaker girl."

"Why did you end it?"

"Because he didn't hold up his end of the deal. He didn't keep his promises to me. He was supposed to write about me, not you, after Shirley Hunsaker's body was found. But all he asked—all he wrote about—was you. He broke his word to me about that. He broke his word to me about a lot of things."

"What else?"

"Personal things."

Suddenly, I knew what was coming next.

"You slept with him."

"Yes."

"And that's really what convinced you to help him?"

"He told me he loved me, and he begged me to do it to help his career."

"Brett Anson doesn't love anybody but himself."

"I found that out."

She looked over at all the pictures and the information on the whiteboard we'd accumulated during the investigation. An investigation we'd worked on together. Her, me and Alex had led the law enforcement task force involved.

"I'd still like to keep working on all this with you," she said.

Could I still work with Bonnie Tatarko after this? I wasn't sure how to answer her. Or exactly what my options were. The Ohio State Police still had primary jurisdiction here, not me or the FBI. Yes, I could go to her boss, Dale Kovach, and tell him what she had done. That would likely take her off the case. But I was reluctant to do that. Maybe because I didn't like the idea of being a snitch. Maybe because I'd bent the rules like Tatarko myself in the past. Or maybe because I realized letting Tatarko stay on the case with me was the best way to keep an eye on her. Keep your enemies—or at least your potential enemies—close to you, as the saying goes.

"I can't stop you from doing that," I said. "You didn't break any laws. I don't like what you did, but it's not illegal or corrupt."

"I'm glad, Nikki. I still want to be friends with you..."

"We're not friends anymore."

"But you said..."

"I'll work with you, Tatarko. But I will never trust you again."

Afterward, I called Ray Terlop, our computer guy back in Washington, to ask him what he'd found out about Brett Anson.

"I've been checking into the guy's past since our last meeting, like you asked," Terlop said.

"And?"

"Nothing."

"What do you mean nothing?"

"I've come up with a big zero on him. I can't find any background—or anything at all—on Brett Anson before he came to the *National Investigator*. No work record, no personal data, no nothing."

"Well, he must have worked somewhere before the *National Investigator*. Some small paper or TV station or website. Maybe even went to journalism school. He told me how he always wanted to be a reporter. So there has to be some kind of a trail Brett Anson took to the *National Investigator*."

"That's what I thought too. But it looks like he just dropped in from outer space or something and showed up at the *National Investigator*. Which probably means—"

"He's hiding his past."

"Exactly. Maybe because of some trouble with the law. Or a messy divorce or lawsuit that he's running away from. For some reason, Brett Anson is covering up so no one can find out who he used to be. Who is that? I have no idea. But I'm pretty certain that he's not really Brett Anson. At least, as far as I can tell. Unless he did really simply drop in from outer space. Because that's the only other explanation. That's all I've got. I wish I could be of more help to you, Nikki."

Actually, Terlop had been very helpful to me with this information.

Even if it was a lack of information.

I'd been suspicious of Brett Anson before this.

Very suspicious.

Now I was even more suspicious.

FORTY-SEVEN

I hadn't been back to see my mother since that first time after I arrived in Huntsdale and talked with her about the Caitlin connection to the new murders.

I'd spoken to her on the phone since then, bringing her up to date when I could on the latest developments in the case—including, of course, the finding of a young girl's body in Caitlin's old bedroom in the house where we used to live.

She was as shocked as all of us by this. Yes, I probably should have gone back in person to talk to her about it. And about everything else going on involving Caitlin much earlier than now.

I felt guilty about that.

She was the only immediate family I had left, and I was her only immediate family.

Still, we were basically strangers, and we had been ever since that summer day when I was eighteen and took my twelve-year-old sister to a town carnival where she was abducted and later murdered.

I still remember the first moment—after my sister's body was found—when my mother, enveloped in her own grief and anguish and anger, lashed out at me by saying: "This is all your fault, Nikki. You're the reason your sister is dead. I hope you feel the guilt about that somewhere inside you. I hope you feel that guilt for the rest of your life."

A short time later, when my father died, she blamed me for that too—saying it never would have happened if I hadn't let my sister die first. He was murdered by the same man who killed my sister, in an effort to cover up the crime.

Maybe my mother was right.

Maybe I was ultimately responsible for both of their deaths.

But I had done my best to make amends for that with my work at the FBI saving other young girls. Young girls like Caitlin. And, by doing this, I had managed to forgive myself over Caitlin.

My mother could never bring herself to do that.

She had been loving and friendly to me though the last time I visited her. But would she be like that again? Especially with all the new things happening to make her remember all over again that I was the other daughter she lost when Caitlin was murdered.

I thought about all that as I knocked on the door of the house where my mother now lived.

"I thought you might be back in Washington again," she said when she saw me standing there.

"I'm still here working on a case."

"The one involving all of these terribly upsetting things about Caitlin?"

"That's right."

I went through all the details of everything all over again for her—specifically the bizarre thing about the mysterious woman living in our old house. The house where Linda Grasso's body had been found in the same bedroom that had once been Caitlin's.

"That woman I met before living in the house—or

pretending to be the owner of the house—turned out to be a phony. She claimed to have met the teenaged girl there who claimed she was Caitlin and left a note. But now, I think she was somehow involved in that murder—or maybe all of the murders—even though I'm not certain about how."

"Why would someone do something like that?" my mother asked. "Why is this happening. Why in our old house?"

"That's what I'm trying to figure out. I'm hoping you can help me."

"I loved that house," she said. "We were so happy back then. Your father and me. Then you came along. And later Caitlin. We had such a wonderful family. A wonderful house. A wonderful life."

She seemed momentarily lost in her fond memories of the past. I needed to bring her back to the present. No matter how unpleasant that might be. For her as well as for me.

"There are still questions about Caitlin's death," I said. "Questions I don't have answers to. Things that don't make sense. I think Dad had some of these same questions before he died. But he never got a chance to find the answers. I want to try."

I brought up again the missing pages in the police report about Caitlin's murder.

"Did he say anything to you before he died about why he might have removed pages from that report?"

I'd asked her this question before, and she'd gotten angry then that I was bringing up traumatic memories for her. But this time she reacted differently. She didn't answer me at first. I thought maybe she was simply ignoring what I was saying because she didn't want to hear it. But instead she was thinking, trying to remember.

"The night before your father died, he said there was something he needed to tell me about Caitlin's death. He never explained what that was. He said he wanted to check more facts to see if he was right. He didn't want to get my hopes up too much. Those were his words, I remember. He said we'd talk about it more when he got home that night. But he never came home. Later that day, I found out he was dead."

I sat there stunned. She had never told me this before.

"Can I look through Dad's stuff again?" I asked her. "All of his records and reports and notes that he always kept. Dad wrote everything down, he always did. There might be something in his stuff downstairs you still have that could help me now."

Yes, I'd already been through it all.

But maybe there was more.

The answer to what my father knew—or at least suspected about Caitlin's death—might have been right here in the basement of this house all along.

"Let me go down and take a look," I said.

"Look at what?"

"The police report. Dad's notes on his cases. Any other documents down there about Caitlin and her murder."

"Oh, all of that isn't there anymore."

"What?"

"It's all gone."

"Gone where?"

She shrugged. I ran down the steps to the basement where I had found all my father's old papers when I was here before. But there was nothing. That area of the basement was empty.

"What happened to it all?" I asked my mother when I went back upstairs.

"He-he took it away."

"Who?"

"A friend."

"A friend of yours?"

"A friend of your father's."

"What friend?"

"Oh, an old friend. You probably remember him. Michael Franze. He's the Medical Examiner in Huntsdale. He said he needed all those old files of your father's for some reason. He took them all."

FORTY-EIGHT

"Why did you come take away my father's records and papers about Caitlin?" I asked Michael Franze.

"What are you talking about?"

"I told you that I found records—including a copy of the police report on my sister's death, with some pages missing—in the basement of my mother's house. I said to you I was going to go back there and look through it all again. That maybe I might have missed something important in those old records and papers of my father's. The next day you showed up at my mother's door and asked to see everything that was there. Then you took it all away with you when you left."

My mother had given me the chronology of how it happened with Franze and my father's records.

"So what was in those papers that was so important to you?"

"They weren't anything important."

"Then why did you race over to my mother's as soon as I told you they were there—and then walk off with them?"

"They were official documents. They include my own medical reports. They belonged in an official file here. Not in a basement somewhere. That's the only reason I had for taking them. What's this all about, Nikki?"

"I'll tell you what it's all about. My partner has a gunshot wound in her shoulder. I almost got strangled to death. Four young girls are dead, one of them right here in Huntsdale. And somehow—as impossible as it might seem—my sister is linked to all of this. Everywhere I look, I keep running into reminders of Caitlin. There's something off base, something wrong about Caitlin's murder. I know I caught the man who confessed to it. But I still feel like there's more. Something I'm not seeing. Maybe the answer is in those records my father left behind."

"But you told me before you already went through your father's stuff there about Caitlin's death. And you didn't find anything."

"Like I said, maybe I'm missing something."

"What?"

"Those missing pages from the report. Maybe there's something there. If I can find them..."

"None of this makes any sense, Nikki."

"Okay, then let me look through all those files again now, just to satisfy my curiosity about them."

"I can't do that. Those are official documents once they're stored here. I'm not allowed to share them with the public. They should not have been in your father's personal possessions. They're for official use only."

"I'm with the FBI, remember, Mickey? It doesn't get more official than that."

"That doesn't matter. I can't share these documents with anyone. Even federal law enforcement. Not without some good reason or a search warrant. And at the moment you don't have either of those things."

"All right, I'll get a search warrant."

"You can't get a warrant."

"Why not?"

"Because you need some sort of justification for a search warrant. Probable cause that there is something in there that could prove to be substantial for your investigation. But there isn't. There's nothing there for you. I don't know why you're doing all this, but you're just grasping at straws."

He was right about the search warrant. I was only bluffing when I said that, just like I had been with Anson earlier.

But I still believed I was right in thinking there might be something important about Caitlin I didn't know in those records.

And I brought up again what I had asked Franze about the last time I was here. Was he convinced Caitlin was really dead? Because it might answer a lot of questions about all the Caitlin sightings and the rest of it if she were actually still out there somewhere.

"Of course, she's dead," Franze said softly and sympathetically to me, like he was talking to a small child or an insane person or anyone else who was having trouble understanding the obvious.

But I still wasn't sure.

So I escalated the conversation even more.

I brought up something that I once thought was an unthinkable thing.

"What would it take to have Caitlin's body exhumed from that grave?" I asked.

He looked at me now like I was truly out of my mind.

"Why would you want to do that?"

"To make sure she's really down there."

He sighed deeply.

"Nikki, do you have any concept of what it's like to exhume a body?"

"No, I've never done it."

"Your memory of Caitlin now is the cute, adorable little twelve-year-old girl she was before she died," Franze said. "But that's not what you're going to find fifteen years later if you dig the body up. Embalming can only do so much. The body—the flesh and most of the rest—begins to disintegrate once it's been underground for a while. Slowly at first. But then at a much more rapid pace.

"During this time, the body will undergo a decomposition process underground inside the coffin. The skin will blacken, then begin to fall off and eventually disappear entirely. The other tissues and the organs in the body will continue to break down and liquify. After fifteen years of this... well, after fifteen years all that would be left of your sister is some bone, teeth and maybe a bit of hair.

"Do you really want that to become the memory of your sister? And what about your mother? Can you even imagine what a nightmarish ordeal it would be for her to have her daughter dug up out of the grave after all this time?

"You need to leave Caitlin where she is in her grave, Nikki. Let her rest in peace. I've known your family for a long time. I was a friend of your father, and I like to think we've been friends too. Trust me on this. Forget this crazy idea of exhuming your sister's body for no other reason than some wild speculation on your part. If you do that, you'll never forgive yourself for it."

"You're probably right," I said.

And I knew he was. Right about it all. Right about not exhuming my sister's body. Right about the emotional distress it would cause my mother. Right that I had no reasonable reason to seek an exhumation or a search warrant for the files from my father in his possession or any of the rest of it. And he was right about him being my father's friend, all the way back to the time when my father was police chief.

But I still didn't trust him.

Not anymore.

Damn, the list of people I wasn't sure I could trust was getting longer and longer.

Bonnie Tatarko.

Michael Franze.

Brett Anson, of course.

Maybe even Dave Blanton, my boss at the FBI in Washington—who might yank me off this case at any time if he got enough pressure from all the controversy I'd stirred up for the bureau.

And my partner Alex was pretty much out of the picture at the moment because of her gunshot wound.

I had no one left to trust.

No one to rely on.

I was all alone.

FORTY-NINE

The next day, we found Susan Stratton.

Finally.

Right here in Huntsdale.

But she was dead.

"Her body was in Grant Woods," Alex said. "The same place where your sister Caitlin's body was found fifteen years ago."

Damn.

The Caitlin connection again.

Everywhere I looked in this case, the memories of my sister Caitlin seemed to somehow turn up.

And now that stretched all the way back to Grant Woods—where she'd been found murdered fifteen years ago.

Going back to Grant Woods was always a terrible emotional ordeal for me. Not long ago, the body of another murder victim —another young girl—was left there too, because of the history of the place with my sister. And now there was a new kind of victim in Grant Woods. Only this time it was not a young girl.

It was a grown woman, a woman who may have—probably

did—play a role in the murders of young girls. A woman who I thought had been a hot lead, our biggest opportunity to break the case. Except she was dead now too.

Chief Earnshaw was the one in charge of the crime scene in Grant Woods.

"The body was found here," Earnshaw said, pointing to a clump of trees that was now marked off in yellow crime tape and crowded with police and forensic people and others combing the area. "She was lying on the ground under one of those trees. Pretty visible to anyone who walked by here."

"Who found her?"

"We did."

"I mean how did you know where to look?"

"We got an email. Said to come out here and look. Said there was a surprise here for us. The email even gave us the exact spot here in the woods where we found the body."

"Cause of death?"

"No visible bruises or marks or wounds on the body, except for the neck. Preliminary report from the medical examiner after examining her was death by strangulation."

"Just like the other four," I said.

"Yeah, I figured that out, Cassidy. We're a little slow sometimes here in Huntsdale. Not as brilliant in crime detection as you are. But every once in a while we manage to figure something out on our own without your help."

Okay, Earnshaw was clearly still angry with me. But that was fine. He knew he had to work with me on this, and I knew he had to, too. That was what mattered. We were a part of his investigation into this murder, whether he liked it or not.

"We" meant me, Alex and Bonnie who had traveled to the crime scene in Huntsdale after hearing the news about Susan Stratton. Plus, an additional person. Connor Nolan was with us too. That was a surprise. I figured he'd be heading back to

Dorchester right away. But he postponed his return and was still here with us now. He didn't say why he did that, and I didn't ask him. But being the crack investigator that I was, I deduced it was very likely because of me. Which was kind of nice.

I asked Earnshaw about the identification of the Stratton woman. He said a wallet with all her identification, credit cards and other personal material was found along with the body.

"Is there any possibility at all the woman whose body was found is someone else, and Susan Stratton or whoever just wanted to throw us off her trail by making us believe she was dead?" I asked.

It was a plausible scenario.

"I don't think so," Earnshaw replied.

He said the dead woman's face resembled the one in the picture from her actress portfolio that had been distributed in the search for her. Whatever chameleon-like changes she'd made in her appearance previously, she had looked like the original Susan Stratton at the end. There would be dental checks and possible fingerprint matches and checking with her next of kin to definitely confirm her identity, he added. But everyone seemed pretty certain this was indeed Susan Stratton.

I looked at the woods around us. The site was about a half mile, maybe a mile, from where my sister's body had been found. Leaving the body here in Grant Woods had obviously been done by the killer because of me. But why? That was a question I still had no answer for.

"Where's the body now?" I asked Earnshaw.

He said it was still here, but had been moved from the crime scene to an ambulance which would soon take it back to the Medical Examiner's office for a full autopsy.

"Can I see it?"

"Why not?" He shrugged.

A few minutes later, we were standing next to a gurney with the body of Susan Stratton lying on it. The bruises on her neck were very pronounced.

"It looks like she was garroted with some kind of a rope," one of the medical people told us.

"Any sign of the rope?"

"No, we didn't find anything at the scene."

"Maybe she was strangled someplace else and then dumped here after she was dead," Alex suggested.

"That's definitely possible."

I thought about how horrible it must have been for her—and the others—to die by strangulation like that. I'd gotten a taste of what that was like from my assailant that night in the abandoned house. But that was only for show by the killer. A demonstration of his power for me. I hoped I never had to endure the real thing like she did.

I looked at the face of her on the gurney. Did she look like me? Could she have passed for me? Well, maybe. She didn't look too much like me here. But she was about the same age as me, the same general features. With all the training she had in changing her appearance for the TV show, it probably wouldn't have been too difficult to make herself look a lot like me. Not an exact resemblance, but clear enough so that people would notice it.

Chief Earnshaw had left us alone with the medical people examining the body while he went back to supervise the crime scene.

But now he came rushing back to where we were.

Something else was happening.

Something big.

"They found a note," he said excitedly. "One of the units at the crime scene noticed it lying at the base of one of the nearby trees. It's about the murder. It's from the killer. And it's addressed to—"

"To me," I said.

"Yes, this is another note to you."

FIFTY

Well, well, well, Agent Cassidy—look where we are now.

I'll bet you're surprised by this latest development. You probably thought Susan Stratton was going to help you find me and capture me once and for all and that would get you even more media headlines for yourself—which I know you love.

You would have tracked down poor Susan at some point, convinced her of the error of her ways—or offered her some kind of plea deal—and gotten her to reveal information that could help you find me.

That's why I did what I did.

Susan Stratton didn't simply "disappear," as you thought, once she heard you were coming to the TV show to question her. She contacted me and told me all about it. She asked me what to do. She was scared and nervous. I couldn't let her meet with you like that, could I? I told her to meet with me instead, and I'd take care of everything. She did, and that's when I made the woman really "disappear." Ha! Ha!

I thought leaving the body in the same place as your sister's was a nice touch too, wasn't it?

Ah, your little sister.

Is she really dead?

Or could she possibly still be out there somewhere?

Another mystery for you to solve.

And now we get to the end of our dance here together. It's been fun, but I have other things to do. Other wrongs to right.

Let me leave you with this thought from the Bible:

"Vengeance is mine, and recompense, for the time when their foot shall slip; for the day of their calamity is at hand, and their doom comes swiftly." – Deuteronomy 32:35

I'm sure you get the message I'm attempting to convey here.

Vengeance.

Vengeance will be mine.

My vengeance against you.

BY THE NAME OF GOD. I WILL SMITE YOU!

And now, until we meet again, I'll say goodbye.

For now.

But our next meeting will be soon.

And, I'm afraid to say, it won't work out as well for you as that last meeting we had in the house where I lured you. Like I told you then, that was only a rehearsal. A dress rehearsal before the final curtain comes down.

Enjoy your hunt for me, Agent Cassidy.

Enjoy all of your final moments.

Because they are all you have left...

"Jesus," Alex said when we'd finished reading the note.

"We need to make sure you're totally protected at all times," Connor said. "Major protection. So much protection that he can't get at you."

Everyone was scared and rattled nervous after reading the note—and the threats in it directed at me.

Even Earnshaw.

"My God, what are you going to do?" he asked.

But I wasn't thinking about that.

All I could think about was two of the lines I'd just read in the note.

The verse quote from the Bible.

And one more.

And I remembered all too well when I'd heard them before.

I read both out loud to everyone.

First, the Bible verse:

"Vengeance is mine, and recompense, for the time when their foot shall slip; for the day of their calamity is at hand, and their doom comes swiftly." – Deuteronomy 32:35

And then the second religious reference in it: "By the name of God, I will smite you."

"So?" Earnshaw asked when I was done.

So the killer wasn't Brett Anson, after all.

And it wasn't anyone else I'd met here on this case.

The killer was someone from my past.

"I think I know who wrote this note," I said.

FIFTY-ONE

"I want to see all the files on a case I once worked on," I said to the person who answered my call at the FBI's headquarters in Washington.

"What's the case?" the woman asked me after confirming who I was.

I told her.

"There's a lot of files about that case," she said. "Looks like a lot of work went into that one."

"Tell me about it."

"How many of the files do you want?"

"All of them."

"Okay, I'm not sure you want them all, but I can get them for you."

"Send me everything you can from the computer files," I said, giving her my email address and contact information in Huntsdale in case she ran into any problems downloading the material for me.

"How soon do you need this?"

"Like now."

A short time later, I was reading—or re-reading for the first time in a long while—our files about The Singles Slayer case I'd worked on a few years earlier.

The Singles Slayer.

One of the first big cases for me at the FBI.

And the one big case I'd never been able to solve.

No matter how hard I tried, I hadn't been able to catch The Singles Slayer.

I went through all the basic details about everything he had done, even though I knew them pretty well by heart even after all these years. Twelve girls murdered over a two-year period. All of them at singles clubs or bars or women walking alone after leaving a date or some event. For some reason, he always targeted single women on their own. Which, of course, is why the media called him The Singles Slayer as the killings went on and on.

I was assigned to a team investigation of some of the earlier murders, once local police realized there was a serial killer out there and requested help. But, even after the bureau joined the search, there were even more killings and the number of victims quickly mounted.

Like Son of Sam back during the '70s in New York City, The Singles Slayer cases changed the behavior of potential victims. Back then, girls dyed their hair blonde or cut it short because Son of Sam seemed to prefer shooting girls with long dark hair.

Here, women desperately did anything they could to avoid being out alone. They stayed close to boyfriends or other people whenever possible. And many of the locations where The Singles Slayer had hunted his victims—the singles bars and clubs—had sparse crowds or shut down completely.

With Son of Sam, it had only been a single place—New York City—that lived in terror of him striking again. But The Singles Slayer caused a national panic. His victims came from

Washington state to the East Coast and Florida, with some killings taking place too in the Midwest and other states in between the two coasts. He was like the infamous Ted Bundy in this regard, traveling the country looking for victims.

All of the victims had died by gunshot. Ballistic tests later showed all came from the same gun. A Bulldog .44 revolver. If we could ever catch someone with that gun, we'd have proof we had the right man. But that never happened.

As the murder spree intensified—along with the publicity around each new killing—the media intensity did too. Why can't you catch this monster? That was the question asked over and over again in the press of the FBI and local law enforcement agencies.

I always felt that was the reason I somehow became the face of The Singles Slayer investigation at some point. I mean I was relatively young and it was early in my career at the FBI when it happened. No reason I should have been the one talking about The Singles Slayer to the media. Giving them our progress, or—as was frequently the situation—our lack of progress.

But, I suspect, the more-veteran people at the bureau didn't want to put themselves in a no-win position like that. They didn't want to look bad in public in front of the TV cameras and reporters. So they picked someone else to do it. Someone they didn't care if the person appeared clueless or floundering or without any real answers in front of the media. A sacrificial lamb to feed to the hungry press. That was me.

The scrutiny of the press wasn't the worst part of the case for me though.

It was the helplessness I felt—over and over again—to help the families of the victims who were looking for answers and closure and some kind of justice from the death of their daughters.

There was the Galvin family, of course. Jeffrey Galvin reached out to me regularly to ask about it. But the Galvins weren't alone. I'd constantly get queries from other parents asking me—pleading with me—for anything I could tell them about what had happened to their loved ones and why.

I never had any answers for them.

Not then.

And not ever since then.

No matter how many other cases I'd solved—big cases, important cases—this one had always haunted me. The murderer that got away. The one time that I failed at my job.

And then, after two years, the killings suddenly stopped. We kept waiting for the next victim, but it never happened. The Singles Slayer was gone. Gone as mysteriously as he had appeared in the beginning. Even though he'd never been caught, there was a feeling of relief everywhere. Including here at the FBI, I guess, once it became clear there was going to be no more murders.

Everyone went back to their lives, and we at the FBI moved on to other cases.

Yes, all those memories came back to me as I read through all of the old files on The Singles Slayer case.

But I was looking for something else. Something specific. Something that had triggered another memory for me when I read through that note from the person who killed Susan Stratton and presumably all four of the young girls.

I finally found what I was looking for.

Deep in one of the old reports on The Singles Slayer case.

At some of the murder sites, The Singles Slayer had left cryptic messages behind—sometimes in magic marker or letters clipped out of newspapers—to taunt all of us looking for him.

I read through those old messages from The Singles Slayer now until I found the one I was looking for.

It said:

"Vengeance is mine, and recompense, for the time when their

foot shall slip; for the day of their calamity is at hand, and their doom comes swiftly." – Deuteronomy 32:35

The exact same quote that had been in the note I just read in Huntsdale.

And the second religious line was there too:

"By the name of God, I will smite you," said a message left with one of the victims.

I called Dave Blanton in Washington, and I blurted out:

"It's him!"

"Who?"

"The Singles Slayer. He's back. We're still chasing after the same guy."

FIFTY-TWO

Dave Blanton wasn't as certain as I was when I first told him about The Singles Slayer connection with the new killings. In fact, he wasn't convinced at all. He pointed out the differences in both murder sprees.

"First of all, the victims are different. The Singles Slayer targeted adult women outside singles bars or walking alone on the street or things like that. This new killer goes after young teenaged girls as young as twelve, seems to befriend them for a period before he kills them, and tends to leave the dead bodies in places like restrooms and turnpike stops. No similarities there.

"Second, the method of killing is different. The Singles Slayer used a gun, the same gun—a Bulldog .44 revolver—in all of his murders. This person strangles the victims to death. Except for the shooting of Alex, there's never been a gun involved. And the bullet wound Alex suffered came from a .38, not a Bulldog .44.

"Third, The Singles Slayer killings took place over a period of like twenty-four months or so. Then nothing since. Why would he stop so suddenly, then start up again and with a completely different way of operating? That doesn't make much sense. What makes more sense is that The Singles Slayer died or went to prison for another crime or something else like that, and that's why the killings stopped. Not that he just took a multi-year hiatus from his murder spree.

"Finally, the new killings seem to involve not just a single man, but at least one—probably two—females working with him. There was never any indication that The Singles Slayer was anything other than a lone, disturbed male. Why would he suddenly begin working with these women on this new killing spree?"

These were all very good questions.

I'd asked these same questions myself after I read through all the files on The Singles Slayer and my notes on the new murders.

But, in the end, I'd come to one inescapable conclusion.

It was the same guy.

Had to be.

The Singles Slayer was back and claiming new—albeit a different kind—of victims.

"The Bible verse is the key," I said to Blanton. "And the reference to God 'smiting' someone. We never revealed that Bible verse to the media or the other line either during The Singles Slayer investigation. It was kept quiet to avoid more sensationalism coming out and to make sure if someone came forward and confessed that it was the right person. No way someone else could just put something like that in this latest note."

"I'm still not sure about this," Blanton said.

"Let me tell you something else, Chief. I don't think using these verses was an accident either. This person isn't stupid. They must have known I'd figure out the connection through the note. He put that Bible verse—the same Bible verse as before—as well as the other religious line in there deliberately.

He wanted me to know who he was. Or at least that he was The Singles Slayer I was chasing. Again."

"Don't forget about something else, Agent Cassidy. Whoever this killer is—whether he is The Singles Slayer or not —he really has upped the stakes in this game or whatever it is he's playing with you. He said he's coming after you. He's targeted you as a victim."

"No one is more aware of that than me."

"We have to get this guy before he gets you."

"I'm with you on that, Boss."

There had been three main suspects we looked at back then during The Singles Slayer killings. All of them were examined very closely because of their background or their actions or because of things they said during our interviews with them.

Their names were Dale Slocum, Joseph Boone and Gary Eaton.

I went through the material I had—and made some checks on line—on all of them.

Dale Slocum got arrested a short time after The Singles Slayer murders stopped for kidnapping a woman, holding her hostage for two days and raping her several times before she escaped. He was captured, convicted and sentenced to twenty years in prison. Slocum was still in jail with a long time to serve. So this couldn't be him doing all of these things that were happening now.

Boone was dead. He drank too much in a bar one night, got behind the wheel of his car and plowed into the back of a big rig truck on a freeway. That eliminated him from the list of possible suspects too.

Which left Gary Eaton. No one had heard anything about Eaton in two years. Interestingly enough, Eaton had been a minister. At some little church in Northern California. It certainly raised the possibility that a minister like him would put a Bible verse and other references to God into a note. That made him a prime suspect at the time. And he still was, as far as I was concerned.

It all made sense.

Bible verses.

And a minister.

Or an ex-minister.

Because Gary Eaton had stepped down from his pulpit at the church, then disappeared at some point after we questioned him about The Singles Slayer. That was certainly very suspicious to us back then. But then the killings stopped, and everyone moved on to investigate other murders and other cases.

I remembered interviewing Eaton at the time. We'd been put onto him by several people in the church who reported inappropriate comments and actions involving some of the women in the congregation. He seemed defensive during that interview, nervous and frankly didn't come across as any kind of a minister I'd ever seen.

Still, we were never able to come up with any specific proof that he was The Singles Slayer.

Maybe we could now, maybe we could prove he was the killer of all these women and young girls.

Both The Singles Slayer killings from the past and the new murders now.

It was Gary Eaton.

Had to be.

I was convinced of that.

All we had to do this time was catch him.

Alex, Bonnie and Connor had a lot of the same questions as Blanton did when I went through it all with them.

Still, Alex trusted my instincts.

So did Connor, I was pretty sure.

And Bonnie finally went along with The Singles Slayer connection theory after some initial disbelief and skepticism.

"Still, assuming you are right about this being The Singles Slayer," Bonnie said, "you still don't know for sure it's this Eaton guy."

"Maybe not," Connor said, "but he sounds like the best possibility."

"We need to find Eaton," Alex said. "But how do we do that?"

"Well, we could let him find us," I said.

"What do you mean?" Alex asked.

"This killer has been playing games with us—and me—for a long time. I think it is time we played our own game with him. He's supposed to be coming after me. Now I'm going to take the damn game to him."

FIFTY-THREE

"Why did you ask me to meet with you here?" Brett Anson asked me.

"I have something I wanted to talk to you about."

"Really?"

"You seem surprised."

"Well, the last time we 'talked' you accused me of being a serial killer who was writing stories about my own crimes."

"I may have overreacted a bit," I admitted.

We were sitting at the bar in a place called The Lightning Rod in Huntsdale. The Lightning Rod was one of the few worthwhile bars in town. It had been around for a long time, back to when I was a teenaged girl growing up here. My friends and I from high school sometimes walked the place, wishing we were old enough to get in.

During the last case I worked on in Huntsdale, I met an old high school friend here to get her help with what I was working on. It was fun for both of us to finally—after all these years—be able to sit at the bar of The Lightning Rod. I figured right now it was the best place for me to meet Anson.

"I don't think you're a serial killer anymore," I told him.

"Because you found out what a nice guy I really am?"

"Because I'm pretty sure I know who the real killer is now."

"What?"

"I want you to write a story for the *National Investigator*. A story based on what I'm about to tell you. It will be a big exclusive for you. The big break in the case that we've been looking for. This could break everything wide open. And I'll give it to you first."

"Why me, Cassidy?"

That was a good question. But I needed to get the information out there through the media. I wanted to make a big splash with it. And no one I knew could make a bigger splash with a story like this than Anson, from what I'd seen. Besides, I didn't have any really close friends or contacts with the press. I did have a relationship with Anson, even if it was a pretty bad one. Still, I knew the guy, and I knew what he was all about. Better the devil you know than the one you don't.

"Do you remember The Singles Slayer case?" I asked him.

"Sure. How many people did he kill?"

"Twelve. Twelve women. All outside singles clubs and bars. Then he stopped. He hasn't been heard from since."

Anson nodded. I could see him trying to put the pieces together in his head. I did it for him.

"It's the same guy," I said.

"The Singles Slayer?" he asked.

"Yes. I think he's doing these new murders too."

"Do you know who he is?"

I told him all about Gary Eaton. How he'd been one of the leading suspects in The Singles Slayer case. About his background as a minister. About the Bible verse in the recent note that matched word for word a Bible verse left before at one of The Singles Slayer murders. About the other religious line that was the same too from The Singles Slayer case. And about Eaton disappearing two years ago just as we were about to move in on him for intensive interrogation about The Singles Slayer murders.

"Gary Eaton is your top suspect in both cases now—The Singles Slayer deaths and the new murders too?"

"Yes."

"Can I call him that in the story?"

"For now, call him a 'person of interest' in the FBI investigation of the two cases. According to an FBI source close to the investigation. Just don't quote me by name anywhere in the piece. Okay?"

Anson took a big gulp of the beer he was drinking. He looked truly shocked. This was not what he expected to hear from me. I had him off his normal cocky sure-of-himself game.

"I can really go with this as exclusive?" Anson asked when I finished telling him about all the rest of it. "Naming this guy Eaton and using all the rest of the stuff you told me?"

"That's exactly what I want you to do. I want Eaton to know that we know all about him. To know we're coming after him. I think this will push him into doing something he wouldn't normally do, making a mistake that will help us finally catch him. I need the media's help to do that. I could have gone to anyone who's in the media, but I came to you. What I really need is someone in the media that I can trust."

"And you trust me?"

"No, I do not."

"Then why tell me all this?"

"I trust your ambition, Anson. I trust you're smart enough to realize that if you do what I want, you'll get a big story. And, even more than that, I promise to give you the exclusive on the rest of this big story when it happens. The story of how we catch this guy. You'll be the first to hear it from me."

The *National Investigator* splashed the story all over its website. The headline:

SERIAL KILLER SHOCKER

Unsolved Singles Slayer Cases Linked To New Murder Spree

There was a big byline on the story: "By Brett Anson." I bet that made him happy. Along with a series of pictures—of some of The Singles Slayer victims as well as the girls from the new murders.

I read the story:

The FBI has now linked the infamous Singles Slayer killings of several years ago to the recent series of murdered young girls, a source close to the investigation told the National Investigator.

"We think it's the same guy," said the source, who has intimate knowledge of the FBI search for the killer. "He's back. The Singles Slayer. Back out there murdering people all over again."

The FBI has identified a suspect—or a "person of interest"—they're looking for, according to the source with close knowledge of the investigation.

He is Gary Eaton, a minister in Northern California who resigned from the pulpit and disappeared more than two years ago—just as authorities were closing in on him for The Singles Slayer killings.

The source said the key now to connecting the two serial murder cases came from a Bible verse and another religious reference left by the killer in a note left behind with the body of the last victim, TV personality Susan Stratton.

"The same Bible verse was used years earlier in a message after one of The Singles Slayer killings," the source

said. "So were other religious references. None of this specific information was ever released to the public at the time. It can't be simply coincidental that it appeared again in this new note. And we don't think it was an accident either. We believe the killer was sending us a signal that he was the same person from The Singles Slayer killings of the past. And that he was now back again."

There are major differences between the two murder sprees. The most obvious being the method of the deaths: Gunshot from The Singles Slayer cases and strangulation in all of the new murders.

But the source said the bureau's working theory is that the killer simply changed his method of murder during his years-long hiatus between the murder sprees.

"We don't know why he stopped The Singles Slayer killings," the source told this reporter. "We don't know why he started killing the young girls now. We don't know why he switched from using a specific gun—a Bulldog .44 revolver— to strangulation. But we believe it was the same person, the same man. We'll find out the answers to all that when we catch him. Confidence is high in the bureau that will be very soon."

"I didn't do this!" Bonnie Tatarko said anxiously to me when she and Alex saw the *Investigator* piece on their website.

"Uh, huh."

"I'm telling you the truth, Nikki. It wasn't me. Not this time. I haven't talked to Anson at all since our conversation about it. You have to believe me."

"I do believe you, Bonnie. Because I know who did give him this exclusive. It was me."

Alex and Bonnie both stared at me in shock. Until I explained it all to them. Told them about my strategy for getting the word out that we knew now who the killer was and how I hoped that might get him to make a mistake we could use to nab him.

"Does Blanton know about this?" Alex asked when I was finished.

"No, I didn't tell him."

"So you just went ahead and did it on your own anyway?"

"I need to make something happen, Alex. This is the best way I could think of to do that."

Yes, I had done what I set out to do.

A lot of people would be reading this article from the *National Investigator*.

I just hoped one of them was Gary Eaton.

Then the next move was up to him.

FIFTY-FOUR

Backtracking the trail of Gary Eaton was not an easy thing to do.

It wasn't at the time he disappeared from any kind of public sight.

And I knew it was going to be even more difficult to track him now two years later.

Gary Eaton had been questioned several times about The Singles Slayer murders. Based on the reports of suspicious behavior we'd received about him. Also because of an eyewitness who identified him from a picture as the man she believed she saw with a gun at one of the crime scenes.

None of this was enough for an arrest at the time. But we felt like we were closing in on him back then. A new interview was scheduled with Eaton where we expected to confront him about everything and, if he gave up anything at all, to move forward with a warrant to search his church and his home.

On the Sunday before the interview was supposed to happen, Eaton vanished.

He announced at the Sunday service at his church that he

was stepping down from the pulpit for "personal reasons," effective immediately.

When agents went to the church afterward, there was no sign of him. The same at his house. Based on his sudden and definitely suspicious disappearance, we were able to get warrants to search both the church and the house. We found nothing tying Eaton to The Singles Slayer murders.

Still, he had run. Was that because of the impending FBI interview about The Singles Slayer case? Or was he hiding something else he didn't want us to find out? At the time, we weren't entirely sure. But now, given the new link with the Bible verses, the former Rev. Gary Eaton was definitely the suspect we were looking for.

I started by calling our San Francisco bureau of the FBI and asking them to send people to the town in Northern California where Eaton had been to look for any clues or indications of his whereabouts now. Where in the hell was he? Maybe someone at his old church would know.

I also got a list of people from our files that we had interviewed about Eaton back then—including some of those who had made complaints against him—in the hopes that they might know something. They did not. At least, the people that we were able to reach didn't know anything more about Eaton. But I kept trying.

I also called Washington and set up a computer search to look for any evidence of Eaton in the cyberspace world. Social media, credit card use, that sort of thing. It's pretty difficult for a person to fall off the radar completely in this digital world of today. Yet, Eaton had managed to do it.

I'd posted a picture of Gary Eaton up on the wall next to me while I was doing all this.

After I hung up with Washington, I looked at it for a long time. Remembering my growing belief at the time of The Singles Slayer killings that he was the man we were after.

He didn't look particularly like a serial killer now, as I stared at his picture. But then serial killers rarely looked the part. They came across usually as normal and maybe even likable people. Maybe even more normal and likable than the average person. Hell, Ted Bundy was damned good-looking and charming, people used to say. That didn't stop him from murdering at least thirty-seven women—probably even more.

Gary Eaton wasn't exactly handsome, but he wasn't particularly strange looking either. Close cropped brown hair, brown eyes, a smile on his face as the picture was snapped. Not the kind of guy you would worry about if you ran into him on the street. Or in church. Or outside a singles club. Until it was too late.

I sat staring at that picture of Gary Eaton for a long time.

Wondering where he was and what he was doing at the moment.

It was later that day when I got a call back from Dave Blanton in Washington. He'd been upset with me about the Brett Anson article, after I told him I'd planted the story about Eaton and The Singles Slayer connection. He continued to say I was jumping to conclusions by linking The Singles Slayer murders to the new killings. I figured I'd get more of the same from Blanton now. But he surprised me.

"You were right," Blanton said.

"About?"

"The Singles Slayer connection. Gary Eaton. Giving that information to the reporter. You were right about all of it."

"What changed your mind?"

"Gary Eaton just used his credit card. Twice in the past twenty-four hours. It's a Bank of America card that has had no activity for a few years. But now it was used to charge items at a gas station and also at a CVS store."

"Where?"

"You're not going to believe this."

"Where, Boss?"

"First in Columbus, then in... well, in Huntsdale."

"Jesus!"

"He's right there with you, Nikki."

I looked around where I was standing. On a street in Huntsdale. Expecting maybe to find Gary Eaton next to me. There was nothing. But I knew now he was here. Right here. Right here where I was looking for him.

"Why would Eaton do something like this?" Blanton asked. "These credit cards were used after the word went out that he was the prime suspect we were looking for in both sets of murders. He must have known that using them would send up a red flag and let us know exactly where he was."

"He did it deliberately," I said. "He used the credit cards after everything I said about him in that article because he knew it would allow us to track him."

"But why?"

"Gary Eaton wants me to know he's here."

FIFTY-FIVE

The first location where Gary Eaton had used his credit card was a gas station north of Columbus, very near to the entrance there to the Ohio Turnpike.

That made a lot of sense.

The first girl's body—the body of Laurie Reddick—had been found at a turnpike rest area not far from the gas station.

Alex and I drove there first to see if we could pick up Gary Eaton's trail from the gas station.

Bonnie had gone back to her state trooper barracks in Columbus beforehand to deal with some stuff there. To be honest, I was just as glad not to have her as part of our investigation at the moment. She'd asked me the other day whether I trusted her again now. I wasn't sure. I guess I'd always have questions about her for divulging secret stuff to Anson the way she did.

Of course, I'd done the same thing later. But her motive was personal, to advance her own career. My motive was to try and catch Gary Eaton and solve the case. There's a big difference there. I wasn't sure if Bonnie realized that yet, but I did. And I could never forget about it.

So I was back with Alex again. She wasn't a hundred per cent healthy. Her left arm was still in a sling from the gunshot wound. But the doctors gave her the okay—albeit reluctantly—to stay on the job with me.

She made a lot of funny remarks to people about the way she looked in the sling. Calling herself "an angel with a broken wing," whenever anyone asked about it. And sometimes doing bad jokes like "I just flew in from Washington, and boy is my arm tired." She made it clear to me though that she was fit for duty and wasn't going to be any kind of detriment to me in her condition.

"It's my left shoulder, I can still shoot anyone with my right hand," Alex said. "Don't worry. If you get in trouble, I can bail you out, like I always do."

Even with one working arm, I was glad to have Alex here with me.

The gas station wasn't much help in giving us any information about Eaton.

Not that I really expected it to be.

No one at a gas station paid much attention to the people who put gas in their cars. They just filled the tank, paid at the pump with their credit card and left.

There were ten gas pumps at the station, and a convenience-type store selling candy and soda and monitoring the pumps in case anyone needed help putting in their gas or paying for it.

We stood outside the pumps for a minute or two, looking at them. Gary Eaton probably was at one of these pumps—standing near where we were now—not long ago. Did he leave behind any evidence or clue? A fingerprint? Some kind of DNA? It would be pretty difficult to check for that, since so many people would have used the same gas pump beforehand and afterward. But I kept open the possibility of having a forensic team come here to check it out. At least that way we'd know Eaton had definitely been here, and he was the one using the credit card.

Then we went into the convenience store and talked to the employees, particularly one woman who was behind the counter.

There was no reason for Eaton to have been inside here. He could have just pumped his gas, paid for it at the pump and left without encountering or having an exchange with anyone inside.

But there was always a chance he had gone into the convenience store to buy a soda or gum or candy or maybe to use the bathroom.

I actually thought there was a pretty good possibility that might have happened.

If Eaton was trying to let me know he was here—which I believed he was doing—then why not make sure that people noticed him inside of the convenience store instead of lying low to keep out of sight?

I showed Eaton's picture to the woman behind the counter, as well as to other employees at the store, and asked if anyone remembered him being there.

"We get an awful lot of people in and out of here." The woman behind the counter shrugged. "Don't look much at their faces."

No one else recognized him at first look either.

We asked the woman at the counter to look up their records of the credit card number Eaton used for the transaction. It took her awhile, but she finally found it. She printed out the receipt and showed it to me.

It said Eaton had purchased twelve gallons of gas at $3.29 per gallon for a total of $39.48. The transaction had taken place approximately forty-eight hours earlier, at 12:58 in the afternoon.

I wasn't sure any of that information helped us, but I wrote it all down in my notebook anyway.

While I was doing that, a young woman who worked in the store approached me and Alex.

"You know, I might remember that person you're looking for."

"What do you remember?" Alex asked.

"Did he have blond hair?"

"Uh, no. Not the last time he was seen."

"Was he a big guy? Like very tall and maybe really overweight?"

Gary Eaton was short and slim.

I handed her the picture of Eaton again.

She looked at it and shook her head.

"I guess maybe I didn't see him, after all."

"Thank you for your cooperation," I said, taking back the picture from her, and decided there was nothing more to find out here.

"Well, that didn't go very well," I said as Alex and I drove back to Huntsdale.

"Maybe we'll have better luck at the Starbucks."

"Maybe."

The Starbucks we were looking for turned out to be in a strip mall about a mile and a half outside the center of Huntsdale. I don't remember that many strip malls here when I was growing up. But there sure were a lot of them these days. This one was located between a pizza parlor and a workout studio. We went inside.

The bad news was that no one working at the Starbucks recognized the picture of Gary Eaton.

The good news is that one of the baristas remembered

details from the specific transaction of the credit card number belonging to Eaton that we asked her to call up.

"Normally one order is the same as the other," said the barista, a small, thin, plain-looking brunette who could have been anywhere from eighteen to thirty, she was that nondescript. "But this one stood out. Because the person made such a big about the milk they wanted in their drink. It had to be soy milk and it had to be two per cent and they wanted Equal sweetener for it instead of Splenda, which we didn't have. It was a bit of a pain in the ass."

I showed her the picture of Gary Eaton again.

"Are you sure it wasn't this man?"

"Absolutely."

"Then what did he look like?"

"It wasn't a he."

"Are you saying...?"

"Yes, it was a woman who made that order."

FIFTY-SIX

"It has to be the same woman I met at my old house," I said to Connor once I met up with him again back at the hotel. "The Stratton woman is dead, she's the only other woman we know of that's in the picture."

"She used Eaton's credit card?"

"I think so."

"Wasn't she taking a chance someone would notice she wasn't a man—like the man's name on the card?"

"Nobody really checks cards like that anymore. You insert the card chip or scan it on the machine. It's all digital. So it wasn't really that much of a chance this woman—whoever she is —was taking."

We were in my room eating pizza. We'd decided to have the pizza delivered here instead of going out somewhere to eat it. Seemed quicker and easier after a long day on the job. Besides, we were close to the bed in my room this way, in case we wanted to go there after finishing up our pizza.

"Why didn't he use the credit card himself?" Connor asked.

"I don't know."

"Maybe he was afraid he'd be recognized."

"No, that's not it. Can't be. He wanted everyone to know that was his credit card being used at the Starbucks. That's pretty damn clear from the way the whole thing went down there with the woman."

"What do you mean?"

"The whole routine the woman went through. A special kind of milk, complaining about no Equal instead of Splenda. That was all designed to make sure the barista remembered her when we came asking about credit cards."

"He wants to let us know he's here. Or rather he wants you to know. Right?"

I nodded.

"He couldn't have been more obvious if he'd left a trail of breadcrumbs to mark his trail."

"And you're going to follow that trail wherever it leads?"

"Of course."

"It could be dangerous."

"Danger is my business," I said as I reached for another slice of pizza. It was okay pizza, not great. Not as great as the pizza I got from my favorite spot in D.C. But even not so great pizza works for me when I'm hungry.

I had a question for Connor.

"What are you doing here?" I asked him.

"Eating pizza with you."

"No, I mean here. In this town. In Ohio. Why aren't you back working at your job as police chief in Dorchester?"

"Do you want me to go back to Dorchester?"

"No."

"Then don't worry about me and Dorchester. I've told them I need some time off. I have it coming. I was originally just going to come here for a day or so to see you. But now I want to stay longer."

"Because I'm so passionate and sexy and all-around mind-blowing for you in bed?"

"Well, there is that."

"What else?"

"Look, Nikki, you're in danger here. A lot more danger than you seem to be willing to react rationally to. I don't want anything bad to happen to you. I want to make sure you're safe. I want to protect you from whatever—from whoever—is out there."

I sighed and put down the slice of pizza I had in my hand.

I knew where this conversation was headed.

But I went there anyway.

"I don't need you to protect me, Connor. I don't need you to watch over me. I'm a big girl. I'm an FBI agent. I'm a professional just like you are. I can take care of myself without you backing me up. What makes you think I can't?"

"Well, I did save your life not long ago." He smiled.

I sighed.

"Connor, I was engaged before I met you. Engaged to a pretty wonderful guy. I thought I was going to marry him. But he smothered me. He wanted to protect me to, he wanted me to get a safer job, he wanted me to be a more traditional wife with a more traditional job for him. I broke off the engagement because I'm not that person. You've got to let me do my job. On my own. The way I want to do it. And I don't need a man—any man, even you—to help me do that job."

Connor leaned over and put his arms around me. He kissed me. Then he looked me directly in the eyes as he spoke.

"You've told me about the people in your past. Let me tell you more about the person in my past. Lauren. I loved Lauren. Even though we were divorced, I still loved her like I'd never loved any other person. And, when she died in that fire, I was convinced I'd never have anyone like that in my life again. Someone I cared about as much as I cared about Lauren. Until you came along.

"I thought about you all the time we were apart, Nikki. I

wanted so desperately to be with you, wherever you were and whatever you were doing, every day during that time. And, in the end, that's what I did. I came here to Ohio to be with you again. And I don't regret that for a minute.

"I'm not sure exactly where we're going, you and me. We have different towns, different pasts, and different goals I suppose in our lives. I don't know how I can ever go to Washington full-time to be with you. Or how you're ever going to be able to be in Dorchester with me. But I don't care about that right now. I'm just glad I'm here with you at this moment. And I want to make that moment last as long as I can."

He kissed me again.

I kissed him back.

And then we fell into bed together.

Our lovemaking was interrupted by my phone ringing.

"Don't answer that," Connor said.

"I have to," I told him, looking at the screen and seeing the call was coming from Dave Blanton in Washington.

"We just got another hit from Gary Eaton's credit card," Blanton said when I came onto the line.

"Where?"

"Huntsdale."

"Same as before."

"Not exactly. This one is from a motel. Some place called the Breezewood Motel. Someone used it to check in there."

"When?" I asked, holding my breath that it was recent enough that we might be able to pick up his trail at the motel.

"An hour ago."

"My God, that means..."

"He's probably still there. Our guy. At the Breezewood Motel."

FIFTY-SEVEN

The Breezewood Motel was located off of Route 33, which was on the outskirts of Huntsdale. There wasn't much else around it. A Dunkin' Donuts across the street and a gas station a little further away. Definitely not a big traffic area.

The motel itself looked like it had seen better days. Or maybe the days had always been bad there. But it sure was a very unimpressive looking place. A one-story building with maybe a dozen units, counting the doors. Chipped paint on the outside. An unmowed lawn that looked like it consisted of more weeds than grass. And a lit-up sign in front—with two of the letters not working—that spelled out: Low Daily Rates: Vacancies Available.

I was with Connor, and Alex who I'd contacted after I got the news about Gary Eaton's credit card being used here to check in not long ago. I'd also called in the local Huntsdale police for backup. When they showed up, Chief Earnshaw was with them. I guess he wanted to get in on a little of the glory if we did catch Eaton in his jurisdiction.

We'd parked out of sight from the front of the motel so Eaton wouldn't see all of us there.

I laid out my plan of action for everyone.

"I'll go in alone, as unobtrusively as possible, to the motel clerk's office to find out if Eaton is staying here and, if he is, get his room number. I'll signal when I have that. Then Alex and I, along with some of you Huntsdale police, we will go through the front door of his room and hope he's still there. If he is, we've got him. Chief Earnshaw, I want you to deploy some of your people to the rear of the motel in case he tries to get out a window or something."

Before I went to the clerk's office, Connor took me aside and said: "What about me? What should I do?"

"Stay in the car."

"I should be there with you and Alex."

"No, you shouldn't. You have no authority here. I can't take that chance."

"What chance?"

"The chance that if this all goes wrong, someone will say that's because the FBI chick had her main squeeze with her."

Connor smiled.

He knew I was right.

Then I began walking toward the clerk's office.

The woman behind the desk there was probably no more than thirty, but she looked and acted like she could be fifty or sixty. Tired eyes. Tired face. A tired look when she saw me coming in. She had mousy brown hair that was uncombed and was wearing some kind of sweatpants outfit that was too big for her. I guess you didn't have to worry too much about impressing the customers with your appearance in a place like this.

I told her who I was, showed her my FBI credentials and said why I was there.

Then I gave her the credit card information for Gary Eaton.

She looked it up and said that yes, someone had checked in using that credit card earlier in the same day. I showed her a picture of Gary Eaton and asked if it was him. She said she didn't know. That she'd only started her shift an hour earlier and someone else was on the desk then.

"What room is he registered in?" I asked.

"Room twelve."

"Where is that?"

"Last room on the left."

"What name did he use when he checked in."

She looked that up in the record.

"Here it is... Gary Eaton."

"Gary Eaton," I repeated.

"Yes, is that who you're looking for?"

"Sure is."

Gary Eaton had signed in using his own name?

After using his own credit card to pay for the room?

It was like he was inviting us to come there and catch him.

Well, that's just what we were going to do.

I went back to the cars parked nearby, briefing everyone on their assignments and again rejected Connor's request to join us going into that motel room. I understood his frustration. I would have felt the same way if I was in his place. But this was finally our opportunity—our big chance—to nail Gary Eaton. The man responsible for The Singles Slayer murders and the more recent killings too. I wanted to make sure that I didn't do anything to mess that up in any way.

We made our way to the door of room twelve as quietly as we could, hoping Eaton didn't notice us from inside. Then we fanned out in front of the door. We all had our weapons out, ready for anything once we went inside.

When everyone was set, I pounded on the door.

"FBI!" I screamed as loudly as I could. "Open up!"

There was no answer from inside.

"Gary Eaton, you're surrounded!" I yelled. "There's no way out for you. Open this door peacefully, or else we're coming in."

Nothing.

"This is your last chance before we break the door down."

Not a sound from the room. Was he out somewhere? Or maybe armed and waiting for us in there? Either way, we had no choice. We had to go into the room right now.

We didn't have to actually break down the door. I'd gotten a room key from the woman at the front desk. I used it now, standing to the side in case he ran out or decided to open fire on us as soon as we went inside.

I turned the key in the lock. The door opened. I pushed it slightly open. Then—on my signal—Alex and I as well as some of Earnshaw's people pushed the door all the way open and rushed in with our weapons ready for whatever Eaton had waiting for us in there.

But we saw nothing at first.

No clothes.

No luggage.

No sign anyone had been here.

Except for the bed.

There was something under the covers of the bed.

I leaned over and pulled the cover back. It was a body. Or what was left of a body. Most of the flesh had deteriorated, and the face was barely recognizable from the person it had once been.

But I recognized enough to know who it was.

Or had been.

Gary Eaton.

He was dead.

Very dead.

And he'd been dead for a long time.

FIFTY-EIGHT

"This man has been dead for at least a year," Michael Franze said to us after examining the remains at the Medical Examiner's offices. "Maybe two years. Maybe, maybe even more than that."

It had been more than two years since the last Singles Slayer murder we'd known about. We always wondered why the killer stopped. Now we had a very good reason why that might have happened. Gary Eaton was dead all this time.

"There was no effort made to embalm or preserve the body in any way," Franze said. "In other words, this body wasn't taken from an actual grave or a funeral parlor or anything like that. I also found dirt embedded in the remains. My most likely theory is that the body was buried in some kind of makeshift grave for a long period of time. Then it was dug up very recently. And left in that motel room by whoever did all this. Weird stuff."

Yes, it definitely was weird.

"How did he die?"

"From the best I can determine after all this time and deterioration of the body, the cause of death was strangulation. I found evidence of scars around his neck, the kind of scars consistent with being choked. Presumably that's what killed him. There was no apparent bullet or stab wounds or other injuries that I can ascertain at this point. I'm going to do a more intensive examination of the remains, but I think this guy had to have been strangled to death."

"Just like all the recent victims were."

"So no surprise there."

"The surprise is that this is the guy who we thought was doing it all. First, The Singles Slayer cases. And now these new murders. Gary Eaton was our main suspect. But now... well, now it's not possible he was responsible for those young girls or for Susan Stratton. He was dead when they were all killed."

"How much do you know about Eaton?" Franze asked.

"He was a minister in California who disappeared mysteriously—no one ever knew why—two years ago. He was our main suspect, the one we were convinced we were after for The Singles Slayer murders back then. And, after that Bible verse and the other religious thing in his last note, we figured Gary Eaton was the key to this whole damn case—all of these murders. Now we're back at square one again."

"Are you certain this is Eaton? Have you confirmed the identity?'

"No, we haven't. Not officially. Eaton had never been arrested so there were no fingerprints to check with the remains, assuming you could even get prints from what was left behind of the skin. We are trying to find some dental records for him we could use to see if they were a match, but nothing so far."

And Eaton had lived alone, no wife or kids or other close relatives we could find. If we did, we'd bring one of them in for a final identification, I guess. So, at the moment, there was nothing official on the ID.

But it was Eaton.

I knew that.

I met him on several occasions when I questioned him about The Singles Slayer cases. I'd been staring at his picture for days now ever since I made the link between him and these new cases.

"This is Gary Eaton. Officially or unofficially, I know for sure who he is."

Alex had been in the exam room with me and Franze, but she didn't say much. She knew Franze and I had a long relationship, so she let me handle the conversation with him. She still did not say a whole lot once we had left Franze and walked out into the waiting area of the ME's office.

I could tell though she was as frustrated and confused as I was by all these recent events.

"Scenarios?" I asked her now.

"We were wrong about Eaton. He didn't kill anyone. Someone else was The Singles Slayer. That was who put those verses in the note connecting those killings with the ones now. Eaton was a victim like everyone else. Not The Singles Slayer."

"Except every other victim of The Singles Slayer was a woman. Why pick someone like Eaton as a target?"

"No idea."

"Alternative scenario?" I asked.

"Eaton was The Singles Slayer. He killed all those women in the past. Then someone killed him. And now that same person is continuing on with a series of new murders."

"A copycat?"

"I guess."

"I like that scenario better, Alex. Someone finds out Eaton is The Singles Slayer, kills him and then begins murdering young girls just like he did. Well, not exactly the same. Different targets—young girls instead of older ones on their own at bars and clubs. Different method of murder too. But close enough to convince us it was the same person doing all of these murders."

"That does leave us a couple of big questions," Alex said.

"Go ahead."

"Why wait until now? If this person really did kill Eaton because they found out he was The Singles Slayer, then left the body underground somewhere for two years or whatever—then why did the new murders start up again now?"

"Good question," I said.

"Second question: Why leave Eaton's body for us to find? Why use his credit cards to alert us? Why dig him up after all this time?"

"He wants to gloat, to show us how smart he is, to taunt us by sending us off in wrong directions—looking at Gary Eaton as our suspect—and then pulling the rug out from under us by letting us find out Eaton has died. Died a long time ago. And telling us that in such dramatic fashion. Luring us to that motel room to find a two-year-old corpse."

"What do you figure comes next?"

"Me."

"He's still coming after you, isn't he?"

"I think that was the point of all this."

"We're not going to let that happen, Nikki."

FIFTY-NINE

If the killer had been one step ahead of me this whole time—and it sure seemed like he (or she) had been—then I needed to figure out a way to catch up.

But how did I do that?

I'd already eliminated Brett Anson as a suspect for murder, no matter how much I despised him for what he had done and the things he'd put me through.

Gary Eaton was out of the picture now, even though I still believed it was very likely he was the original Singles Slayer killer who murdered the first twelve women.

The other two suspects for The Singles Slayer case from back then had airtight alibis—jail and death—meaning neither of them could be the one I was looking for.

So who then was still out there doing all of this?

And why?

I thought about this for a long time after Alex and I left Franze's office, discussed it at length with her and went back over and over everything I knew about the two murder sprees. Looking for some kind of clue or hint that I had missed.

When I was finished, I had come to one inescapable conclusion about the person we were desperately looking for.

That conclusion was: I had absolutely no idea who it was.

There was one thing I was pretty sure about though. The killer was close. Had to be here in Huntsdale to drop Gary Eaton's body in that motel room. The notes had made it clear I was the next target. I was in Huntsdale. Ergo, the killer must still be here too.

But where?

Well, presumably staying at a hotel in the area.

Not likely it would be the Breezewood Motel, but we went back and checked it out again. The woman we'd talked to before was gone. A teenaged boy was on duty. He seemed as tired and bored with the job as she did. Maybe this was her son.

It didn't take long to determine that the Breezewood Motel was a dead end. There were twelve rooms in the place, and ten of them were vacant. The other rooms were occupied by an elderly couple who both required walkers to get around and a local Huntsdale man we discovered was there for a tryst with a barmaid he'd met at a strip club the night before. Nobody who fit the profile of the killer we were looking for.

Huntsdale was a small town, so we didn't have too many hotels to check. Maybe about a half dozen within the town itself, and a few more on the highways nearby. Alex and I split them up to check out. I thought about asking Connor to help too. But I still didn't want him taking an active role in the investigation. He didn't belong to law enforcement here, which meant he didn't really belong working with Alex and me or any of Earnshaw's Huntsdale police officers on the case.

One problem, of course, was that we didn't know exactly who we were looking for.

"We have no name, we have no clue as to what the person looks like and we're not even sure this person is here," Alex said. "Or, if they are, we can't be sure they checked into a hotel or motel in the area. This gives new meaning to the term 'searching for a needle in a haystack,' doesn't it?"

"I know, I know. But I can't think of any better idea at the moment."

"Me either."

"I do think the person we're looking for is still here somewhere."

Alex sighed.

"Okay, let's go look then."

Two hours later, neither of us knew anything more. Alex texted me that she'd struck out everywhere she went.

I had the same experience at the hotels and motels where I checked. No bodies in the hotel lobby. No one running through the place waving a machete or a gun or a rope to strangle people. No one who signed in by identifying themselves with the name of The Singles Slayer. Okay, I knew it wasn't going to be that easy. But I'd hoped we would find something—anything at all—to give us a clue where to look next. Instead, we had drawn a big zero.

I went back to my own hotel. It was the last one on my list and thus, my last chance. I tried to keep my hopes up that this hotel would be different. I knew it was a long shot, but there was a certain logic to the killer staying at the same hotel I was at in order to be close to me.

Even though I still had no idea who I was looking for, I asked the clerk behind the front desk to show me a list of recent guests who had checked in.

I read through it all—asking the clerk questions when I could about the ones he remembered—without much success.

I was just about to give up when I saw one name that did look familiar. Galvin. The entry showed only the last name. I asked the desk clerk to check on the whole name. He said it was

Jeffrey Galvin. That was the same name as the father of Sara Galvin, the long-ago victim of The Singles Slayer. I looked at the rest of the information for Galvin. He'd used his driver's license as ID to check in. The driving license was from California, the same state where the Galvin I knew lived.

What in the hell was going on here?

Was it just a coincidence that Galvin—or someone that sure sounded like the Galvin I knew—was here now?

Had he showed up here because he heard I was closing in on The Singles Slayer from the news?

A lot of questions were running through my head as I got on the elevator. I made my way to the room listed for Galvin at the front desk. I knocked on the door. I yelled out to anyone inside. Then I knocked again, very loudly this time. This time I felt the door open a bit from the force of my knock.

I reached down to my side and took out my Glock 19M. I wasn't sure exactly why I was doing that. But better to be safe than sorry, I thought to myself. I pointed the weapon directly ahead of me now as I stood at the door.

Then I pushed the door all the way open and went inside.

It was dark. Except for a light coming from a table next to the bed. I found a light switch on the wall by the door and clicked it on. Then, with my gun still ahead of me, I looked around the place. It was empty. I checked everywhere, including the bathroom, No one anywhere at all here.

No clothes either, no baggage.

Just like the room at the Breezewood had been.

Except there was no body on the bed in this room. The bed looked freshly made, and it appeared no one had slept in it or even sat on it since housekeeping was here.

Which left only the light coming from the table next to the bed.

As I moved closer, I saw it was coming from a computer

screen. The monitor was lit, and there was a screen saver on the screen.

The screen saver was a picture of me.

I pushed one of the keys on the computer.

As soon as I did that, the screen saver picture of me disappeared and was replaced by a Word document file.

There was a list of seven documents in the file.

Five of the document titles were the names of the murder victims—LAURIE REDDICK, REBECCA BURGESS, LINDA GRASSO, SHIRLEY HUNSAKER and SUSAN STRATTON.

Another one had the name of SARA GALVIN, Jeffrey and Doris Galvin's murdered daughter.

But it was the remaining file—the one on top of the list—that I clicked on before any of the others.

The one that said AGENT NIKKI CASSIDY.

I knew this was going to be bad even before I read it.

But it was even worse than I thought it would be.

Much worse.

I read the words that were on the computer screen in front with a growing sense of horror and dread and fear...

SIXTY

Hello, Agent Cassidy,

Well, here we are again.

You and me, we have quite a history.

But this is the end of it I'm afraid—this will be the last time for you and me to be together.

I actually feel a bit sad about that, but you will feel even worse. And that makes me feel better about everything that's about to happen. Because I am about to achieve what has been my goal from the very start: to destroy you and everything that you have and everything that you love.

Have you figured out who I am by now, Agent Cassidy?

Don't worry.

I will reveal all to you very, very soon.

All the answers you've been looking for. Even the answers about your poor little sister Caitlin. I can tell you many things about Caitlin. I can tell you everything you want to know about Caitlin. Won't that be fun?

Since you're reading this, I know you took the bait I left for you as a trail. The name of a victim from the one case you never solved: The Singles Slayer case. Maybe you don't think much about The Singles Slayer anymore—with all your big headline-making arrests in more recent times—but I do. No, I will never forget The Singles Slayer.

Now is time for us to meet in person.

You and me.

Well, actually there will be three of us.

You.

Me.

And your mother.

Because I am at your mother's house with her right now.

Not the old house, where poor Linda Grasso met her end.

We are at her new house, and—as you might expect—your mother is very anxious and very nervous and very, very afraid at the moment.

So come to your mother's house and see us, Agent Cassidy.

One last time.

I'll be waiting for you...

I grabbed for my phone and punched in my mother's number. There was no answer. It went straight to voice mail. I left her a message saying it was urgent that she get back to me right away, even if I wasn't sure it was possible for her to do that. Then I dialed her number again. And again. Still no answer.

I frantically called Alex.

"He's got my mother," I screamed into the phone when Alex came on the line.

"Who?"

"The killer. He just left me a note saying that. Said he's at her house. I'm headed over there now. Meet me and bring me as much help as you can find in a hurry."

"Are we talking about the house on Stockton?"

In my panic, I realized I hadn't made clear to her what house I was talking about.

"No, where she lives now." I gave her the address. "It's in Chillicothe. About fifteen minutes away. Call the Chillicothe police on this too. Get them over to the house right away."

"Where are you?"

"At the hotel."

"Let me pick you up there, we'll go to your mother's together."

"I can't wait for that. I'm on my way now. Meet me there with everyone else. I can't let anything happen to my mother, Alex. She's all I have left of my family."

"Do you know who the killer is?" she asked.

"I think so," I said. "I'm not sure, but I think I do."

"Who?"

I told her.

"What does this guy Galvin look like?" Alex asked when I was finished.

"I don't know. I've never met him."

"But you said you'd been in touch with him a lot of times over the past two years ever since his daughter's murder."

"I was in Washington, he was in Los Angeles. I never handled his case directly, other agents out there did. But he began texting me after I went on TV to talk about the investigation. I guess he became fixated on me as the symbol of the FBI—and the FBI's inability to solve the case—and he's been texting me for information ever since. That's the only way I know Jeffrey Galvin."

"Jeez."

"Just get to my mother's as fast you can, Alex. I'm headed to my car right now."

I had already left the empty hotel room and was running down the hall to the elevators before I hung up the phone. There was only one elevator that seemed to be working. And it was several floors away. I waited for a few seconds, then went to the stairs. I was only on the sixth floor, so it was quicker. I raced down the steps and was soon heading out of the hotel lobby toward the parking lot to my car.

It was another rental, and it didn't have an ignition key like I was used to—there was a button to push to start it that was programmed to match a key fob in my handbag. But I was in such a state I started frantically looking for a key. Then, when I finally realized I didn't need one, I still had trouble starting it because I needed to step on the brake at the same time I pushed the ignition button. Finally, it started.

I started to shift the car into gear to drive away from the hotel parking lot toward my mother's house.

That's when I heard a noise.

Coming from the back seat.

And I realized I wasn't alone in the car.

Suddenly, I felt something tightening around my neck.

"You're finally here," a voice said. "I've been waiting for you. I've been waiting for this moment for a long time."

I struggled to breathe or to reach for my gun, but it was no use. I couldn't do either one. I was immobilized.

"I'll bet your partner and a lot of other police are headed toward your mother's house right now," the voice said. "So they're not going to be able to help you. I lied to you about where I was. I've lied to you about a lot of things. But then you've lied to me, haven't you? You've lied to me for too long. Now it is time for you to pay the price—for you to be punished —for all your goddamned lies."

There was a scary laugh.

The tightening around my neck got worse, and I could barely breathe.

Then everything went black.

SIXTY-ONE

When I opened my eyes and regained consciousness, I saw a man's face.

I recognized the face because I'd seen him many times before.

Brett Anson.

"You," I said.

He was pointing a gun at me.

My gun.

I realized he'd taken it from me.

"Surprised?" he asked.

"What about Jeffrey Galvin?"

"That's me too."

Suddenly it all started to make sense. Sort of. Jeffrey Galvin and Brett Anson were the same person. I thought they were both on my side. But now I knew how wrong I was. I'd been chasing the killer, but the killer was right here with me the entire time.

I looked around. We weren't in the car anymore, I was lying against a tree in a wooded area. Not just any wooded area. It was Grant Woods, the same place where my sister's body had been found a long time ago. Anson/Galvin was sitting on a rock with the gun pointed directly at me.

"You had it right when you first suspected me, but for the wrong reasons. You thought I was doing it to get big scoops and advance my journalistic career. You had it backwards. I was doing the journalistic thing as a cover for my real target. First those girls, and now you."

"What about my mother?" I asked. "Is she…?"

"Your mother is fine. I never really saw your mother, I don't even know for sure where she lives now. But it was a clever ruse, huh? I'll bet there are all sorts of police swarming around her house now. Looking for you and for me. But here we are. All alone. Just the two of us."

"Why? In the name of God, why do all this?"

"It's for Sara."

Sara Galvin. His twenty-two-year-old daughter who had been gunned down by The Singles Slayer at the beginning of that murderous spree. The one case I had never solved. Looking back now, I should have seen the level of frustration in Galvin as we kept striking out in our search for the killer.

Why can't you catch him? he would rage at me sometimes in his texts back then. *That's supposed to be your job. Do your job!*

He was right.

But I never did accomplish that for him.

So he did it on his own.

He explained that to me now.

"I found that monster. You couldn't do it. Or you wouldn't do it. But I did. I tracked Gary Eaton down without you. I made him pay for what he had done to Sara. He confessed to killing her, he confessed to all of them. Then I killed him. An eye for an eye. It felt good, Agent Cassidy. It felt real good."

I'd heard of these things happening before. A crime victim's family or loved one turning vigilante to deliver what they called justice to the person responsible. Losing faith in the law enforcement and justice system to do the right thing. Instead, taking action on their own. It was understandable in some cases, I suppose. Yes, Gary Eaton—as The Singles Slayer—had been a monster. But, like the old adage goes about the danger of chasing monsters, Jeffrey Galvin had become a horrible monster himself.

I wondered how Galvin had managed to track down Eaton as The Singles Slayer who murdered his daughter, but I didn't ask him this. I was more interested in the rest of it. And I knew I wanted to keep him talking. Because once he was finished talking, I was going to be his next victim.

"I saw you on television," he said, gripping the gun tighter now as he kept pointing it at me. "All that stuff about your heroics and the cases you solved and the girls you brought home as an unstoppable FBI agent. Even before all this happened in Huntsdale. The big, big media star. The woman who always caught the bad guy. Except for the one who murdered my Sara.

"I still remember that night Sara went out. My wife and I, we weren't worried about her going out. I mean she was a grown woman, she wasn't a kid anymore. If she wanted to go out for a night with her friends at some club, it was no big deal. Sara promised me she'd be home before midnight. She gave me a kiss on the cheek, and then she went out the door. We never saw her again.

"Whenever I saw you on TV or read about you, it was always about the cases you'd solved and the girls you'd either saved or found justice for. Well, all I could think of was why hadn't you done that with my Sara? Why couldn't you find justice for her too? Why couldn't you find the goddamned Singles Slayer who snuffed out her life that night. It gnawed on me and it ate away at me until I couldn't take it anymore. Just the sight of you on TV or in a newspaper or magazine or an internet picture sent me into a rage.

"And so I decided that I would make you pay. I would make

you suffer, just like I had suffered. I knew all about your sister and the questions and emotional turmoil you had about that from the news stories. I used that to get to you. To make you start asking even more questions about your sister. To do everything I could to make you think that somehow your sister might still be alive.

"That's how it started. With the note from her, then the woman who looked like she might today if she were alive—and all the rest. I wanted to make you believe—I wanted to give you hope—that your sister was still somehow alive. That she was waiting for you to rescue her after all these years. That you could finally get rid of all the guilt you've felt about her death.

"I wanted to build that hope up in you as much as I could, which is what I did. And then, once you truly believed Caitlin could possibly still be alive, I would take that hope away from you. Your sister is dead, Cassidy. And now you're going to join her."

I was still lying against the tree where he had put me. The rope noose he'd used was still around my neck where he left it. How long had I been unconscious? Enough time for him to drive me from the hotel parking lot to here in Grant Woods a few miles away.

"Okay, you wanted revenge against Eaton. You were mad at me. I get all that. But why kill all those other people. Those young girls... they did nothing to you."

"It started out of necessity. The Reddick girl—who I'd found and recruited to go to your house—got suspicious and I was afraid she'd tell someone what I was doing. She never even went to your old home. She just took the money I gave her and spent it on clothes and jewelry and stuff. That story from the fake Maureen Wilcox about her showing up at the door was all made up. Reddick was supposed to appear at other places claiming to be Caitlin Cassidy too. But she had the money, and she tried to run instead. So I killed her because of that and to keep her quiet. Then I had to choke the other girl who helped find that body so she didn't talk either. And on and on. There was Shirley Hunsaker, which just seemed appropriate. And, as for Linda Grasso, I wanted the body of a dead girl for you to find in your sister's old bedroom. So Linda had to pay the price."

"What about the actress, Susan Stratton?"

"Ah, yes. She wanted to become famous. She was frustrated by her small role on the TV show. When I found out about the ability she had to make herself look like anyone, even you, I realized I could use her in my Caitlin plan. I promised her I'd get her big publicity for her career with the *National Investigator*, and she was excited about that. She had no idea she was involved in anything criminal. I convinced her she was just playing a part for a story I was working on. Then, when she heard you were coming to question her about murder, she panicked and called me to find out what to do. So, as you can see, I had to keep Susan Stratton quiet too."

"She was one of the two women who made appearances involving the Caitlin stuff. Who was the other one? The one I met living at my old house?"

"My wife."

Of course, Doris Galvin. I should have known that.

"And she was part of all this? She was okay with helping you to kill all these people?"

"She's my wife. She does whatever I tell her to do. Including murder."

That didn't make a lot of sense. But neither did the rest of what Galvin was telling me. Except I knew it was all true. Somehow, his grief and frustration over his daughter exploded into a rage of revenge against everyone he believed responsible for it, including me. I guess that might explain what he did to Gary Eaton. But it didn't explain any of the rest of it. There was no possible explanation for that, but I asked him about it anyway.

"Like I said, at first it was just going to be Laurie Reddick. I killed her because I had to. But then after that... well, I began to enjoy it. I mean I'd lost my daughter. Why shouldn't these other girls be sacrificed too? Why shouldn't other people feel the pain like I did? It felt good after each time I killed one of them. Especially knowing that you couldn't figure it out. That gave me even greater satisfaction. To outsmart the great FBI agent Nikki Cassidy. Who couldn't catch my daughter's killer, and now couldn't catch me. That made me feel so good. It still does."

I could see now he was almost gloating.

"And now," he said, "now the best is yet to come."

SIXTY-TWO

I desperately tried to think of some way to buy more time.

By now, Alex and the others would have gotten to my mother's house and seen that I wasn't there. Alex would know something was wrong, and she'd go looking for me. Sooner or later, she'd think about Grant Woods and search for me here. But that likely would happen too late to save me.

No, I was on my own here.

All I could do was keep him talking.

It would help me stay alive a little longer.

"How did you manage to become a journalist so easily?" I asked, hoping that would interest him enough to keep a conversation going. "You were a lawyer in Los Angeles. A big-time lawyer. A successful lawyer."

"I was a very successful lawyer. I could always convince people of what I wanted. And so I convinced people I was a reporter."

"But people go to journalism school for four years to get a job like yours. And you just walked into being a big star reporter?"

"It was actually really easy." He laughed. "Especially at a

place like the *National Investigator*. They don't care about your background. All I had to do was break a big story or two for them—stories that I created by the way—and they loved me. I started working for them six months ago, and yes... now I'm their star reporter."

Which explained why Alex and me and the computer people in Washington could find no background on Brett Anson.

There was none.

He simply created the persona for the *National Investigator* to do what he wanted.

"It didn't hurt any that the editor of the *National Investigator* is a woman," he said. "Let's just say she was impressed by my charms as well as my exclusives. She and I, we hit it off pretty well."

"Like you and Bonnie Tatarko?"

"She was very impressed by me too."

"And Susan Stratton?"

"I have a way with the ladies. Except with you. All that charm of mine never worked on you, did it? I wonder why. I mean sleeping with you—before I eventually killed you—would have been a nice bonus. Well, too late to worry about that now. It's time to finish this. Stand up."

I stood. The rope was still around my neck, which made me feel strange. But there was nothing I could do about that. He motioned me over to a spot in the woods a few hundred yards away. We walked over there. I recognized the location right away. It was the exact spot where Caitlin's body had been fifteen years ago.

"They're going to find you dead too, just like your sister was, right here," he said. "Not a suicide, even though they might think that at first. Despondent FBI agent who can't catch serial killer takes her own life, blah, blah, blah. But then they'll see the marks around your neck. And realize you couldn't have done that to yourself, under the circumstances. You couldn't strangle yourself with that rope, someone else had to do it. That's how you're going to die, Cassidy. Strangulation. It will be long though, and it will be painful.

"Like it was with the others, except this time I'm going to draw the game out—I'm going to enjoy it—for even longer. Each time that rope cuts off your air, and then you get a few precious breaths back, you'll be moving ever closer to death. At some point, you'll wish for death to make the ordeal stop. Laurie Reddick did that, actually pleaded with me to finally kill her and make it all end. I look forward to you doing that too before you finally die.

"Hell, it will be a great story for me in the *National Investigator* too. Think about that! I accomplish what I wanted with you, and I advance my journalistic career too by breaking the big story again. I mean I thought I'd probably go back to law when this was all over. But now I'm going to be a big media star too, just like you were.

"Yes, it's going to be a win-win situation for me."

We were at the spot now. The place where Caitlin's body had been found. Now my body would be found here too, unless I came up with something to stop that. I had to do that somehow. I couldn't let this happen. I was *not* going to let this happen.

"Sit over there," he said, pointing with the gun—my gun—to a large tree limb on the ground.

I sat.

He moved quickly behind me, grabbed ahold of the rope that was around my neck and pulled it tight until I was gasping for air. He held it like that for a while, then loosened the rope again. I gasped for air.

He wasn't ready to kill me.

Not yet.

He was going to play this game—cutting off my breath,

having me pass out at some point, then reviving me again—until he was ready for the final moment when he ended it all.

That was Jeffrey Galvin's game with murder. Well, I needed to play my own game with him. To change the rules of the game.

"Are you ready?" He laughed. "Here we go again."

This time the tightening of the rope was worse, but I made it seem even more difficult for me to stay conscious than it really was. Gasping for air, like I was dying. When I did that, he released the rope again.

"Wow, that was quicker than I expected to get you to this point," he said. "I can't wait to see what you do this time."

He squeezed the rope around my neck again. Tightly, but not tight enough to make me black out like I did in the car or that night at the house.

Except he didn't know that.

Because I acted like he had.

I clawed at the rope even more desperately than I had before, gasped for air like it was the last breath I would ever take and—as quickly as possible—fell limp and rolled myself off the tree limb onto a spot on the ground. Not just any spot on the ground though. A specific spot that I had noticed while I was sitting there.

There was a rock. A large rock. Not too big for me to pick up in my hand easily, but big enough to do damage to my target. I fell onto the rock now, grabbed ahold of it under my body and then heard a surprised Galvin bend down to check me out.

"Get up, you bitch!" he was screaming. "We're not done here yet."

He grabbed at the rope around my neck to try to pull me up, and that's when I turned around and smashed him in the head with the rock. Blood poured from his forehead, and I knocked the gun out of his hand. It landed on the ground several feet away from us.

He yanked on the rope to try to subdue me, but I could tell he was hurt now. I saw the gun lying in some tall grass tantalizingly close. I struggled to try to get to it, with him pulling on the rope in a desperate attempt to tighten it even more around my neck. I still had the rock in my hand, so I hit him with it again. But he held onto the rope and squeezed it even tighter. He knew now he needed to finish me off quickly.

I reached out for the gun.

Not quite close enough.

I pulled together every bit of strength I could find this time even though the rope was cutting off almost all of my air.

I didn't have much time left.

I made one more lunge for the gun.

I got it this time.

I whirled around and shot Jeffrey Galvin before he could kill me.

The rope around my neck suddenly loosened, and I was able to take several deep breaths. Galvin was lying on the ground next to me. There was a growing splotch of blood on his chest, and a stunned look on his face.

"You win, Cassidy," he managed to murmur as blood began to come out of his mouth too.

"Nobody wins," I said.

Then Jeffrey Galvin/Brett Anson died.

SIXTY-THREE

We found Doris Galvin a few days later a longways away in Idaho.

Or rather Doris Galvin found us.

She walked into a police station in Boise and surrendered. Once she was in custody, a contingent of FBI and other authorities descended on the spot to question her. They discovered she had been living in an RV that she had driven across country from Ohio after her husband died.

"I tried to run," she told us. "But I realized it was too late for that. It's over. My life is over. It was over the moment I lost my daughter, I realize that now. Without Jeffrey, there's no reason for me to keep going. I'm too tired to run anymore. It just doesn't matter for me at this point. Nothing matters."

Under intense questioning, she did fill in some of the holes in what we knew about Jeffrey Galvin and everything he had done to avenge his daughter's murder.

She talked about her husband finding Gary Eaton, getting him to confess he was The Singles Slayer and about how he brought him back alive at first to their house in Los Angeles, then kept him in their basement for days.

Jeffrey Galvin starved Eaton, kept him without drinking water except for a few sips each day he needed to keep him alive. He had tortured Eaton mercilessly during this time, she said. And strangled him over and over—leaving him just a few precious breaths of fresh air before releasing his hold. Then he'd strangle him all over again, repeating the process like a water torture until Eaton was a blubbering wreck pleading for some kind of mercy.

He got him to tell everything he had ever done in great detail—including the Bible verses Eaton had left with victims at the time, and that Galvin would use again later to get my attention.

Finally, after Galvin decided the proper revenge had been carried out against the man who murdered his daughter, he delivered the final stranglehold to kill Eaton. Once he was dead, Galvin put the body in his car, drove it to a park in the same area and buried Eaton's body there.

Doris Galvin insisted she had nothing to do with the killing of Eaton, it was all done by her husband. She said he was very strong, as evidenced by his ability to strangle people, and she was afraid of him herself. That he threatened to strangle her to death if she tried to stop him from doing any of the things he was doing.

Despite this, she maintained that she had continued to plead with him to stop the killing of the new victims, but that he refused to listen.

It was clear to me—and everyone else—that she was desperately seeking some kind of plea deal by cooperating in any way she could at this point. She probably would get a deal too, at least one to help her avoid the death penalty. Even though there was no real need for her testimony in a court of law since her husband was dead. But she helped us to get the whole story, even if it was her version of it.

"I noticed a frightening change in my husband as it all went on," she said. "At first, this was just about revenge against the man who killed our daughter. I understood that. I felt the same rage as he did. And I felt that law enforcement—the people who were supposed to bring this horrible man to justice for doing what he did—had let us down."

She looked at me when she said that.

"But, as time went on, Jeffrey seemed to be enjoying the killing for the sake of killing. I think it gave him a sense of... well, a sense of power. Power he never had before when he was waiting for some word on the case. Power that he was able to do it on his own. To catch and kill the monster that was Gary Eaton when no one else could do it.

"He became obsessed with you," she said to me. "To outthink you, to have you go off in the wrong directions, to prove he was better than you at doing all this. And, most important of all, to make you go through the same kind of torment we had done by injecting all the things about your dead sister in the case.

"That's why he did all that with your sister. Making it seem like she was still alive. Getting that actress to look like she might be her today, all these years later. Putting me in your old house where you lived. Leaving one of the bodies there. He wanted to torment you. He knew how important your sister was to you, how emotional you were about her loss. He played on that.

"Every time he did it, either taunted you or killed another girl to keep you chasing futilely after him, he gloated afterward. That's the only explanation I can give you to describe the way he acted. He gloated about the things he was putting you through. I'm sure he was gloating right to the very end. When you killed him."

That confirmed the same kind of thing I had picked up from Galvin during those last minutes in Grant Woods.

So a lot of what Doris Galvin told us was probably true.

Interestingly enough though, she never expressed any remorse or sympathy for the dead victims.

Once it was over, Bonnie Tatarko came to see me one last time.

"Are we good, you and me?" she asked.

"Sure."

"I mean it, Nikki."

"We're good, Bonnie."

I wasn't exactly sure if I was good with Bonnie Tatarko or not. She'd betrayed my trust. But I was happy to let bygones be bygones. Besides, I figured I'd never see her again. Except then I found out I might be wrong about that.

"Just so you know, I've applied for a new job in law enforcement," Bonnie said. "I think I have a good chance of getting it."

"Where?"

"With the FBI."

"The FBI," I repeated.

'Yes, I found out there's an opening in the Cleveland bureau. I submitted my application to Washington. I'm hoping for the best. I could use as much help as I could get though. Can I use you as a reference? Would you recommend me for the job?"

I wasn't sure whether I wanted to recommend Bonnie Tatarko for a job with the FBI or not. I'd have to think about that some more. But I'd worry about that when the time came.

I was still in Huntsdale.

And Connor was still with me.

Sort of.

That is we were still sharing the same bed, even though we hadn't worked out anything new about what was going to happen once I went back to Washington.

But we'd made a pact not to talk about it.

At least for now.

Instead, we would just enjoy each other's company.

Which is what we were doing when he brought up my near deadly encounter with Galvin again in those woods—along with some of the other scary stuff that had happened to me during this case.

"You take too many damned chances."

"It's my job."

"No, you can do your job without putting your life on the line as much as you do. I don't want anything to happen to you, Nikki. I worry about you. Because... because I love you, Nikki Cassidy."

He kissed me then.

I kissed him back.

"Do you really mean that?"

"Of course."

"Then prove it."

"How exactly do I do that?"

"If you really love me, truly love me, then you'll do anything I ask you to do to prove that love, right? No matter how difficult it turns out to be."

"I suppose."

"Okay, then I'm giving you the ultimate test. My mother. You're coming with me to meet her."

SIXTY-FOUR

The last time I brought a love interest of mine home to meet my mother was before a big dance my senior year in high school. It did not go well. My mother interrogated the guy about his past, his present and his future plans like I would interrogate a murder suspect. By the time we got to the dance, he was barely speaking to me. I never saw or heard from him again.

I probably should have brought Greg Ellroy—my former fiancé—here when I was trying to break up with him, but couldn't figure out exactly how to do it. I spent a long time before I was able to end that relationship. Five minutes for Greg Ellroy with my mother would have accomplished it much faster.

Now I was going back with Connor Nolan—the current love interest in my life—and I wasn't sure how that was going to work out.

But I needed to see my mother before I left Huntsdale, and it just seemed easier for me to do that with someone like Connor at my side.

"She goes between hating me because she blamed me on some level for the deaths of my sister and my father and then loving me because I'm all she has left of a family," I said to him before we went inside. "There are times when she seems to drift away and thinks that Caitlin is still alive. I remind her that Caitlin is dead and my father is dead too. Sometimes she gets mad at me when I talk about Caitlin or my father, especially when I question her about the details. Other times she begins hugging me because I'm still here. It can be a tough situation dealing with my mother."

I told Connor about bringing my long-ago high school date to meet her so I could prepare him for the worst.

"I promise not to get mad at you like he did, no matter what your mother says."

"I just hope you feel that way when this is over."

"It'll be fine, Nikki," he said soothingly.

And it was.

Connor was charming to her—hey, he's a charming guy—and she appeared to like him right off. Especially when he told her he was a police chief like my father used to be. That seemed to have a real impact on her. For whatever reason, she decided Connor was a good guy. The same conclusion I'd already come to myself.

"It's always nice to meet a friend of my daughter's like you. A police chief, huh? How interesting. My husband was a police chief too. He was the police chief right here in Huntsdale for many years.

"I know, Nikki told me all about him. He sounds like he was a terrific man."

'Oh, he was," she said.

She told him some stories about my father, too, a few of them I hadn't even heard before. Connor laughed when appropriate, looked sympathetic when that was the right response. I could definitely see my mother really liked him. They were getting along famously. Getting along so well together that I almost felt left out of the conversation.

There was another reason I had come back to see my

mother before leaving Huntsdale though. To bring her up to date on everything that had happened with Caitlin on this case. To make sure she understood how Jeffrey Galvin had simply used Caitlin to torment me about her memory.

"I saw Caitlin again," she said when I was finished.

"What?"

"She was standing outside my door here."

That was the story she'd told me the last time I was here.

"Mom, like I explained, that was an actress. She made herself look like Caitlin might look today. Other people saw her like that too. It was a ruse to get to me, to get inside my head. But she was simply an actress playing a role. And she's dead now too."

"I knew about that woman. I heard about the death on the news, just like I heard and followed everything you've been doing. But this time it wasn't her that I saw there. It was Caitlin."

"We went through all this the last time I talked with you." I sighed.

"No, this just happened a few days ago. After that woman died. Caitlin was there again. Big as life. For just a minute. Then she was gone again. Why did she leave me again so quickly? Why would she do that?"

She looked anxiously at Connor and me for some answers. He didn't reply. I didn't know what to say either. My mother was clearly being delusional. That was the only possible answer.

Or was it?

There's been so many questions that popped up about my sister since I'd been back in Huntsdale.

The other "sightings."

The supposed note from her.

Okay, a lot of this had been a way for Galvin to play mind games with me.

But did he do all of it?

If my mother really had seen someone here who looked like Caitlin might today, it could not have been Susan Stratton. Because Galvin had told me he never even knew where my mother lived now. So what—and, more importantly, who—did my mother see recently outside her front door?

And then what about the reference to me as "Nik"—a name no one ever called me except Caitlin. How could anyone know that? There was never any explanation. Doris Galvin said she was told by her husband to tell me that the girl had referred to me as "Nik" instead of Nikki—because that was Caitlin's pet name for me back then. How would he ever have found that out unless someone told him. But who?

Meanwhile, there was still the mystery of the missing pages that had disappeared from my father's official police report on Caitlin's murder. The report that Mickey Franze had taken from my mother's home when I told him that copies still existed there.

What was really on those missing pages?

I went back to see Franze again before I left Huntsdale.

"I've been thinking a lot about that conversation I had with you about Caitlin," Franze said. "About your doubts and concerns you never found out the whole story. Well, maybe you're right."

He didn't seem nervous or defensive about discussing this topic like he had in the past with me.

He told me he was going to tell me everything he knew.

And I believed him this time.

"Your father was acting strangely at the end. What you told me about your mother saying he'd made that reference to knowing more about Caitlin the day he died. He said something similar to me. That there was more to what happened with

Caitlin than anyone else knew. He made me promise never to repeat that to anyone. And I never have, Nikki. Even to you. Until now.

"I think you deserve to know everything there is to know about Caitlin after all this time. Your father was my friend. I just want to do the right thing by you for him. I wish I could help you more. But your father never told me anything more specific while he was alive. I've always wondered what secret he might have been holding on to about Caitlin.

"That's why I went to get those reports he kept on the case at your mother's place. I was hoping they might have some kind of answers. I don't have any answers yet, just questions like you. I suppose you will never be able to answer those questions about Caitlin. You'll never be completely sure."

"There is one way for me to be sure about Caitlin," I said.

I didn't have to say anymore.

Franze knew what I was talking about.

And, in the end, he agreed.

SIXTY-FIVE

I didn't want to do it.

But there was no way I could not do it either.

I had to be sure about Caitlin, one way or another.

I waited with a mixture of anticipation and dread as workmen at the cemetery raised her coffin out of the grave where it had been for the past fifteen years.

I thought about how many times I had stood at this grave and "talked" to my sister there. Even though I knew it was a one-way conversation, it still always made me feel better.

I thought about my memories of her as an adorable twelve-year-old girl—running around the house, giggling and gossiping with me in our bedrooms late at night and... well, just being Caitlin. My little sister. The sister I was supposed to grow up with.

I thought too about what Michael Franze had said about the condition of a body after fifteen years in a grave. How it would look more like a skeleton than the Caitlin I remembered.

The workmen had the coffin up out of the ground now and began working to open the top. We moved closer.

I was ready for anything.
Or so I thought.
Until I looked down and saw what was inside.
The coffin was empty.

A LETTER FROM DANA PERRY

I want to say a huge thank you for choosing to read *The Lost Ones*. If you did enjoy it, and want to keep up to date with all my latest releases, just sign up at the following link. Your email address will never be shared and you can unsubscribe at any time.

www.bookouture.com/dana-perry

This is the third book in a new thriller series of mine featuring FBI agent Nikki Cassidy. The first two were *The Nowhere Girls* and *Last One to Die*. In this book, like the first two, Nikki is chasing a serial killer of young girls while at the same time still trying to answer nagging questions about her own twelve-year-old sister's death years earlier. And once again, Nikki is drawn back to the small town in Ohio where she grew up and which still holds so many deadly secrets for her. Nikki is a flawed character – tough, smart, honest and dogged, but still trying to redeem herself from the mistakes she's made in the past. I like Nikki Cassidy. I enjoyed spending time with her writing these books. I hope you enjoy reading about her just as much.

If you liked *The Lost Ones*, I would be very grateful if you could write a review. I'd love to hear what you think, and it makes such a difference helping new readers to discover one of my books for the first time.

I love hearing from my readers, you can get in touch with me on social media or through my website.

Thanks,

Dana Perry

www.rgbelsky.com

facebook.com/DanaPerryAuthor

x.com/DanaPerryAuthor

PUBLISHING TEAM

Turning a manuscript into a book requires the efforts of many people. The publishing team at Bookouture would like to acknowledge everyone who contributed to this publication.

Audio
Alba Proko
Sinead O'Connor
Melissa Tran

Commercial
Lauren Morrissette
Jil Thielen
Imogen Allport

Data and analysis
Mark Alder
Mohamed Bussuri

Cover design
Jo Thomson

Editorial
Helen Jenner
Ria Clare

Copyeditor
Jane Eastgate

Proofreader
Nicky Gyopari

Marketing
Alex Crow
Melanie Price
Occy Carr
Cíara Rosney

Operations and distribution
Marina Valles
Stephanie Straub

Production
Hannah Snetsinger
Mandy Kullar
Jen Shannon

Publicity
Kim Nash
Noelle Holten
Myrto Kalavrezou
Jess Readett
Sarah Hardy

Rights and contracts
Peta Nightingale
Richard King
Saidah Graham